I0654275

GOING *for the* GOLD RING

R. THOMAS ROE

Going for the Gold Ring
by R. Thomas Roe

Signalman Publishing
www.signalmanpublishing.com
email: info@signalmanpublishing.com
Kissimmee, Florida

© Copyright 2013 by R. Thomas Roe. All rights reserved. No part of this book may be reproduced or transmitted in any form or by any means, electronic or mechanical, or incorporated into any information retrieval system, electronic or mechanical, without the written permission of the copyright owner.

This is a work of fiction. Names, characters, places, and incidents are either the product of the author's imagination or are used fictitiously, and any resemblance to actual persons, living or dead, business establishments, events, or locales is entirely coincidental.

Cover design by Duncan Long
www.duncanlong.com

ISBN: 978-1-935991-99-1

Library of Congress Control Number: 2013938594

Signalman
Publishing

Also by R. Thomas Roe

The Gaelic Letters

Palm Beach Gold

Searching for America

Finding America

The Alabama Rebel

Introduction

Carousel rides of old were special for children. The young ones were drawn in by the blaring organ music joined with cymbals, bells and chimes that announced the brightly painted wooden ponies awaiting them. The children stood with mouths agape and eyes wide focusing on the pony of their choice while they waited for the carousel to pause so they could mount their chosen steed. As they handed their ticket to the attendant, they would run to their wooden racer staring up at the charging expression of speed and strength exhibited by the flaring eyes and nostrils of the fierce animal, give it a cursory pat and then crawl up onto the saddle. As the organ music again commenced and their charger began to rise and fall, their faces would flush with excitement and they would hold on for dear life as they petted their trusty steeds and gave words of encouragement while the carousel built up speed. As the ponies made their circular transit bearing their riders on to victory, there was a gold ring suspended along the route that was almost within reach of the young riders' outstretched hands. The gold ring was a trophy for whoever succeeded in possessing it—but it required courage and superior effort to secure the ring and stay on the pony. Those who succeeded earned the respect of their peers, parents and a free ride.

The phrase going for the gold ring applied to those young or old who showed great courage and spirit to achieve a goal. This novel follows the saga of two who sought the gold ring and the barriers they encountered.

R. Thomas Roe

"The thing with kids is, if they want to grab for the gold ring, you have to let them do it, and not say anything. If they fall off, they fall off, but it's bad if you say anything to them."

—Holden Caulfield, ***The Catcher in the Rye***

Chapter 1

Trey woke up with the morning sun shining on him and turning the room into an oven. It was July in Minneapolis, the one month when high temps and humidity frequently combined to make it almost unbearable—and this month was especially warm. The rest of the year in Minnesota was unpredictable, ranging from oppressive humidity to freezing temperatures. The July heat and the hungry mosquitoes created a bad combination, and right now Trey had a mosquito buzzing around him that he could not seem to target. Why the hell he had rented a room in a house without air conditioning was beyond him, but if he had he would be paying even more than the little amount he could afford now.

His thoughts reminded him that he was three days past due on the rent and the house witch was going to land on him today or tomorrow for sure. He lay in his own sweat, pondering how he was going to come up with the monthly rental payment of thirty dollars for his room. He had gone to sleep thinking about money and he woke up thinking about money or rather, the lack thereof. He had been renting here for the four years of night school at Walker College of Law, and had been handling the rental payment without major problems for most of that time, but that was when he had a job. He had lost the last job during test week four weeks ago. Since then he had been trying to decide what to do about it. He had not been fired, the company just shut down so the job loss carried no particularly bad stigma, only that he was now out of funds and had to come up with a solution soon.

He needed this small ten-by-ten room; it was his home. The one stable part of his life he liked was this room. It was comfortable and it held everything he owned except for his car, but then he didn't totally own his car either. He and the bank owned the car. As for the room, it was just a bedroom. Nothing more. The bathroom was down the hall and he shared that with three other men who were undergrad students at the college. Two of the men were just back from the war. One was a severely wounded, wheelchair-bound vet, and the other was his brother and caregiver. The vets from the war spoke a different language. Vets hung with vets and the younger students hung with their crowd. There was no animosity involved. They were just different people. For one thing, the vets in the college studied and took college very seriously.

Right now vets were not foremost on Trey's mind. He needed a job. The only good thing going for Trey right now was that he was between girlfriends and that saved him some cash. He didn't have to pick up the tab for anyone and could concentrate on getting back on his feet. He had also now graduated from law school and that was no longer a priority so he could concentrate on somehow earning enough money to pay for his keep.

Trey had interviewed with three law firms in the city and all three had turned him down flat. Mid-level or lower scholastic standing in an evening law school did not grab their attention. Trey did not want to take a job outside of the legal field if he could help it. If that appeared on his resume, it would not help him when he interviewed for a legal job full time. Interviewing for any job, part time or otherwise, that paid money was going to start in the coming week and Trey could only hope that he could find something before his few remaining bucks dwindled to nothing. He was already hitting on his credit cards for food, gas and other necessities and knew that was coming to an end. That would be just as soon as the bill came due again and he lacked the funds to pay it. That could also hurt his chances of gaining employment if his potential employer checked his credit, which they would most likely do.

As Trey pondered his financial situation, he wondered how much money he had spent in the bars last night. He had bought lovely Chris Sutton a number of drinks, even though she was with Don Macy, and many for himself as well at the graduation party. What a waste of money. Chris should have been buying him drinks as she was employed, but there was no way that was going to happen. There were ten guys after blonde-haired, well-put-together Chris Sutton and she didn't have to buy any guy drinks. Furthermore, she didn't appear to have any interest in buying Trey Stark anything. What the hell was he thinking? That was his food and rent he was throwing at the bartender. He had gotten smashed which was not his normal style, but it was a big night. Formal graduation from night law school. Four years of hell at night crawler tech and this was the final gathering of the fourth year students. All of the class that remained after four years was graduating, including Trey Stark, and he was going to make the most of it. He had spent most of this last year in "crim law" staring at Chris Sutton's back, neck and rear end four rows in front of him in class, and he was going to give that one final shot if at all possible. It was like a mountain climber staring at Mount Everest forever without reaching the very top. Last night he was headed for the top but then ran out of cash and also good lines as the alcohol took its toll. *Well, live and learn.*

Trey rolled over in the bed trying to find a spot that was not already wet with his sweat. As he did so, he thought he should get rolling as there were many things he should be doing. It was obvious to Trey that he was going to have to earn some money in order to keep his room and buy food. Even if he were successful in finding a legal job, the money would not be coming in for at least a month or more. A few years back he had worked at a company loading trucks for a somewhat decent hourly wage. He would go back there and see if he could line up a part time job.

Part time was what he needed right now if he was going to be interviewing with law firms. Part time was even harder to find these days than a full time job. This added to the dismal thoughts going through his mind as he located the clothes he had scattered around his room the night before. He took a couple of aspirins to deal with his pounding headache that his evening's activities had brought him. When he was ready to go, he placed a call on his phone to Walt Clark, his fellow classmate at Walker. They had been partners in moot court and worked together quite well—in fact, they had won their case. Walt was pretty much the same as Trey: fairly sharp, usually broke, and working the field looking for the right job. They had been together the night before at graduation and then at the Rooster's Nest, their favorite bar, where they had all gone to celebrate. As he listened to the phone ringing for his friend Walt, Trey was a bit surprised that he was still able to use his own phone service. He knew that was about to end for non-payment of his bill and he had to take care of that soon. If he lost his phone service it would severely limit his job opportunities; hard to look for a job without a phone.

Walt Clark answered the phone on about the seventh ring and it was obvious that the call had just awakened him. "Ya-lo. Clark here."

"Walt, let's get some breakfast. I'll pick you up in five, okay?"

"What the hell time is it?"

"Almost ten, Walt. Be there in five."

Trey slipped out the front door of the rooming house without being seen by Mrs. Storm, the landlady, and drove his car over to Walt's rental pad, parked and waited for Walt to appear. After a few more minutes, Walt walked out of the house making his way slowly to the car. As he opened the car door, he mumbled something about money.

"Walt I am damn near flat broke so you had better have some cash. I am not the bank. Those days are gone."

"We are all broke, Trey, especially after last night. What the hell were we trying to do? Chris Sutton turned a profit but the rest of us are in poverty. You were throwing money at her but I didn't see her throwing anything at you and she was just hired by the prestigious law firm of Fuller and Brown. Talk about a bunch of dumb shits."

"Got that right, Walt. It's all over now. I am down to serious broke and I have a ton of bills to pay. I have to find a job, any job, damn soon. Any ideas?"

"None here, Trey. I was hired by that cheese-ball law firm that I told you about, but I don't go to work until next month. I could use a short-termer right now. I'm worse off than you are, though. I have school loans of over fifty thousand dollars. What the hell was I thinking? I should have become a plumber."

"I'm right with you, Walt, thirty-seven thousand for school loans and another ten here and there. What a bunch of B.S. Then you go out and interview, and the guy just looks at you and laughs when you tell him what your grades were and where you went to school. On top of it, we have the Bar Exam coming up in about three weeks.

What a joke and the joke's on us."

"Let's go over to the diner—cheapest place I can think of. But before we drop Chris Sutton, I have to commend you. She was sort of buying your program."

"You must be on drugs. I did not get that impression. I wish it were true, though. Which one of my hokey-ass lines seemed to be doing the trick?"

"I just had the impression that she was more interested in you than she was in Don Macy. Why the hell that is, I don't know."

"Interesting."

They found a parking place directly in front of the diner, which was very unusual, and when they walked in the hostess pointed them to an empty booth. They were on a winning streak and Walt commented that this must be their lucky day. The diner was a popular eatery for both St. Thomas University and Walker law students. Both Trey and Walt had attended both schools and had been eating at the diner for years. They had stopped at the front of the diner to wait for the hostess to seat them; they weren't going to violate the diner rules by grabbing a booth on their own. That was a great way to get into trouble, ending up spending the entire evening waiting for a waitress to appear. As they sat down in their booth, one of the vets on Trey's floor at the rooming house told him his towel was hanging over the shower stall in case he was looking for it. Trey thanked him and hoped it would not become a floor mop before he retrieved it. The clientele at the diner brought in students of all ages, including the vets. It specialized in low cost but fairly healthy dinners for students as well as the general public. Both Trey and Walt were well known in the diner and as they sat waiting for a waitress, they were greeted by an older, heavy-set woman who congratulated them on their graduation and handed them menus. Her name was Maud—Trey did not know her last name—but she was always a friendly face in the diner.

"Well, you boys look as though you celebrated after your graduation. Hope you had a good time."

"Maud, we did have a good time, at least that's what my wallet says. Never again, Maud. We are turning over a new leaf as of today."

"I'm sure. Enjoy. Wave when you are ready to order."

At breakfast the two discussed possible employment opportunities. That took only a few minutes and both concluded that they would check the want ads later for anything and then prepare a short talk for the interview on how they had always wanted to work in a warehouse. They would not mention anything about law school. That would be the kiss of death for quick employment as menial laborers, part or full time. Employers looking to hire warehouse workers were not totally stupid. They wanted warehouse workers that wanted a long-term career in a warehouse, not just for a few weeks until they finally found a job in a law firm.

After they had finished the Saturday special at two-fifty a copy, Trey mentioned the advice his father had given him when Trey had told him he would be looking for a job with a law firm. "Get this, Walt. He told me I should become a nurse as the pay was decent and I could practice law on the side. That way I could earn enough to survive. He must have been panic-stricken that I was going to be moving back into the house."

"Trey, not a bad idea if you could handle the bedpans. Not for me. Your father obviously preferred a son who was a nurse emptying bedpans to a son who was unemployed. Actually it is not a bad idea. Maybe you could become a non-bedpan emptying nurse if there is such a thing. If so, I'd take it on. Nurses get hired. New lawyers from night law schools don't. Fact of life."

"Four years right down the drain—maybe not, though. Hell, you got a job. Maybe I can find one somewhere. My problem is they are not too dazzled by my grades. Like one guy said to me, 'Why should I hire you when I can find a hundred guys who were in the top third of their class in real law schools?' You know what I told that guy?"

"I give, what?"

"I told him those hundred guys didn't have half the fun that I had. I thought it was funny but the stiff dork wasn't laughing. That was sort of the end of the interview. I will have to drop that from my repertoire. You should have seen his face; that was the best part. He just stopped talking, mouth open, and stared at me. I could see what he was thinking—this guy can't be real."

After breakfast, Trey returned to his room and pored over the classifieds for "Help Wanted." There were no openings listed for law firm or legal work, which he did not expect to find, but there were a few openings for full or part time labor at minimum wage rates and Trey wrote the numbers down for future reference. He would also check the locations, since driving distance could be a factor with the rising cost of gasoline, plus his car was becoming less dependable every day.

He also looked up the phone number of the company he had worked for a few years prior when he found himself in a similar situation. That was outside work, from midnight to eight in the morning. He had almost frozen to death until he had made enough money to purchase some thermal boots. But that was during the winter, and wintertime in Minnesota was a real challenge, especially with outside work. It was even colder at night and that was when he was out there loading the trucks. The boots helped a lot but he still was frozen most of the time on the job. He still had the boots so at least he didn't have to buy another pair but he sure as hell was not going to need them for a few months.

It was hard to dress warm when the outside temp hovered around twenty to thirty below zero most of the time between the hours of midnight to eight a.m. The wind was the real killer. When it was thirty below and the wind was blowing at twenty to thirty, the wind chill was way the hell down there. Well, he wouldn't have to worry about that for a while.

Trey went through the phone numbers he had written down and began with the few listings that sounded as though they could be inside jobs. As he later learned, they were all outside jobs. Employers that had inside jobs at minimum wages did not have to advertise. All they had to do was to answer the phone. The first two jobs were located approximately twenty miles from his home so he noted them as undesirable. The pay would barely cover his gas costs. His pig car loved to swig gas. The third was fairly close by but when he called, they had already filled their quota of new hires. Finally he called his former employer and they were willing to take him on as a full time employee. No part time work available but by that time he had figured out that part time would not give him enough cash to even start to pay up some past due items. He was to start Monday evening, again on the night shift and the work was outside loading the trucks. The night shift was what Trey preferred even though it was colder work in the wintertime; it permitted him to do some interviewing during the daylight hours. Night interviews were not an option when working days.

Trey drove over to his law school to research job opportunities in the library. There were some employment opportunities tacked to the board in the library. These were generally the least desirable legal jobs in town and were usually avoided by all graduates in the top four-fifths of the class. They were the sort of jobs you didn't want to have on your resume a few years down the road when you were again interviewing for a real law firm job. Nevertheless, Trey wrote down the company names and phone numbers so that he could call them later if he had no better luck elsewhere. Trey then went to the legal directories and began reviewing the law firms in Minneapolis and Saint Paul. He wrote down the names and telephone numbers of firms that he considered potential targets. He avoided the so-called blue chip firms as he was well aware that he was not a potential candidate for them. He also steered clear of the larger law firms regardless of their rating. He wanted to get into a smaller size firm of under ten attorneys, if at all possible. A smaller firm, in his mind, would not be as involved in office politics as much as a larger firm with thirty bottom dwellers fighting for recognition.

Trey spent the better part of the day working in the library, stopping by the diner for a sandwich before returning to his room. Maud waited on him and suggested a meat loaf dinner that was receiving high praise. She also told him he looked better than the last time she had seen him.

"Why, thank you, Maud. I feel a heck of a lot better now than I did then. I should be cured by tomorrow."

"Sure hope so, Trey. Enjoy."

After dinner he returned to his room and the landlady was waiting for him when he entered the house. She looked at him with a frown on her face and said, "Trey, your rent check is not here. Why not?"

"Mrs. Storm, I will be late this month. I lost my job a couple of weeks ago but I just lined up another one. I'll have my rent money in about a week after I start and I'm starting that job next Monday. I should be okay after that."

"Don't let that happen again, Trey. We all have bills to pay."

"Thanks, Mrs. Storm. Won't happen again."

Trey made his way upstairs to his room somewhat relieved that he had dodged another bullet. He thought about calling the phone company as he knew they were about to cancel his service and right now that would be the kiss of death as he had the phone number on all of the resumes that he had sent out or was going to be sending out. He would wait another day and then call them. He did not want to be promising too much in view of the fact that he owed a number of service providers funds that they were after. His credit cards were about to be blocked and he needed them for his very survival. One thing about the credit cards was that they would be calling him soon and he could make promises to them at that time. They usually called before actually shutting down the credit. Hopefully he could come up with the minimum payment due when cash started to roll in.

Trey laid down in his bed, tired from the activities of the day not to mention the hours spent in the bars the evening before. He was pleased that he had made some progress in resolving his many financial problems but still had a long ways to go. He thought about the forthcoming Bar Exam that would determine his eligibility to become a "real lawyer." The entire process was beginning to bore him. He had less than a month to finish his review for the exam and had been reviewing over the past semester as he had taken some of the test subjects four years previous and undoubtedly forgotten a great deal. He had always done quite well in tests, but the new Bar Exam was considered a very high hurdle to pass. Among the all right or all wrong answers of the multiple-choice questions were most right or least wrong correct choices. He was taking a refresher course at the present time to assist him in dealing with the new exam. Hopefully that would prepare him sufficiently. He could not imagine what he would do if he failed the test. With the time intervals between Bar Exams, he would be looking at a delay of approximately a year in becoming licensed if he failed the test. That was the primary motivation for his getting serious about his review work. He had seen some progress in doing the review work. The multiple-choice questions under the new format were very difficult and he was going through a learning process as he was now doing better on them than he had been doing when he first started.

As he pondered the possibility of failing the Bar, it reminded him of his conversation with Walt in the morning. Maybe he should have become a nurse. He had no great driving ambition to be a lawyer. That was just something that he had considered as at the time nothing else was looming on the horizon. Trey had known a few lawyers and he had a generally favorable opinion of the profession but no driving thirst to actually become a lawyer. It was a wonder he had passed all of his courses and arrived at this point with the limited interest he had in becoming a lawyer. As he thought about the time in his life when he was formulating his opinion on a legal education, he recalled that what had initially interested him was his desire to do research and investigate issues searching for data that supported something he was interested in. He knew that was important in the legal profession and he did enjoy that. He had worked on a few projects in his schooling where he had to delve deeply into issues with library research. He surprisingly enjoyed that, which made him think he would possibly enjoy legal work. He knew product liability practice involved much research. Telling people that he was studying law always received a favorable response and maybe that was his prime motivation. He had doubts about his decision to go into law but he also had no other vocations that appeared better for him.

The whole concept of aptitude for one career course over another was a mystery to Trey. *How the hell do I know what I would be good at or would enjoy. For that matter what is more important, being good at something or enjoying it? What the hell does a young guy know about life that would tell him where he should go?* He had taken tests for aptitude in high school but some of the suggestions were almost comical. He had no idea what had produced the half dozen career fields the tests indicated. Interestingly, law was not one of the suggestions.

On top of that, it did not appear when he finished his undergrad that he was all that employable. Now that he was finishing law school with his new accreditation that had produced most of the enormous student loan that hovered over his head he was no more employable than when he had finished his undergrad.

Why the hell did I ever decide to become a lawyer? Maybe I wanted to run for governor or congress or something. I had never really thought about the type of work I would be doing. Never yearned for it. Isn't that what you are supposed to do when you want to become something? You are supposed to yearn for it. I never yearned for anything other than Chris Sutton and I apparently flunked that course as well. Yearn wasn't even in my vocabulary. Well, I'd better yearn to get myself out of this mess I'm in now. Saturday night and here I am. Crashed in my pad. No date but what the hell would I do if I had one? No money, no babe that wants to ruin her evening with Trey Stark. God, I'm in a horseshit mood.

Trey finally picked up a novel he had started weeks before and never finished. He read for a while and then fell asleep seven pages in. He was sleeping soundly when the phone rang. He dreamed the phone was ringing and finally realized it was. When he picked up the phone, it was Walt Clark asking him, "What's up? You going out tonight or are you going to rot in your pad?"

"I don't know. I don't think I want to get hammered again. I'm too broke to go to a movie. Maybe I'll just stay here and read or wait for Chris Sutton to call me."

"Yeah. That makes sense. Maybe I'll do the same. We can both wait for Chris to call. Maybe one of us will get lucky."

"I'd suggest you buy a lotto ticket. Chances are much better."

"Okay, I'll see you at breakfast at the diner. Say about ten. Okay?"

"Sounds good."

Trey rolled over and slept soundly until sometime after two a.m. when he awoke and realized he was still dressed. He threw his pants and shirt in the chair and crawled under the covers. He thought about Chris Sutton for a few minutes and then was sound asleep.

Chapter 2

The next afternoon being Sunday, Walt and Trey were sitting out at the patio bar at the Lakeside Bar on Lake Minnetonka, the usual Sunday meeting place for the younger set from the west side of Minneapolis. The two weren't talking. They were nursing their beers while checking over the young ladies that were crowding into the bar. Some of them they knew but most they did not know. As they stared out over the crowd, Walt spoke up. "Well, what do you know? There is Chris Sutton. Do you suppose she followed me here? She's with that dork, Don Macy. Shall we invite them over? They seem to be looking for a place to sit."

"I know where Sutton can sit. Wave them over if they look your way. You can talk to Macy and I will chat with Chris. Oh, by the way, I'm not buying any drinks. I'm not even drinking anymore today. I don't want to give the wrong impression. Maybe we can shame Macy into popping for a few rounds. I don't recall that he was a big spender Friday night. I should lay off of Macy. I think we hate him mainly because he was the top student in our class. Really not a bad guy."

Their two former classmates spotted them sitting at their table and headed their way. As they approached, Macy asked if they could join them and Trey told them to have a chair. Chris commented that Trey looked much better today than he did the last time she saw him Friday evening.

Trey replied that he had been very tired Friday evening as he had been burning the midnight oil studying for the Bar refresher. Chris just smiled and said, "Yes. That will do it. I've got to start hitting that harder now. We will be taking the Bar in just a few more weeks, Trey."

"Yes. I could use a few more months. I've been at it most of this semester but that has been a bit here and a bit there."

Macy just laughed. "The Bar is a piece of cake. I'll worry about that next month. Remember, about ninety percent pass the damn thing. Can't be too hard. Look at the competition and then relax."

Chris said, "Easy for you to say, mister number-one-in-the-class. Some of us have to study."

Trey thought a moment and said, "The problem is that if you flunk you lose about a year out of your life before you are again on speed. That is what bothers me."

Chris looked at Trey and said, "Good point, Trey. That has always been my concern as well. Maybe we should study together."

Walt now began bumping his shoe against Trey's leg.

Trey thought about what to say and finally commented, "I hate to say it, Chris, but I have to study alone. I just don't do well in the group study scene. I'd be glad to meet with you every now and then to share progress notes and so forth. I'm going to start studying big time tomorrow and will be for the next three weeks until the exam. The part of the exam that concerns me is the new multiple-choice test. I have been working on the practice exams for that and I swear, I'm looking at four correct or four incorrect answers—and which one is the right answer, I have no idea. Yet, I am making some progress as I am doing better on the practice quizzes as time goes on. As for the essay portion, that does not bother me half as much."

Chris nodded. "I totally agree. I have looked at some of those questions and they are tough. When you are downtown, Trey, give me a shout. You know, I'm at Fuller and Brown and we can have lunch. You can tell me how to deal with the multiple-choice. I can use all the help I can get."

"I'll do that, Chris. I have picked up some clues on how to get by them but then that may just be my imagination. I have looked over some of my corrected practice exams and examined the wrong answers, and sometimes I see the clue that I should have seen when I took the exam. On the other hand there are many that I got wrong and I can't see what was so good about the correct answer. I also have to find a job. Congratulations on lining up your job. That is a good firm from what I hear."

"Yes. Fuller and Brown—Old Fags and Bags. I am told I will eventually be working in the litigation department so I'm mighty pleased. Hate to flunk the Bar and get canned right off the bat so I have to work on the exam. If you don't call me, I will give you a call and maybe we can have lunch and go over what we are coming up with."

"Sounds good to me, Chris. Macy, I suppose you have about ten firms fighting to hire you, right?"

"Not that many, Trey. I think I'm going to go with Taylor Caldwell, also in the litigation area. They've made a pretty decent offer and I like the sound of the practice areas they work in."

"That's great, Don. You did good work at Walker and it paid off."

The four sat around talking for another half hour before Don Macy offered to buy a round of drinks. Trey said he was not drinking but as the waitress came up to take their order, he decided he would have just one as he had to get home. Walt said he would join him, as he had to leave as well.

When Trey and Walt were driving back towards Minneapolis, Walt spoke up and said, "I can't believe you turned down Chris's offer to study with you. I would have been all over that."

"Walt, I am at a point in my life when I can't screw around with some things. Studying for the Bar with Chris Sutton would be screwing around. I would be thinking of ways to get her in my clutches and I would get the all-time lowest Bar score. Thanks, but no thanks."

"Yeah, maybe."

"Walt, why did you decide to become a lawyer and go to law school?"

"Parental guidance. No real reason. My degree in sociology was not producing too many job offers, at least not offers that I would be willing to take."

"Sounds as though you were as motivated as I was. Now we sit here with student loans up the ying yang. Not too smart."

Trey had his first appointment at one p.m. the following day. He removed some spots from his one and only time-worn suit and wiped off his one pair of shoes. His tie was beyond repair and he tried to clean off some of the larger, more noticeable stains and let the rest go. He put some resumes in his briefcase and some business cards he had printed up in his shirt pocket so he could leave a few with whoever he was talking with. After putting two dollars worth of gas in his car, he drove to downtown Minneapolis for his interview with the Gailsworth Law firm. This was a fifty-member law firm, much larger than what he was most interested in. They held themselves out as a business law firm but were more into collection and debt practice than anything else. When Trey told the receptionist that he had an appointment with Mr. Travis, she handed him a questionnaire to fill out and deliver to Mr. Travis when he met him. It was obvious to Trey that this Travis guy was the regular interviewer and most likely this was about all that he did for the firm. Hell of a life.

After a forty-seven minute wait, Trey was finally admitted to Mr. Travis' office. Trey handed his completed questionnaire to the interviewer and was told to take a seat at the chair directly in front of his desk. Trey glanced around the sparse office half expecting to find a single burning light bulb directly over his chair. The office had the appearance of a storeroom—bare furnishings, small desk, wooden chairs, cheap artwork on the walls. No plush furnishings here. Travis was wearing a suit that was showing more wear and less care than the one that Trey was wearing. For a moment Trey wondered why Travis had not bothered to clean off the three food stains he could observe on the front of his suit coat. He thought about suggesting a rag and cold water as a solution but passed on that.

After a brief review of the questionnaire, Travis finally spoke. "Mr. Stark, what brings you to the Gailsworth firm? I see you just graduated from Walker. I assume you would like to work for our firm. Why have you selected our firm?"

Trey thought, what a damn stupid question but he quickly put together a response. "Well, sir, I have heard that the Gailsworth firm is a very good firm to work for. I have a strong interest in business law and all aspects of it, including debt practice, and I would like the opportunity to show you that I would be a good addition to your staff wherever you placed me."

"That is commendable. I note that your standing in the class was in the lower half. Is there a reason why you did not do better scholastically?"

"Sir, I had to work my way through night law school and I was working approximately fifty hours a week besides carrying a full load at the school. My parents were not doing very well financially and needed my help. Had I not been obligated to help them out, I would have undoubtedly been in the upper third at least. I am fairly intelligent and have always excelled academically."

"Hm, interesting. I note your undergrad grades were barely passing, however."

"Yes. Again I was working outside eight hours a night loading trucks and carrying a full load at Normandale Junior College. That was a very tough school that prided itself in making high demands on the students. If I had wealthy parents paying my bills like the rest of my classmates, I would have been an honor grad, but such was just not the case. My dad used to say, 'If you want to go to school, you are going to have to pay for it on your own.' I did pay for it on my own and as a result, I was working close to forty hours per week in high school, college, and law school."

"Mr. Stark, what do you think about working in the area of collection practice? We do have openings in that area and you could possibly fit in there."

"I would be honored, sir, to work in the collection area for the Gailsworth firm. I have always considered it everyone's primary duty in life to pay their bills on time. My credit has been impeccable and it bothers me that I have to pay higher prices for goods due to the fact so many people today are not paying for the bills that they have incurred. It actually makes me angry. I know that I am paying part of their bill when I buy something. That really angers me and I would consider it an opportunity to go after those deadbeats."

"Very interesting, Mr. Stark. I like your enthusiasm for that type of practice. I will provide your information to Mr. Stone, who will be making the selections. I made a note of your enthusiasm for that particular area and I think he will like that. I have your phone number and if everything goes fine, we will be calling you for a follow-up interview."

"That would be great, Mr. Travis. Thank you very much for taking the time to interview me. I would greatly appreciate the honor of working for the Gailsworth Law firm and let me assure you, you would never regret having hired me. Thanks again, Mr. Travis."

Trey had another appointment at three p.m. and fortunately it was not too far from the Gailsworth firm as he had spent more time there than he had estimated. Within a matter of minutes he was in the lobby of the Chesterton Billings Law firm. This was a mid-level firm in Minneapolis with concentration in the litigation and Business Law areas. There was no mention of their being involved in debt practice or the collections area. Again this was a slightly larger firm of seventeen lawyers, but Trey knew two of the associates that were working there had graduated from Walker, so he put it down as a possibility. Some firms would not interview Walker grads, which did not make a lot of sense as it was a fine school and known to turn out competent lawyers. The fact that it was primarily an evening law school was what they hung their hat on to allow them to discriminate. Trey did not follow the logic of that but that's the way it was.

Trey was not given a questionnaire to fill out from the receptionist but was told he would be meeting mister so and so in a few minutes. As Trey sat down in one of the chairs in the lobby, he realized he could not remember the name of the interviewer. He would have to check his name tag if he had one and make a note of that. Not a good start. As the minutes dragged by, Trey hoped that he was not looking at another forty-seven minute wait as he had experienced at the Gailsworth firm.

Trey began wondering again why he had ever decided to pursue a legal career. He had grown up in Minneapolis and became a bit serious about his future when he was a student at De La Salle High School, which was a Catholic Christian Brothers school that had been educating Minneapolis young men for close to a hundred years. They had become co-educational some years back before Trey had started to attend. It was there that Trey first considered the law practice as a profession for him. After a number of years it just became for him the course of study that he would pursue. He'd had some experiences at De La Salle that made him consider law as a vocation. He had been on the debate team for one semester and found that interesting but primarily by reason of the research involved in preparing the arguments.

Trey's parents were non-committal about Trey's interests in the legal field as they were aware that law school could be an expensive course of study that they would have to financially support at least to some extent. His parents were not wealthy and neither of them had attended college so they had mixed feelings as to his intention to move on to college after high school but they were generally in favor of his further education. Trey's father, who had not even attended high school, was in charge of inventory in a retail chain operation. He did not make a great deal of money but he made enough to provide for his family. He had always tried to impress upon Trey, as he was growing up, the benefits of work and saving money.

Trey took some of this training to heart but only enough to prevent an argument. Trey's parents, Dan and Mary Stark, led simple lives with minimal outside diversions. They had sufficient money for the necessities of life but very little for the occasional pleasures that came their way. While they were not flush with cash, they were much better off than Trey had portrayed them in his interviews, but nevertheless Trey was not lavished with gifts or experiences in life that a young man may have wished to pursue. Trey did not enjoy the experience of summer camp or travel to areas of the country that some of his friends enjoyed. He did not regret not having these experiences, as he was well aware of his family's fiscal limitations. One thing Trey learned from his father was to take advantage of the knowledge contained in books, both fiction and non-fiction. Trey was an avid reader and had always been impressed by his father's grasp of knowledge that came from the many books that filled bookshelves around the house. His father was always short of funds but he managed to accumulate a sizeable library.

As Trey thought about his upbringing, he was aware he had received a great education at De La Salle, which being a private school was an expensive undertaking for his family. Many of his less fortunate or non-Catholic friends were students at Washburn, the public school that provided education for a good share of the students in south Minneapolis. He regretted that he had not been a better student at De La Salle but back then he just wasn't as focused on that as he should have been. He particularly regretted his lack of focus as he now sat in the law firm lobby awaiting his interview. He checked his watch and noted that he had been waiting thirty-seven minutes. He wondered if they kept Don Macy waiting this long for his interviews. He doubted it. Trey did not really dislike Don Macy. He attributed his attitude towards Macy as a product of some envy and to the fact that Chris Sutton seemed to be attracted to Macy. Trey did not appreciate Macy's somewhat imperious manner of lording his high law school grades over the other students. Macy suffered a bit from a case of arrogance that irritated Trey, and Walt was of the same opinion. As Walt frequently said, "He's just not like us."

After another twenty minute wait, Trey was about to doze off when he realized someone was calling his name and when he looked up there was a young appearing suit searching the lobby for him. Trey snapped up and announced he was Trey Stark. The young man smiled and told Trey to follow him to his office.

As Trey was seated in the office for his interview, the young man introduced himself and prepared a notepad and pen to take notes from the interview. While he did so, Trey studied his interviewer. Trey figured he was not much older than Trey and must be a fairly recent law school grad as well. Trey did not recognize him however, which told Trey that he was not a Walker grad. He was wearing a good quality unblemished suit and appeared comfortable and confident in his superior role to the hungry applicant who nervously awaited his questions, which then commenced.

"Mr. Stark, I understand you are here interviewing for a job. Did you bring a resume with you?"

"Oh, yes. Here is my resume…sir." He had already forgotten the fellow's name.

The interviewer reviewed the data on Trey's resume and then looked up at Trey and asked him why he had sought an interview with the Chesterton firm.

Trey told him that the firm had an excellent reputation among the students at Walker and he was interested in the areas of practice that the firm participated in. Trey mentioned that a number of students from Walker had worked for the Chesterton firm in the past and some were there at the present time.

The interviewer, whose name was not coming back to Trey, mentioned that he was aware the firm had hired some of the students from Trey's school but they also interviewed graduates from the University of Minnesota, Harvard—where he attended law school—and schools around the country. "Trey, why do you think our firm should hire you to join our staff?"

Trey had the definite opinion this guy was no way in hell going to hire him for anything so he responded in jocular fashion. "Because I am a smart young guy that will make a lot of money for the firm. I like to work. I don't B.S. and I have a cousin that was just in a serious accident, seriously injured, and I am sure I could bring that case into the firm."

The interviewer sat back in his chair with a bit of a stunned expression on his face, probably from the fact the hook was halfway down his throat. Trey could tell that he was trying to think of what to say. Now Trey had the impression that the tables were turned and now he was the interviewer.

Finally the interviewer spoke. "Interesting. I doubt your cousin's case would be of interest to the firm, but tell me a bit about it."

Trey was not about to tell him anything about the accident because the story was B.S. but he was going to ride this pony all the way to the barn just for the fun of it. He was tired of being played with in these interviews. "Well, I don't want to reveal too many facts or you will have your runners out trying to pick up the case. I will just say it appears my cousin, who is in his twenties, will be paralyzed for the rest of his life and the accident was not his fault. Oh yes, and there is a pile of insurance on the other side. That's all I will say about it. Now, what else can I tell you about my qualifications for a job here?"

"First of all, Mr. Stark, we do not have runners. Secondly, there would be follow-up interviews before you would ever be hired by this firm and I would suggest that you not mention this case in future interviews if you even have them. We do not hire on the basis of what connections our applicants may have or may not have."

Trey noticed the emphasis on "not have" but figured that was all for show. He would just add to the story a bit. "Oh, I was not men-tioning my cousin's case in hopes of getting a job. I just thought you might find it interesting being a lawyer and all that I would likely be bringing some business to the firm. No, I wouldn't do anything like that."

"Let me just get some information from you. The address and telephone on the resume are good at this time, I assume."

"Yes. All of the information there is current and correct."

"I note your grades were not spectacular. Any reason for that?"

"I was working full time all through undergrad and law school, which kept my grades down. I had to put myself through law school, was working around fifty hours a week, and had to provide my par-ents with part of my income to help with their money problems. If it were not for that, I would have been on the Dean's list all of the time. I barely had time to study."

"Okay, Mr. Stark. We will take a look at your resume and if the firm is interested, someone will be calling you for a follow-up in-terview."

"Great. Thank you, thank you very much. I am a good worker and would like to have the opportunity to show you what a good worker I am. Thanks for the interview."

That evening in the diner, Trey described the two interviews to Walt. Walt thought his comment to Gailsworth that he wanted to go after those deadbeats was priceless. "Trey, if they check your credit, they will see that you were pulling their leg."

"Walt, I don't really give a damn. It's a skanky ass firm but I may have to take them up if they come up with an offer. They apparently need attorneys for their collection work and I do believe they will call."

"You might as well not even talk to Chesterton. Your cousin story is not going to float."

"They may bring me on board for a month or more and I can string them along for a while. They may forget about the cousin after a while."

"I don't think so."

"Well, it was fun."

"I suggest you drop the B.S., or word will get out and you will never get a job."

"Yeah, maybe."

In the following days, Trey worked the night shift loading trucks from midnight until eight in the morning and then interviewing most of the mornings with occasional afternoon interviews when he could not reschedule them for the mornings. His grades were killing him in these interviews. A few of the interviewers told him that his grades put him out of the market but he could possibly get a job in collections or in the insurance industry and he should try them. Trey thanked them all and figured there was no way in hell in this market that he was going to find a job in a regular law firm. After a while he decided he would concentrate on studying for the Bar Exam as the time was drawing short and skip any more interviews unless he was called in for follow-up interviews. It was most important that he pass the Bar on this attempt; another year lost would be disastrous. If he did not get a law firm job, he would go out on his own.

Chapter 3

During his second week interviewing, the Chesterton firm did call him back for a follow-up interview. At first he decided not to call them back as it would just be a dead end street. But after further thought, he decided to see what they had to say. When he returned to their office for the follow-up interview he was not kept waiting. The receptionist buzzed a Mr. Wilson and within twenty seconds, Trey was seated in the very impressive office of Mr. Douglas Wilson, who was listed as a partner in the firm. Various awards and Bar Association certificates adorned the walls of his office along with photographs of Wilson in the company of known figures in the state, including the governor and some in the national political scene.

Wilson had a copy of Trey's resume and discussed some of the items recorded thereon. He then leaned back in his chair and asked him what type of work he wanted to get involved with at the Chesterton firm.

Trey was a bit awed by the apparent results of his "cousin story" and was beginning to think Walt was right in his warning that this could have adverse effects. "Well, sir, I would like to get into litigation as that is where I believe I would be best suited. I think product liability would be very interesting. I am good at research and I know a good product liability attorney has to be good at that. Furthermore, your firm has a good reputation and I would like to be part of that."

"Trey, Connie tells me you have a cousin that had a very unfortunate accident. How is he doing now?"

"He's doing better than he was so we are hoping that he may avoid the more serious consequences it appeared at first that he would have. Much better."

Wilson was now staring at Trey trying to figure out what was going on with the cousin story. He was a very busy attorney and had been "sigged" onto this interview solely for the possibility that it may involve a good case for the firm. He did not like wasting his time on B.S. "So you are telling me that it does not look like your cousin will suffer paralysis as a result of this accident, is that right?"

"That is what we are hoping, but one never knows. I get the information third hand so I may not know for some time what the final outcome is."

Wilson decided to get right down to the basics. "Trey, if your cousin did end up with serious disability, do you think you could bring the case to the firm, or is that out of the question?"

"I think I could, but then his parents might have other ideas. They all know I am out in the legal world now having just graduated from Walker and they have always had confidence in my opinions. I can't see them taking it to someone else."

"Where is your cousin now?"

"Oh, he is still in the hospital. For sure—I don't think they will have any quick answers on his condition. That is the message I am getting."

"What hospital is he in, Trey?"

"Well, I hesitate to say as I don't want people bothering him before he's ready for that."

"Trey, I would suggest that we have our investigator gather facts on the case as time is moving and you don't want evidence to be lost because no one investigated the case."

"Oh, Mr. Wilson, I have taken steps to preserve all of the evidence. Photographs, names of witnesses, information on the instrumentalities involved in the accident—I've preserved all items of evidence related to the accident. I have been working on that full time. So don't worry about that. No, sir."

After another suitable pause, Wilson continued the interview. "Have you had any job offers so far from other firms?"

"I have had two offers from P.I. firms that I am currently considering. Both offers are decent but I think they are both interested in my cousin's accident and I want to go with a firm that wants to hire me for me and not for what I could bring to the firm right now. I will bring more than that case in the future because I am a hustler and I will get the cases."

"Who are the P.I. firms that made the offers?"

"Oh, Mr. Wilson, they requested that any offers from them were to be held in strict confidence and I assured them that would be the case."

Wilson could see that he was getting nowhere and decided to bring the interview to a close. "Trey, I'll be frank. Your grades are… not impressive, but I get the impression that you are quite a cagey guy. You have the makings of a good litigator. Your story about your cousin is very interesting for two reasons. One, it sounds like it could be a good case for the firm. Also, it sounds like a great B.S. story for a young attorney to get hired by a decent law firm. Now I am sitting here wondering which it is but both of the interpretations leave me with a good impression of you. I like people with imagination who want to be litigators and I think you fit in that category. I'll tell you what I will do. If your cousin's case ever evolves, call me and I will hire you on the spot and let you assist on the case. If it is B.S., and you have not been hired by anyone as I think that is also a very likely outcome, call me and I may take another look at you. Is that a deal?"

"That's a deal, Mr. Wilson. Thank you. Thank you very much. I most likely will be in touch sometime in the future."

"Yes, Trey. I believe you will."

That evening in the diner, Trey told Walt of his follow-up interview with the Chesterton firm. Wilson impressed Walt. "You are lucky you ran into a guy with a brain. Most of these law firm dorks that handle the interviews are brain dead. They get all wrapped up in your grades, your connections, how polite you are and that is it. This guy thinks. Your B.S. story impressed him. So, now what are you going to do?"

"I've already decided. I have stopped all interviews and I am studying for the Bar. I have got to devote every spare minute to that. If I don't get a job, I will open my own shop either in my home or somewhere else. I expect a job from the collection firm, Gailsworth. If they offer me a job, I will call Wilson for a meeting. I will tell him the story is all B.S. and commend him for the way he handled this. I will tell him I want a job with Chesterton in P.I. work. I don't care about the pay as long as I can live on it, but I will talk about that months later when he can see how I produce. If he does not hire me, I am going to work in collections until I get my bills paid. Then I will see what is available or maybe go out on my own. That's my plan and I'm sticking to it. May even become a nurse."

"I guess I can throw away my crutches then, Trey. I figured your story would work its way down to them coming to see the cousin who was miraculously now able to stand and walk with crutches. I had it all figured out, right down to throwing the crutches aside and screaming, 'I can walk! I'm not paralyzed!'"

"Walt, that would be worth seeing. I swear to God, if a law firm saw that performance, they would hire both of us."

Maud served them their dinners and commented that both of them would make excellent attorneys. "Just keep your spirits up, boys, and you will do just fine. I can spot winners and you two are winners."

"Maud, that is the nicest thing anyone has said to me in a very long time. Thanks. It's due to the fine food at the diner if we have any good qualities. When we become rich and famous, we will still dine at the diner, right, Walt?"

"You damn betcha'."

Trey finished all but two interviews that he had scheduled previously, and dropped the cousin story from his repertoire as Trey knew that just led to problems and he had enough of those already. None of his interviews appeared fruitful. They always ended with suggestions he look for work in the insurance industry or in collections. It was a week after his interview at the Gailsworth firm when his phone rang. It was Mr. Travis calling him to see if he was still available for work. Trey answered that he was and Travis told him to come in for a follow-up interview and the likely possibility that he would be offered a job in their collections area. Trey thanked him profusely and made an appointment for the following morning at ten a.m. for an interview with a Mr. Stone in the collection area.

Trey pondered how to handle this situation where he was fairly sure that he would be offered a job but he could not turn them down as his creditors were becoming more difficult every day to give him more time to pay his bills. He would try to delay a starting day at Gailsworth for a week or two to give him time to deal with Chesterton and also to have the time to study for the Bar. He met with Mr. Stone at the appointed time, and by eleven a.m. he had an offer at a wage rate that with some organization on his part would get his debts at least under control within a year or so. He then returned to his room and planned his call to Wilson at Chesterton.

Trey called Wilson that afternoon and made an appointment for an interview. His appointment was for the following afternoon at two, which meant that he would get only a few hours sleep before his interview. The next day he tried to sleep when he returned to his room after loading trucks all night long but kept thinking about how to handle the interview and consequently never did sleep. At two he was sitting in the Chesterton reception area and was quickly routed to Mr. Wilson's office.

Trey walked in and Wilson was sitting at his desk smiling. "Good afternoon, Mr. Stark. I hope you have been doing well."

"Not too badly, Mr. Wilson. I appreciate your seeing me again. I have some things I would like to tell you and then a request I would like to make."

"I'm all ears, Mr. Stark. Are you bringing us a case?"

"Not exactly, Mr. Wilson. As you most likely suspected, there is no cousin and no case. Let me explain that a bit. The reason the story came up is your interviewer was about the third dweeb in a row that was interviewing me. He may be a good guy but he just hit me wrong. It was apparent to me that there was no way in hell he was ever going to put his stamp of approval on me with his signature. I thought I might as well have a little fun in the process. Unfortunately the story then took off on its own. Now I would very much like to work for the Chesterton firm. I know that I would be a good, effective litigator for the firm. I am fully aware that my grades do not ring bells for me but what I would like to offer is this. I would like to join the firm at a wage that would allow me to survive. That is it. Low ball on the salary with a review say in six months to see if I deserve more, which I believe I would. Minimal cost to your firm.

You could even label me as temporary help so you didn't get nailed on the cost of any benefits or whatever. That is about it. Any questions that I might answer?"

Wilson was smiling as he pondered what to say. "Interesting. I thought the cousin story was phony but I enjoyed it. Not many potential employers would have enjoyed it but I'm sure you thought of that as well."

"Yes, I did. I dropped that from my program in my other interviews."

"So, where are you in the interviews? Have you been hired yet, or pondering a number of offers by chance?"

"I do have an offer but not one I would like to accept. I may be forced to, though, as funds are limited, so to speak."

"So, what are your intentions?"

"I would like to work for Chesterton under the terms I just mentioned."

"I see. I will have to think about that. We are not so hard pressed that lowering the cost to hire someone would be a major consideration for us but I will consider it. My initial reaction is that we will not be hiring you, at least at the present time. I do like you as an employee and may consider you in the future, given more time to consider your application. I suggest you take the job that you have been offered and look me up in a year or so and we can discuss this again. That is the best I can do at this time."

"Thank you, Mr. Wilson. I will contact you again in the future and if you feel that you could use my services before then, please give me a call at the number on my resume. I would very much like to work for Chesterton and I know I would do well here. Thanks again for seeing me today."

The two men shook hands and Trey left the firm. He had not been hired but in view of what had taken place, he had not done too badly. He would call Gailsworth when he returned home and accept their offer of employment.

Trey made arrangements with Gailsworth to commence work the following Monday morning. When he appeared at the firm for his first day of work, he was shown his new office. His office was a small cubicle similar to ten others in the back of the work area. His desk was a sheet of three-quarter-inch plywood built on a fairly stable stand with a double file cabinet built into one side. A very used computer was sitting roughly in the center of the desktop; it was not exactly an impressive office. There were other young attorneys, male and female, busy making telephone calls and filling out contact data on their calls to clients, creditors and others involved in the payment or non-payment of debts owed to their clients.

Trey was considered on training status with regular pay, which would last for a two-week period where he would learn the methods used by the firm to collect funds. Only a few of the clients were people or companies that had performed a service and had never been paid. Most of their files were purchased on the debt market for pennies on the dollar. The firm bought them by the thousands, and upon collection represented a solid profit for Gailsworth. There were companies that marketed only bulk debt accounts and these eventually went to companies or firms such as Gailsworth. All of the debts they purchased were bought at huge discounts and had already been massaged by debt collectors across the country. The debts Gailsworth was purchasing represented the last gasp attempt to produce money from the debt. Surprisingly enough, there were sufficient collections produced by these debts to amply reward the collection agent. A satisfactory collection on these accounts ranged anywhere from five to ten percent of the balance owing.

Trey spent one solid week training along with three other new collectors, learning under the supervision of Ted Abramson who had been with the firm for a number of years. Abramson had a regular office so most of the group learning sessions occurred in his office. One of the other three trainees was not an attorney but had worked in collections previously. Of the other two, one was a female that had attended law school out of state and the other was a graduate of Lambert College of Law, another night law school in Minneapolis.

When Abramson had the trainees in his office for his initial session he impressed upon them that the secret to making money on collections was a matter of time expenditure. Minimal time on files was the name of the game. Let the deadbeat know they would be paying no matter what else they may believe. Then they would get a default judgment in the event the debt had not yet been reduced to judgment. When those steps were completed, they would tell the debtor that they or other family members are liable on the debt, whether they are or not. Typically, they would let the wife know that she must pay the debt if her husband does not. If the husband had passed away, the wife was told she was liable at law for his debts and must pay on this debt. The same general rule applied to parents of the debtor.

One of the attorneys asked why a wife should have to pay for her husband's debt. Abramson's replied, "She should if she thinks she must under the law. It is your job to tell her that she is liable under the law, whether she is or not. Look," Abramson said, "tell them anything that you have to in order to get the debt paid. They don't know whether they have to pay or not and they know if they hire an attorney to fight the case, that will cost them a ton. Tell them that as well. Let me also remind you," he went on, "your pay hinges on your success at collecting on the debts. If you are a real winner, you will be compensated on the basis of a percentage of your receipts. Some of our attorneys have made thousands every month in collection bonuses. Let me also warn you not to waste time in listening to excuses why they have not paid. We don't care why they haven't paid, they just need to pay the bill. For those of you that may think our tactics are not fair or legal, let me tell you that the deadbeat's spouse and children benefitted when the deadbeat incurred the debt. Don't kid yourself that they did not. They will pretend to know nothing about it while knowing full well they enjoyed the stereo, the TV or the car as much as old deadbeat did. Just collect the money and let someone else cry for them."

Abramson showed the trainees the forms they would be working with in their work. Many were legal forms that needed to be filed with the courts to reflect the debt and its reduction to judgment. Some were for law firm reports to keep tabs on the attorney's performance. Abramson explained that all of the forms were in the file cabinets at their desk as well as a clipboard, pens and scratch paper. His final words of advice carried the message that if a collector was not producing results or was not meeting quota, they were rapidly terminated. It became apparent to Trey that he was going to have to hustle in order to earn the income that he knew he was going to need to reduce his own student loan and credit card debts and keep up with his other expenses. He made it a point to rapidly learn the collection tactics that worked so that he could pay his own bills.

Finally the day arrived when Trey had to take the Bar exam. He made arrangements with the Gailsworth firm to be absent for the two-day exam and as was their policy, he would not be docked his normal pay for the two days absence. The exam was held at the city auditorium and approximately five hundred applicants for the testing appeared on the scheduled date. The first day was devoted to the multi-state or multiple-choice phase of the exam. The second day would be essay questions, which in Trey's mind would be the easier part of the exam to pass. Trey went to the exam in the company of Chris and Walt. Trey and Chris were fairly confident of passing the test based primarily on the number of hours and days preparing for it whereas Walt was not confident at all. He was the same way in law school and usually when it was all over, he had some of the highest grades on his exams. Trey expected that his friend Walt would do quite well with the Bar Exam. At the end of the first day, Trey had no idea as to how he had done. There was not a single multiple-choice question that he was confident he had answered correctly. Walt was of the same opinion. They stopped at the diner on the way home for a sandwich before returning to their homes for some last minute cramming.

Chapter 4

The following day after the exams were over a number of them went over to the Rooster's Nest for a beer and some relaxation. Chris and Don Macy were among those present. A number of the usually successful students from Walker voiced their opinion that the test "wasn't bad." Trey mentioned that he had no idea as to how he had done. Chris and Walt both agreed. Macy thought the exam was a "piece of cake" and most likely they had all passed it with flying colors. It would be at least six weeks before the test results were out so there was no sense in worrying about it. That was the position of most of the test takers. A few of the students who had graduated from Walker with Trey asked him how things were going at Gailsworth. They were all employed at reputable law firms and considered Trey's job at Gailsworth to be the bottom of the barrel. Trey knew what they were up to but could care less. Trey figured that he would succeed somewhere in the practice of law. It was just a question of where. "Laugh all you want, kiddies. I enjoy my current situation."

After two weeks of intensive training, Trey was turned loose in his cubicle to make money for the firm. He was given a stack of files representing well over one hundred separate debts dating back a number of years. He soon learned not to waste time on determining what gave rise to the debt. That was irrelevant with respect to the main target, getting the debt paid. He did quickly review the facts giving rise to the debt, at least initially, with the thought in mind that others who had been overlooked by previous collectors might be liable. He soon learned that was not the case. The files had been meticulously massaged by many collectors before they landed on Trey's plywood desktop. Furthermore, in reviewing some of the files, Trey soon learned that a significant number of the alleged debtors denied their liability for the debt. Not all of the denials appeared groundless but Trey ignored the arguments raised as spurious responses of deadbeats trained by years of experience in dealing with collectors.

Trey's office consisted of a computer with an internet connection and a word processor, printer, telephone, pencils, pens, stationary, and his metal file cabinet that had obviously made the rounds. His chair was a worn out number on wheels with a slight tilt to the left and no back pad. It had one once but no longer. Overhead fluorescents provided light for all of the cubicles. His office was obviously a bare bones operation. He would not be conducting any interviews with clients on leg off cases in his less than forty square foot office.

Trey had been working in the Gailsworth firm for two weeks before he actually commenced work on a file. His first file involved an elderly woman who had been married to the original debtor for a number of years. Her husband had passed away five years prior to Trey coming in contact with the file. The amount involved was originally two thousand seven hundred dollars, which had grown to seven thousand plus dollars due to the accumulation of interest charges on the account pursuant to the terms of the original sales contract on the purchase of a used automobile. By the time Trey acquired the file, the automobile involved could qualify for collector status under the State's licensing laws. The file materials contained current addresses and phone numbers of the decedent's surviving spouse and two of his grown children.

Trey spent more time reviewing the file prior to contacting the debtor than he knew he would be spending in the future. He wanted to know the file well in order to counter any of the defenses that he knew he would have to fend off. Without prior experience in this business, he had best know the file. When he was prepared for the call, he had a work sheet in front of him with the debtor's telephone number and residence address. He also had a list of standard responses he should make if the debtor raised certain defenses. He noted the widow lived in Bloomington in a rental apartment. She lived on social security payments and the assistance of her two sons who also lived in Bloomington. They were also potential targets but according to the file materials, they did not appear to have assets of any consequences but they were both employed and had been for a number of years. Trey dialed the widow's telephone number and soon a Mrs. Preston picked up. Trey identified himself as an attorney for Mid-Central Federal, who had been the creditor on the account. He informed Mrs. Preston that he was in the process of filing a judgment on the debt and she was listed as the creditor.

"Mr. Stark, I know nothing about the debt you are calling on. That was my husband's and I was not involved."

"Mrs. Preston, you realize you are liable on the debt by reason of the fact you were married to Mr. Preston, right?"

"My sons tell me that I am not and if you file anything against me, we will sue your pants off."

"Your sons are mistaken, Mrs. Preston, and we may sue them if they continue to obstruct justice."

"I don't have any money anyway, Mr. Stark. You can't get blood out of this turnip, you know. You are wasting your time with me. I am also told you can't garnish my social security payments so you are just out of luck, but keep talking Mr. Stark. I find this amusing. "

"Where do you bank, Mrs. Preston? Maybe we should talk to your banker."

"I don't have a banker, Mr. Stark. Next stupid question."

"What kind of car are you driving now, Mrs. Preston?"

"I don't drive. Do you have any intelligent questions?"

At this point in the conversation, the phone was taken over by what Trey assumed was one of her sons. "What are you up to, you jerk ass? This woman has absolutely no funds, no assets and never was a signer on that debt. Why don't you do your homework? If you keep bothering her, we are going to sue your ass. Not your company's ass, your ass, junior. How would you like that, jerk? Then we will find out where you live, what car you drive, where you bank and we will own your ass. You will be our yard boy, got that, junior? We be crackin' the whip on your white ass. Now say goodbye as we are hanging up and if you call back we will sue you for harassment and you will be workin' in my backyard tomorrow."

Trey leaned back in his chair and reviewed the call. It didn't sound like an opportunity-filled call to him. He saw absolutely no potential for any sort of recovery on that file. Furthermore, he could see himself dodging process servers on a clear-cut harassment case. He would talk to Abramson about how to handle this type of case.

Trey took the file and his notes and made his way to Abramson's office. He was in and had Trey come in and take a chair. Trey related his experience on the file and then said, "Ted, when I run into this on a file, it strikes me that there is no way in hell we are going to collect a penny on this debt and furthermore I may become somebody's donkey doing their yard work to pay off my judgment. What do you say?"

"Some really do look bleak. Look at it this way, if you sued her, she would have to hire an attorney and that could cost her an opening bill of at least five hundred dollars. I would be tempted to sue her and then tell her we would take the five hundred and would give her a release on the file. Most people would take that rather than get involved in an ongoing lawsuit."

"Yes, but what if they sue me in the process?"

"Trey, we have people here that would defend you from such a suit."

"Who pays the judgment against me if they are successful?"

"They would not be successful, Trey. We bury them in discovery and soon they just want out. We have never had to pay off any harassment suits. Ever. Don't worry about it."

"So you are saying I should go ahead with collection attempts on the judgment, right?"

"Absolutely. Have Martha find out where she banks. Martha knows how to do that. Then lay a garnishment on her bank account. Her social security check goes there for sure. Tie it up and then tell her we will take four hundred to close out the entire matter. If she has a brain at all, she will pay the four hundred or her sons will. Somebody will."

Trey followed Ted's advice and a week after filing a garnishment on her bank account, his telephone rang and it was one of the Preston boys. He was livid and recited a number of four or more letter epithets followed by Trey's name. When he had run out of breath informing Trey what he was going to do with him after they put the dress on him and tied him up to the tree bent over backwards, Trey suggested that a simple solution to the entire problem would be to settle the claim for a fraction of what was due. That was followed by a pause and then a question.

"How much are you talking about, jerk?"

"Mr. Preston, let's relax. How about seven hundred and I will release the garnishment and send you a release on the entire seven thousand eight hundred dollar debt. I am hoping I can get that approved but I don't know. I am sympathetic to your mother's case and will do what I can but I am new here and that may not work. What do you say, can I tell my boss that all I can get on the file is seven hundred. Help me out here."

Trey's proposal was followed by a lengthy pause and finally the woman's son said he would consider it if Trey could get that arranged as they were tired of fighting this business, which had gone on for years.

Trey took down the contact information on the son so that he could get back to him if the offer was approved, which he knew was already approved.

A week later Trey had received the settlement check in the amount of seven hundred dollars and he had sent out the release and withdrew the garnishment. He thanked Mr. Preston profusely for his cooperation in bringing this matter to a close. Trey assured him that he had to argue at great length and threaten to quit his job before the company finally gave in and went along with the settlement.

The next four weeks for Trey included some recoveries and a number of failures to recover on the majority of the files that he had pursued. His net recovery for the month was seven thousand dollars, well above the average for the firm. Abramson was impressed and promised Trey that he would be on a bonus with one more month of activity such as he had experienced in his first month. Trey had learned a great deal from his first month on collections. The first rule he learned was not to waste any time on listening to the reasons of the debtors for their non-payment. They all had their reasons and some of them were very good. The second lesson learned by Trey was not to shoot for the moon—that would just produce resentment and no cooperation from the debtors. He had to take what he could get and then get the hell out of there. Five hundred dollars on a ten thousand dollar debt was much better than fighting forever and getting nothing. Scare the hell out of them, settle quickly, and move on to the next file. Following the lessons Trey had learned put him well ahead of the average collections the following month as well.

During the two months that Trey was improving his situation at Gailsworth, he was no longer interviewing unless firms were calling on follow-ups and none were. After a day working the files at the firm, Trey would stop at the diner for a sandwich, talk to Maud for a few minutes and return to his home for the evening. He was becoming more anxious all the time to learn whether he had passed the Bar Exam or not. If he had passed it, he could then devote his time and thoughts to his future life as an attorney.

Trey called Chris and inquired as to how she was doing and she was making progress as well even though she had to work longer hours at her new law firm job. The final month before the Bar she had received permission to work only half time in order to spend more time studying. Those days were now long gone and she was pondering her fate with the Bar as was Trey. She met Trey for lunch on a few occasions and they talked over the good and bad points of their respective jobs. Chris enjoyed what she was doing but it was basically research grunt work and the firm had not yet assigned her to work in litigation. They kept indicating that she would be assigned there shortly but nothing was happening. Trey assured Chris that she had passed the Bar as she had always been a top student at Walker and had studied sufficiently to pass the Bar. They should be hearing the results in the next month or two as to whether they passed or not. Trey was fairly confident that he had as he had done fairly well on the practice exams and he attributed that to his long time experience of success at taking exams. As he told Chris, "That was what got me through law school."

The two were seeing each other more on a regular basis as time passed. Their conversations focused on their areas of practice and what each one was learning but also personal conversation was creeping into what they talked about. Chris mentioned that she and Macy were still good friends but that was all it was. She also asked who Trey was taking out and when he said "no one" she expressed surprise.

"Just been too busy, Chris. Besides, you're the only one I would be interested in and you have been pretty tied up by Mr. Macy."

"Yeah, sure, Trey. Like my phone has been ringing off the hook. Give me a call sometime. I'd be glad to go out with you."

"I will do that, Chris, if you would not be embarrassed to go out with a debt collector. Amazingly I am doing quite well at it. I hope it does not become habit-forming. Not quite why I went to law school." Trey then told Chris he was hoping to get his bills paid and then would possibly open his own practice. He felt that he was just one of those guys that worked best on his own. He had a hard time getting excited about making money for other people. Chris mentioned that it was Trey's independent attitude that had paid off for him in law school. Trey laughed and said that was what also had gotten him into trouble occasionally.

As time passed for Trey, he was becoming a bit more enthusiastic about getting into private practice. He figured that when he had saved up enough funds to finance his own practice, he could do some interviews and if they did not pan out he could open his own shop. If he was getting short of funds, he could always get involved in the collection area to finance his practice. He seemed to have a talent for making that pay off. He could stick with that part time for Gailsworth or he could set up his own collection section in his own law firm. He was fairly sure Gailsworth would give him a part time job if he needed one. There was also a possibility that he could work for the Chesterton firm as he thought his relationship with Wilson could pay off. Unfortunately it would not pay what Trey figured he could bring in with his own debt collection practice. He would have to give that more thought in the future.

In Trey's meetings with Chris over lunch, she had expressed her desire to get into private practice on her own at some future date. She had mentioned more than once, "Trey, we should consider opening our own office at some time if and when issues work out."

"Great idea, Chris. I will keep that in mind. I don't know if you would care to be somewhat involved in the collection area as I am considering using that to fund my practice."

Chris paused and said, "Hm, I would have to give that some

thought. I can just hear what my parents would be saying about that—not good. But, let's see what happens. I'm starting to get the idea that I am becoming the firm donkey in my present job and I want more challenges than I'm presently getting."

"I would enjoy working with you, Chris. I think we would get along very well. Let's see what happens."

On the weekends, Trey now had funds available for some entertainment but he kept that to a minimum as he wanted to use his time and money more efficiently. He was not hitting on Chris as she and Don seemed to still have a relationship going but he kept seeing her occasionally for lunch and sometimes a beer after work. A friendship was growing there but Trey had his mind now more on his career than anything else. Trey's weekends usually involved a Friday evening spent at the Rooster's Nest where many of his former classmates including Walt hung out telling stories or bragging about the great files they were working on in their law firms. There were only a few of the class that were still out on the job hunt but Trey was now not one of them. Everyone knew that Trey was working with the Gailsworth firm but no one brought that up. That was not considered a feather in Trey's hat, but with his bonus every month Trey was now making considerably more money than any of his classmates. His income had gone up so remarkably that he was no longer thinking of giving up his golden goose. He had now decided to build up a bankroll to finance his own operation when he opened his own firm. He had even figured that he too could buy up bulk bad debts and use that source for cash flow while advertising for personal injury work. He might even hire a collector or two to work the files while he expended his energies in expanding his business.

When Trey received the letter with his Bar Exam results showing that he had passed with scores in the top third of the candidates, he gave Chris a call and she had received her good news as well. The two of them congratulated one another and made arrangements to go together to the swearing-in ceremony to be held in the auditorium. The failure rate on the exam was below ten percent, which was about average for Walker.

As they drove over to the auditorium, Chris mentioned that she was saving her money for the day when she opened her own law office. "This working for other attorneys is definitely not the way to go. I just do not feel as though I am learning anything other than shortcuts to the Post Office."

"I'm in saving mode as well, Chris. Let's stay in touch and see what happens in the future. Maybe it will work out. The collection practice does pay the bills and I intend to keep that going in my own firm while I build up revenue from private practice."

"Well, you've gotta do what you gotta do, so let's see what happens, Trey."

After Trey had been working at Gailsworth for a little over a year and was a member of the Bar Association, he began to give thought to Douglas Wilson at the Chesterton firm. He finally gave him a call and suggested they have lunch, which Wilson immediately agreed to. When they met, Wilson was very curious as to how Trey was getting along and what he was involved with. Trey told him that he was with the Gailsworth firm, which Wilson immediately interpreted as a go-nowhere job. Trey informed him that he was making a ton of money on his bonuses and when he had sufficient funds available, he was considering opening his own firm doing collection and personal injury. Wilson was amazed that Trey was doing as well as he appeared—he was very well dressed and had a new air of confidence.

Trey inquired as to whether there were any open slots at Chesterton that he could fit into. Wilson said there could be but not at the pay level that Trey was currently making. Trey thought about that and then said if the job was interesting he could make some sacrifices. Trey was more curious about the possibility of working for Chesterton than actually interested in leaving his lucrative position at Gailsworth. Wilson finally told Trey that he would hire him into the firm if he wanted to join up but that Trey had what sounded to Wilson like a very good plan with much more independence that he would not have at Chesterton. Trey told Wilson he would think about it and let him know but he doubted he would leave Gailsworth at the present time. When they parted after lunch, Wilson wished Trey well and told him to stay in touch.

Chapter 5

In the time that Trey had worked at Gailsworth, he had developed a computer system for working the debt files. The system was all automated from the time a file came into the office until the time the file was closed. A file was opened and closed within a six-month time frame, which precluded files from settling in for life. He had learned that the files that made money for the firm did so in the first three months of their life there. After six months, very few files ever generated any money; anything older than six months was generally considered a loser. Trey used the program only to handle his files and did not discuss it with Abramson as he intended to copyright the program when he finally left the firm. At the end of his first year with the firm Trey was promoted to supervisor status and placed in charge of four collectors. Within two months of his promotion, he fired two of the collectors who did not show promise. Of the other two, one was very good and the other marginal. Trey figured that when he left the firm, he would take the good collector with him. As a supervisor, Trey's income increased with the percentage he received from revenues generated by those collectors working in his department combined with his own earnings. He had continued his own collection efforts, which were producing more revenue all the time.

He called Chris one Friday afternoon and suggested that they head over to the Rooster's Nest for the five o'clock crowd, which was comprised mostly of former Walker students. Chris readily agreed and Trey said he would pick her up in his car. When they strolled into the bar, his classmates took in the scene and raised their eyebrows. Chris was now working full time at Fuller and Brown. Most of their classmates who were seated in the bar had passed the Bar, including Walt. Macy was sitting in the bar and commented so everyone could hear, thanking Trey for bringing Chris over.

Trey replied to him that he was there to help.

Chris added, "I waited all afternoon for you to call, Don, and nothing. So I accepted Trey's offer."

Macy seemed to take it all quite well and Trey concluded that their relationship had apparently not been as heavy as everyone thought. The Walker group stayed intact until about eight o'clock when they began drifting out.

After a while, Trey suggested that he and Chris find a restaurant somewhere and have dinner. Chris thought that was a good idea and they headed for Charley's. The restaurant was packed as it was Friday evening but the maître d' recognized Chris and found a table for them. Trey commented that he was going to have dinner with Chris more often. He had been spending way too much time at the diner.

"Trey, I don't mind the diner. I could have gone there as well. I am not locked into the fancy restaurant."

"I know you aren't, Chris, and I like the diner myself, but every now and then I like to see who is eating at Charley's or the White House or wherever."

"I agree, Trey."

The two talked over their progress in their respective jobs and Trey said that he was actually enjoying the debt practice. He added that the money he was making was overcoming anything that he did not like about it. He was not going to take it up as a career, but for the time being it was working out just fine. Chris said she was enjoying her job at "fags and bags" other than the fact that her work was not particularly challenging, they wanted to work her too many hours and they were always bitching that she was not booking enough billable hours. Trey asked Chris if she was going to stay in that line of legal work or if she was going to get into some other area such as litigation.

"First of all, Trey, I enjoyed it more when I was studying for the Bar and I was working half time. I went from half time to time and a half after the Bar. I would enjoy the work if it were something other than researching boring topics. I enjoy litigation. You are involved in something with a focus, such as winning the case. With research, it just never seems to end, and if it does you never hear about it.

They keep telling me that I am going to be moved to litigation but nothing seems to happen. "

In celebration of his passing the Bar and becoming a licensed attorney in the State of Minnesota, Trey decided to take a week off. He had been burning the midnight oil for years it seemed and he wanted a few days to kick back and decide on his next move. His employers at Gailsworth were concerned that they might lose him and were offering him a promotion that would put him on par with Ted Abramson, complete with a plush office along the lines of Abramson's. Trey had a lot to think about during his week off and decided to go to San Francisco. He had never been there and knew that he would enjoy it. He had read much about the city and also wanted to visit Jack London's ranch out by Mount Tamalpai, which London mentioned in *Seawolf* and some of his other writings. When Trey had been a young boy, he read many of Jack London's writings and attributed the source of his interest in literature and adventure to London. He had always admired Jack London's life filled with adventure and writing novels. The very occasional writer such as London made a lot of money but the other twenty million starved. As Trey frequently said, somewhat tongue in cheek, if there had been more money in writing he would have taken it up.

Trey made arrangements with the firm and soon was headed west on Delta Airlines on a non-stop to San Francisco. As the plane climbed out from Minneapolis and headed west towards California, Trey looked down on the snow-covered farm lands of Minnesota and thought how much more attractive the mountains of California would be combined with the ocean and harbors surrounding San Francisco. He may find it difficult to return after seeing that.

This was the first time that he began to relax. His life up to this point had been surviving one challenging crisis and getting ready to face another. He had a drink on the plane and reviewed his life up to this point. He was doing very well in the collection business and was saving a large sum every month. He was starting to design in his mind what his office would look like when he opened his own firm. He knew that could be a tough grind with minimal revenue from the personal injury and DUI practice but if he hung onto some of his collection business, he could deal with that as well.

He was very comfortable sitting in the airplane with the engines providing a steady drone that soon had him dozing off. He woke up a few times when the pilot spoke on the intercom system that they were passing some point of interest. After what seemed to Trey like a short period of time, the pilot announced that they were letting down for their landing in San Francisco and they were number one for the approach. It was late in the afternoon as the plane flew over San Francisco and the Bay waters, and he had a brief view of the city and its surroundings. It was an impressive sight. Trey was somewhat familiar with the history of the city and finally seeing it brought to mind many of the stories of adventure and conquest that comprised its history. In the week he was going to spend there, he wanted to absorb as much of San Francisco as he could take in during the time allotted. Trey had always been an avid reader of historical fiction, other than the time spent preparing for the challenges of the Bar and his financial difficulties combined with the employment search and then getting situated at Gailsworth. He had still found time to read a number of Jack London's novels as well as Melville and Conrad, which had further inspired his basic search for adventure and challenge.

Trey had a reservation for a room at a small hotel just off Union Square. He rented a car at the airport as he wanted to visit a number of places and was soon ensconced in his hotel room down in the theatre district. There was a decent appearing bar on the corner by his hotel with the name "Jack's" in large neon letters over the front. After an excellent dinner in a small café, Trey headed for the bar. There were only a few people present when Trey walked in but the bartender informed him that it would be packed later on in the evening when the music started. Trey noticed a piano in the only open space in the bar and the bartender said, "Yes, that is the music. The guy is good." Trey said he didn't know how long he would be there but he might just hang around as he enjoyed a good piano player.

Trey sat at the bar, ordered a beer and sorted out his plans for his visit to San Francisco. He would take the trolley down to the waterfront tomorrow and take in the sights there. As Trey put away a few more glasses of beer he began to relax and enjoy the thought that his life was finally taking shape. He was making good money at Gailsworth but it was not the job that he wanted for his life's work.

He would either have to open his own shop as he had planned or work for another firm but that could be hard to take for an independent-minded guy. Trey was not very good at playing the role of the subservient employee. He had learned that in some of the temporary jobs he had taken up over the years.

He had worked for Montgomery Ward on University Avenue selling fishhooks and fishing gear for a short while during his undergrad years. He was given a quota of five hundred dollars a week of sales that would equate to about a truckload of fish hooks. His manager constantly reminded him that he was short on his quota week after week. Trey just looked at him wondering if he really thought he could bust five hundred a week in fish hooks. While he had been employed there, he had been accused of theft by the department head. Apparently five dollars was missing from the till and his boss figured he had taken it because Trey did not appear sufficiently concerned that five dollars was missing from the till. Trey told him that when he started stealing it was not going to be five dollars' worth. That comment did not reduce the manager's suspicions that Trey was the culprit. Trey was insulted by the small amount involved; they obviously did not consider him to be a big spender. He quit that job shortly after being accused, especially right after he spotted one of the "Monkey Ward" security dicks hanging his ass over the shelf above the storage area beyond the sales floor keeping an eye on him and other thieves through a ventilator.

As Trey sat in the bar, he thought about his time at Monkey Ward and what a jerk his manager had been. He had no desire to repeat that experience and he knew that many law firms were no better than Monkey Ward at hiring unimaginative managers. Furthermore, Trey had an attitude problem that irritated some managers. He appeared way too comfortable for them. They wanted him to appear less confident and more worried about his job. He walked too slowly, they told him; they actually told him that; they wanted him to speed up his movements and hustle while at work. He was told that by one of his employers. Trey tried to tell them that hustling was good but that had nothing to do with how fast you walked, but was never able to get the message across.

As Trey drank his beer in the bar, more people were coming. Trey enjoyed studying people in bars, and this evening was especially enjoyable. All kinds came to bars and that was one of the few reasons that Trey enjoyed being in a bar. You could meet anyone in a bar, some he didn't enjoy meeting, but he had to use some common sense in the process. Trey considered himself a good judge of character and had not had any bad experiences thus far. He was more careful around women than he was around men. Women could get you into a barrel of trouble if you didn't keep your guard up. Very few, very normal, hard-working, young women went into a bar alone. If they were alone, red flags fluttered for Trey. They were the kind that would claim you raped them or stole from them or would harass you with phone calls forever. He generally left them alone and let them harass other guys. One thing he noticed about the young women and men in this bar was that they were all quite well dressed. He assumed most of the clientele worked in the buildings surrounding the bar and had come here directly from work. They were an intelligent-appearing group of people. Quite possibly similar in background to a Friday's crowd in Minneapolis in the hours at the end of the workday.

Finally the piano man came in, arranged his music on the piano, and approached the bar where the bartender already had a fresh glass of beer ready for him. Trey studied the piano man and estimated that he was around his late forties or maybe even fifty. Trey wondered what life experiences had left him in this bar at his age instead of in some more comfortable situation with much better pay. He most likely worked here primarily on tips and Trey made it a point to get some smaller bills so he could tip the man. When the piano man began to play, it was very apparent that he enjoyed playing. He was not bored at his work. Maybe that is what kept him working at the keyboards. He had a good touch with the piano. He didn't hammer out the tunes; rather, he played the piano with affection. He had a soft touch—maybe that was why the few women in the bar were so focused on him. Even the younger gals seemed mesmerized by him. He was a decent-looking fellow but obviously no longer a very young guy. Trey had regretted that he had never learned to play a musical instrument. He had tried piano when he was a kid but just couldn't get into it. When his teacher passed away that was his excuse to quit.

Trey was enjoying getting slightly sloshed from the beer. He had been in work mode for so long that he had forgotten how to relax. The fellow next to him commented what a good piano player the piano man was. Trey commented that he was not an expert at judging piano players but he did enjoy the music this fellow produced. The guy only commented that some were better than others. The fellow was silent for quite some time and then spoke up again. "You a tourist here in San Francisco, or on business?"

Again, red flags rose up for Trey. He wanted to say, "No, I'm a cop," but that might present a problem, particularly if this guy was a real cop. "No, just visiting some friends in the city. Supposed to meet them here but so far they haven't shown up."

"There's another bar just down the street. They may have been thinking of that one."

"Well, they can figure out that I am not there and try this one."

The fellow turned his attention back to the piano man and Trey figured he was no longer a subject of interest. About that time an attractive young woman came in the bar and sat right next to Trey. He thought this was an interesting bar, wondering how long it would take for her to strike up a conversation. It didn't take long. In time, she said the piano man was one of the best in town and she wondered how long this bar was going to be able to keep him.

Trey commented that he enjoyed his music and hoped they would keep him. He threw that in to make it appear that he was somewhat of a regular at the bar but then he thought she obviously has been here before and had tagged him as a newbie. Without any preamble, she asked Trey where he was from. She had obviously pegged him as a tourist or transiting businessman. Trey told her he was from Minneapolis and she said she had never been there. He told her it was a nice city. He left it there hoping she would find another target.

As the time passed, the bar continued to fill to the point that it was standing room only around the bar. They were packed in two deep behind Trey and he was not about to give up his seat to anyone, even if he had to take a leak. Most of the crowd was about Trey's age, with an equal mix of male and female. Most of the women that came in the bar were with other young women or male friends. They were fairly well dressed and appeared personable and intelligent. Trey assumed that many were attorneys or other professionals.

As Trey studied the young men in the bar, he wondered how he appeared to others in the bar. Probably quite the same but Trey knew that he was not the same. He had always been different. As his friends said, he had a different drummer. That was why he went to work for Gailsworth and then was quite successful even though it was a collection firm. Most attorneys he knew would avoid a collection firm like the plague. Yet he was even now thinking of starting a firm with part of it involved in the collection business. Well, he was different but he was doing quite well and as far as he was concerned that made it all worthwhile. Trey also knew that he was fairly intelligent, but he also attributed most of that to his common sense. He had a knack for being able to figure out problems that brought him the most benefit, something many people were incapable of doing—those who knew him had commented on that at one time or another.

Trey thought about Don Macy. He had the reputation of being a brain in law school and Trey agreed, Macy did pull down the best grades. When he spoke in class, people listened. Trey respected Macy for applying himself in law school. As Trey frequently said, never criticize someone for doing well. Macy was no dummy, but yet, Trey was not that impressed by him. He always thought that Macy was book smart but a little short in the area of common sense. Not glaringly so, but his common sense level did not match his scholastic performance. He suspected that Chris probably thought the same thing; he viewed Chris as someone with common sense akin to his own. He had another sip of his beer and thought of Chris. He probably should have offered to bring her along on the trip. He wondered what she would have said. He had never made a real move on her but as he drank his beer he resolved that he would when he returned to Minneapolis. He always thought that she had some interest in him. Nothing she had said, just the vibes that he got from her. He liked her style and everything else she brought along with her.

He wondered why he had never made a move on her. She associated with Macy, but it did not appear to be some hot romance, just a matter of convenience. He wondered if he was afraid of making a fool of himself but quickly dropped that. He was not one to worry about how he was appearing to someone. He was not shy around women but he had always held Chris Sutton in a special place and was careful about how he dealt with her. Well, it was time to stop being so careful and to start being smart. Possibly she was wondering what his problem was as well.

When he had bought the diamond ring for himself, Chris asked him if he was engaged. He knew she was 'ragging' him but he stopped her with his reply that he had bought the ring for the one he loved. For a moment Chris paused. Then she smiled and said she figured that was it. He should have come back with something like, "When I make my move, Chris, I will get a bigger one for you." That would have brought her to a halt. Well, next time. Trey knew that he was better at coming up with great replies two days after they were needed than the day when they should have been sprung. He excused himself for the tardiness, though; he was aware that was the same for most people.

The young woman that spoke to him earlier in the evening had been involved in conversation with the fellow on her other side but he had since left. Trey turned towards her and she was looking directly at him with a smile on her face. Trey commented, "The place has definitely filled up. When I came in, I was about it."

"Yes. This is Friday night and it always fills up. Very popular place."

"Are most of these people out of the office buildings around here?"

"I would say so. I recognize a number of them. Generally the same crowd every Friday evening."

"Do you work in this neighborhood?"

"Yes. I work for a law firm up the block."

"Interesting. And what sort of work do you do for them?"

"I am an attorney. I work in real estate and business law. How about you?"

"I'm a lawyer myself. I work in business matters." Trey was not eager to bring out that he worked in collections. Then he would have to explain that he was making a wad and that would clearly sound like B.S.

The two talked at length and Trey explained that he had just taken the Bar Exam in Minneapolis and had attended an evening law school. The young woman had also attended a night law school in San Francisco and commented that there were a million lawyers running around the city. Pay here was not that great. Trey figured that she brought that up thinking that he was in town in hopes of moving to San Francisco and getting a job in one of the local firms. Trey told her that it was not too great in Minneapolis either for a beginning lawyer. Trey had changed his opinion about her after they had talked for a while. At first he questioned that she was a lawyer but she answered his questions and that confirmed in his mind that she was telling the truth. She also asked a few questions about the practice in Minneapolis probably for the same reason. Trey figured they were probably about the same age but she had been practicing longer so maybe she had a few years on him. At times he wondered if she was not also in the collection area as she seemed like a fairly normal person, not playing any elite lawyer games with him. He told her he was only in town for the week and asked her what places she would recommend that he visit while there.

She mentioned a few bars and then mentioned the Fisherman's Wharf and the cruise boats to Sausalito and Alcatraz. "They are very popular with the tourists in the summertime and I have done them both at one time or another. This is a good time to tour as the tourists are not here seeing as how the kiddies are in school. The Top of the Mark Hopkins Hotel is another popular spot. Nice bar and you get a great view of the city. The theatres right down the street from here are usually presenting good fare. Our restaurants are world famous. There is a lot to do. I think you will enjoy your visit."

He thought about asking her to show him around but he was not that attracted to her and so far she had not offered. He would pass on it for now. He told her what his name was and asked her name. She told him it was Stephanie but did not add a last name. That was fine with him. They chatted for another fifteen minutes or so and then she said she had to leave. She was meeting friends at another bar. She wished him luck and said she usually stopped in the bar in the evenings for a drink before going home so would likely run into him again. That was fine with Trey. When she left a guy took her chair and that was the end of Trey's socializing.

Trey paid his tab and then walked up to the piano player and put a five-dollar bill in his tip cup. The piano man looked up at him, smiled and thanked him. Trey returned the smile and said, "Thank you. Your playing reminds me of an old friend. Would you…play it again, Sam?"

"What would you like to hear, Humphrey?"

"How about 'As Time Goes By.'"

"You are on the ball, Humphrey. You should have brought Ingrid with you."

Trey smiled and said, "I will do that on my next visit. I have been regretting not bringing her on this visit."

As Trey walked towards the exit, a bar or two of the melody was playing out, softly, with feeling. Conversation in the bar ended as the piano man sang the lyrics,

You must remember this, a kiss is just a kiss…

Trey stopped walking towards the exit, turned around and listened as the piano man performed at the piano. Trey stood and listened to the words of the song as they wound down to the famous lines:

It's still the same old story, A fight for love and glory, A case of do or die.

The world will always welcome lovers, as time goes by.

As Trey left the bar, the patrons were applauding the performance of the piano man. The old classic had obviously appealed to the majority of the patrons present in the bar. Trey again wished that he had brought Chris with him on this trip. He would certainly do that the next time he visited the city by the sea and when he was again here, he would ask the piano man to play "As Time Goes By."

Within minutes he was back in the room in his hotel. He went through the tourist magazines in order to make sure he was aware of the tourist spots he should be sure to see while he was there. He noticed the clock said it was ten in the evening, which was not late but it was midnight on his Minneapolis time and he was very tired.

After reading for awhile, Trey fell asleep and slept like a rock until eight in the morning. That was unusual for Trey as he was normally up and around by six in the morning.

Chapter 6

Trey left his hotel around nine in the morning and found a small café down the street that was serving breakfast. He bought a paper and read the local news to see if there was anything of unusual significance that he might find interesting. Just the local events that occurred in any large city and Trey figured he would finish his breakfast and walk on down to Fisherman's Wharf. He could possibly take one of the tour boat trips that Stephanie had mentioned. He walked down the steep hill from the café and checking his map headed in the direction of what he figured would take him to the main part of the wharf where the tour boats departed from. After a lengthy walk he was at Fisherman's Wharf enjoying the aroma of the ocean and the salt air. There were many people walking around the shops and restaurants surrounding the wharf but they were mostly couples or singles, most likely like Trey in town on business or possibly on a vacation. It was a nice day to be walking around as the temperature was moderate and there was no sign of rain. He saw the ticket booth for the tours and was soon talking with the ticket seller, who informed him that he would not need a reservation in order to get on the Alcatraz tour and sold him an open ticket for any tour during the weekdays. A weekend tour would require a reservation. He could get on the Sausalito cruise anytime as business was a little slow this time of year, but he had already decided he would drive over the Golden Gate Bridge and visit Sausalito the same day that he was going to Jack London's home in Glen Ellen.

He studied his map to figure out how to fill out his Saturday. He saw that Golden Gate Park covered quite a space on the map just to the south of where he was and he had read about the famous Japanese Teahouse at the park. He would need his car to deal with a visit to the Park and he could also take in the Cliff House and the Marina as well. He had been told that the Marina was where all the runners in the city went for their morning run. He would go back to his hotel room and pick up his running gear, get his car and he could visit the park and then change in his car for a run. After a lengthy walk up the steep hill to his hotel from the wharf, Trey gathered his running gear and drove down to the Golden Gate Park. He followed the signs to the Teahouse, parked the car and walked over the picturesque bridge and up to the Teahouse. He had a cup of tea and a fortune cookie, which told him his future was filled with enjoyable surprises. Trey figured that must mean Chris was coming his way. Trey observed the other patrons of the Teahouse and assumed they were very much like him—in town for a short visit and had read about the Teahouse in one of the hotel tourist publications. They seemed to be enjoying their visit as he was enjoying his.

When he left the Teahouse he drove to the Cliff House Restaurant, which was built high on the cliff overlooking the ocean, giving the patrons a very good view of the seals down on the boulders below the restaurant. He was getting a very good impression of San Francisco and the weather was perfect. The temperature was around 78 degrees, sunny with a cool breeze coming in from the ocean.

When he had changed into his running gear and finally found a place to park his car—no easy task—he took off for a run in the Marina. There were hundreds of runners out as it was a Saturday and apparently many did not have to work. The runners were balanced with both men and women. Young women that Trey saw running were in very good shape. A much finer looking batch of women than he was accustomed to seeing running around Calhoun or Harriet in Minneapolis.

Trey liked the city very much and was impressed by the architecture, the hills and beauty of the waters surrounding the city, but most of all by the people, who were very friendly and seemed to be enjoying themselves very much. He could easily live here. He would have to think about that, as it was a very attractive concept. On the other hand, he was aware that every attorney that came to the city had the same thought.

When Trey finished his run, he went to his car and took out a novel he was reading and a large towel. He walked up to the green where others were sitting on the grass reading and spread out his towel, laid down and began reading *Of Human Bondage* by Somerset Maugham. Trey was about halfway through the novel and thought about his comment to his close friend, Walt, that it should be a training manual for all single guys. He was deep into the novel and enjoyed it thoroughly. It was so relevant, particularly for guys between the ages of about 25 and 40, which certainly included himself. They could really be stupid at times and this novel pointed it out in spades. While Trey was reading a young girl who had been running walked up to him and asked him what he was reading. She said she had noticed him laughing and was always on the lookout for a good book. He told her this was not so funny as it was humiliating and he gave her a bit of the plot. She thought for a moment and then said, "I believe I read that before. It was well written, but I thought it was a bit depressing."

Trey thought a moment and said, "I suppose from a female point of view it would be. From a guy's point of view—and I have only read about half of the novel—it is a humiliating story of the stupidity of men. It is so humiliating for this poor guy that it is comical. What a dork he is."

"That poor girl—what was her name, Helen or Mildred? Something like that—what a life she led and many women lead that same dead end life. Not this girl. No way, Jose."

The two discussed the book for some time and Trey was enjoying her company. She was intelligent and had a very good sense of humor, which he always looked for in anyone. He figured she was a few years younger than he and she was in very good shape. He looked at her running shoes and saw that they were a good quality pair of Nikes and had some miles on them. She obviously took her running seriously. "I take it you are a regular runner, right?"

"You bet. I'm in the running club at USF and we hit it pretty hard."

"USF is what? I'm from Minneapolis. Not checked out yet on San Francisco. Let me guess—is that the University of San Francisco?"

"You win the prize on the first row. Yes. I'm a third year student there in liberal arts. Majoring in Literature."

"I take it you live here in the city, right?"

"All my life."

"I'm just here for a week. Wanted to get away for a short trip and picked Frisco. I'm very impressed so far. Beautiful city. The people seem very friendly. Know anyone that wants to hire a brand new attorney? I'm sure they are very rare here. Just joking. They aren't rare anywhere and certainly not here."

"I don't know but I would assume someone, somewhere…would maybe, possibly, want to hire another lawyer." As she said this, she was laughing.

The two talked about running and other matters of interest to Trey and in the process he learned that her name was Sandy. She was a very cute girl and Trey was about to ask her to be his guide in the city when she informed him she had to get back to her room and start studying for exams that she had been taking in summer school. She wanted to graduate after three and a quarter years and could not screw up these exams. He thanked her for spending some time with him and said he would be looking for her at the Marina while he was here in San Francisco. She wished him an enjoyable stay and soon was gone. Trey watched her as she left and thought to himself, *What a sweetheart.*

That evening, Trey went to the Mark Hopkins Hotel and took the elevator to the Top of the Mark bar that Stephanie had mentioned. It was a beautiful view of the entire city and Trey was able to find a booth where he could sit and enjoy the city. He soon realized that he was getting a view of the entire city as the room was very slowly revolving, giving him a new viewpoint constantly. *This is great*, thought Trey. *The next time I'm coming out here, I'm bringing Chris along, for sure.* Trey had a couple of drinks and then figured that he had better taper off as he had to drive his car back to his hotel parking ramp and did not need to get a DUI while he was on his trip. He should have cabbed over to the Top of the Mark; if he had done so, he could enjoy another drink or two.

The following morning, Trey had decided that he was going to drive over to the Jack London Park across the Golden Gate and take in a tour of the home that London was building at the time of his death but never lived in as it had burned down in the process. There was a bookstore there together with the actual home that he lived in that was referred to as the cottage. The home he was building was known as the Wolf House and was virtually completed when it was engulfed in flames. The only part of it that remained was the stone foundation that Trey visited after he toured the museum and bookshop. He didn't actually tour Wolf House as there was a very large rattlesnake parked at the stairway leading up the concrete wall of the house. Fortunately others there pointed the snake out to Trey as he was not used to them and this snake was quite camouflaged by its coloring. Trey was able to walk around the structure and see the general floor plan of the foundation from higher ground.

Trey then drove to Sausalito and had a beer at a bar that was situated along the waterfront near the ferry pier. The bar was crowded with the younger set that he had seen frequently in his visits to bars and restaurants in the San Francisco area. There seemed to be more socializing seen on this trip than he was accustomed to seeing when making the rounds in Minneapolis. Sausalito was a very interesting community. The buildings and homes were built right along the shore of San Francisco Bay. Trey spent some time in the bar talking with a couple from Indiana who were also taking in the sights. Trey had the definite opinion they were fairly recently married as they seemed very involved with one another. As he thought about it after driving back to his hotel, he concluded that they possibly were just quite happily married. The thought amused him as he questioned his ability to spend his entire life with one person but he did realize that many people preferred it that way.

Driving back to his hotel, Trey thought how enjoyable it would be to live in San Francisco but he also was aware that like anyplace else, it too had its negative points. He had noticed that home prices were through the roof and taxes were another matter. He concluded that nothing was perfect and he would stick with Minneapolis for the immediate future although taxes there were high as well. After reading some more of his novel, he took a snooze for over an hour and then went out for dinner. He found an Italian restaurant a short walk from his hotel and spent two hours there enjoying an excellent dinner. Again, people-watching was great in the restaurant with a number of young couples out socializing and enjoying one another. He walked back to his hotel and read for another hour before again falling into a deep sleep.

Trey spent the following three days taking in the sights of San Francisco, including a tour of Alcatraz, which he found very interesting. For the prisoners there, seeing the beautiful city so close by must have been a tremendous temptation. By the end of the week, Trey had seen most of the more significant points in the city and was ready to start getting back to Minnesota. He had thought a great deal about where he was going in his law practice and was not completely satisfied with his current situation. He was embarrassed to say that he was employed by the Gailsworth firm. He was very pleased with the money that he was earning but it wasn't good to be a bit ashamed to mention the name of your employer. Everyone knew that Gailsworth was the firm that was written up in the newspapers every now and then for shoddy practices going after widows and orphans to pay bills that legally they were not obligated to pay. Trey did not want to spend the rest of his life dodging questions as to where he worked. He had used tactics to recover funds on debts that he was not proud of. He didn't even want to tell Walt all the details of his work.

As he thought of his work at Gailsworth he could only conclude that he was not the same, naïve, good guy that he was when he started there and that was only about a year and a half ago. Lately he had been turning down some debtor files as just way beyond the pale but they were very few. On one of them, he had an insurance company file where he was instructed to recover the funeral costs paid out to a family on the death of their son in a car accident. The burial costs were paid out in error; the policy was not meant to cover funeral expenses. Trey reviewed the file and noted that the son was an only child and was ten years old at the time of his death. He delayed action on the file and finally packaged it up and sent it back to the company with a note that he was not going to work on that file. Obviously the family had suffered greatly and to tell them that they had to repay the cost of burying their son was just too much. The insurance company then stopped sending files to Gailsworth for collection, which was just fine with Trey. Abramson was aware of the incident but said nothing. He most likely would have pursued the file but didn't want to antagonize his number one collector by criticizing him for sending the file back.

As Trey flew home he thought about what he was going to do to clean up his present situation. He had to leave Gailsworth and either get into a better situation or start his own firm as he had considered previously. He would chat about it with Walt and some other close friends to get their input. Then he would decide what to do. Whatever he did, he would plan it out to make sure he had all the bases covered. No hasty decisions here.

He also thought more about having a regular girlfriend. He was tired of the bar scene and was well aware from his San Francisco trip that almost everyone that was in the restaurants or out and about in the city was coupled up except for him. Trey had considered where he was going in life and was well aware that he did not fit into the common mold. What the hell was wrong with him? He had always been a loner and was well aware of the fact that he preferred it that way. Did that make him abnormal? He did not think so, but knew other people considered it a bit strange. He was not even sure that he ever wanted to get married. He doubted he could make that work as he thoroughly enjoyed his own life and did not need an advisor. He did admire some couples but very few. He noticed in most couples that he saw a certain level of tension a great deal of the time. He wondered if it was really there or if he was assuming it was to justify his views on marriage.

Chapter 7

When Trey returned to Minneapolis and stepped off the airplane onto the catwalk into the terminal, a blast of frigid January air hit him and reminded him of what he did not like about living in Minnesota. The outside temperature was around twenty-five degrees below zero with a twenty-knot wind, which produced a wind chill of around thirty-five degrees below zero or lower. When he found his car in long-term parking, it was covered in snow and ice. Apparently earlier snow had melted and then frozen onto the car, making it very difficult to remove. The windshield wipers that were frozen to the windshield had to be cleaned off and then the windshields had to be scraped to get the ice off so that Trey could see to drive. After fifteen minutes of preparing his car to be driven, Trey got behind the wheel and turned the ignition key. He was successful in getting one half of a grunt out of the starter before it became silent. Obviously the battery had succumbed to the cold.

A fellow was getting in a pickup a row behind Trey and Trey approached him requesting a jumpstart "for ten bucks." The fellow agreed and minutes later, Trey was sitting in the car with the engine running, praying for it to warm up the car. Trey was freezing. He had not dressed for the Minnesota weather when he had left on his trip. After about ten or fifteen minutes, his defroster had cleared a small hole in the windshield about the size of a fifty-cent piece so that he could see ahead, or somewhat ahead. Trey waited another five minutes or so with his teeth chattering until he had better visibility and then proceeded to make his way back to his condominium. It was a cloudy, dark day in the city with a strong wind blowing the snow over the ice-covered roadway. As Trey's car proceeded down the road, it was like driving over a washboard as the tires hit the accumulated frozen ice covering the road. Trey had to reduce his speed in order to maintain control of the car and to improve his comfort level on the rough road. Trey thought about the difference driving here and his pleasant drive up towards Glen Ellen to visit Jack London's home. That had been a very enjoyable drive and quite a bit different from what he was now experiencing.

An hour later, after he had unpacked his bags, settled in the condominium and was beginning to feel the living room warming up, he called Walt to see if he wanted to get dinner someplace. Walt was agreeable and the two met at the Rooster's Nest for a drink first. The bar was crowded as it was Friday late afternoon and Trey saw a number of people that he knew from school. Trey told Walt how impressed he was with San Francisco and the many places he had visited on his trip. Walt said he had never been there but would put that on his to-do list after listening to Trey.

When they were at dinner, Trey brought out that he had been thinking of leaving his job at Gailsworth.

"So you want to get away from all the money you make there and into the poverty wages all of us are getting. Have you considered that?"

"Yes, I have. I haven't figured that out yet. I do like making the money. I thought I could open my own shop and continue the collection business to support the cash flow I will need while building up the general practice aspects of the firm. I think that would work."

"Maybe, maybe not. Trey, I would not want to work in a collection firm and I think you could be branded as that if it was part of your operation. Don't just go by what I have to say on this. I just have a bad view of the collection area; been reading too many articles in the Star Journal about the little old ladies being badgered by the big dirty law firms working the collection game."

"Walt, I have the same opinion and I think most other people, lawyers as well, have the same view. I am tired of dodging the age-old question 'where do you work?' I'm ready for a change."

"Trey, if you come up with a good option, let me know. I could use a change myself. Being a high-class office boy is not why I went to law school. When they have to send something to the post office, guess who they always call for?"

"Life is not fair, Walt." Trey switched topics, asking Walt what else was happening in the city while he had been gone.

"Not a hell of a lot, Trey. Oh, some kid is in deep 'kimchi' to say the least. The stories vary but the kid says this black kid came up to his car at a stop sign and tried to open his car door. The black kid then pulled out a gun and told him to unlock the door. The kid driving also had a gun, figured he was being carjacked, opened the car door and shot the black kid. The black kid died. The gunner was white. There were some local hood witnesses who said the black kid had no gun and was just hitchhiking to—guess where—school, of course. They swore he was on his way to school. Others said he did have a gun, but no gun was found when the cops got there. The newspapers are hanging the white kid and now the Reverend Shamile Armstrong of media fame is coming to Minneapolis to lead a rally to ensure that justice is carried out. Like I say, the kid is in deep 'kimchi.'"

"Interesting. Other than that, anything else going on?"

"No. I did the Minnetonka tour last Sunday. Nada, Zip, Zero. I did see Chris there with a couple of girls. No Don Macy. Maybe that is history as you suggested."

"I thought I should have invited her to Frisco. I do believe she might have gone. Woulda, coulda, shoulda, you know."

The following day while Trey was in his office looking over the new batch of collection files that he was to be working on, he decided that he could no longer pressure people into paying bills that many of them were legally not liable for. He could justify going after some of them as they had obviously benefitted from the loan that was now in arrears. If there were any connections, he would continue to pursue the loan. If not or if the connection was too tenuous, he would not handle the file. He was going to hang it up at least for the Gailsworth firm. He knew that it was never smart to leave a job until another one was lined up but there was another rule that also came into play, and that was to not stay at a job when he could no longer perform at one hundred percent. He had a solid reputation with Gailsworth and when he left, he wanted that to be there after he was gone. He never knew when he might need that contact again. He also had to consider the fact that he stood a good chance of continuing collection work on his own after leaving Gailsworth.

He would have to pursue some files there that he was now refusing to pursue. Well, that was life and he would have to deal with those files when he was faced with them.

Trey went to Abramson and announced that he was leaving the firm. He would annotate unfinished files so that whoever took them over would have the benefit of his views on how they should be handled. Abramson was very surprised and hated to see Trey leave the company. He was the heavy hitter in collections and it would be a long time before they found another one like him. Trey thanked Abramson for his support and told him to call upon Trey if he had any questions on any of the files he had worked. The two ended the conversation on very good terms. Trey stayed in the office for another week just clearing up files and making sure that his cubicle in the firm was well prepared for his replacement. He left a document detailing generally how he worked the files and what the golden rules were for successfully doing the job. He deleted all references to his operating system that he had created as he was well aware that he could very well be involved in collection work in the future and would want to have it with him.

A few days after he had given his resignation, he called Chris and suggested they have lunch as he had things that he wanted to talk to her about. She said, "I would love to have lunch with you, Trey. I thought maybe you had fallen off the map after you passed the Bar Exam."

Trey explained to Chris that he had taken a trip to San Francisco, a city he had never been to, and enjoyed it very much. "I'll tell you all about it, but I suppose you have been there twenty times."

"Never have, Trey, but you can tell me all about it tomorrow."

Trey met Chis at Friday's for lunch and she, as always, looked great. Trey was glad to be sitting down with Chris and the two were soon involved in a lively conversation. Trey told her all about his trip to California and that he had thought of her as he sat at his table at the Top of the Mark Hopkins hotel. Chris smiled when he told her that and said, "Next time you go out there, give me a call and I will join you. Your trip sounds great and I've always wanted to visit that city. It seems so beautiful, built right on the bay and the ocean."

"Chris, I will do that. You would enjoy it, believe me." Trey then went into the issue that generated his request that she join him for lunch. He told her he had given notice to the Gailsworth firm and the reason for his decision. She thought his decision was very noble in view of the great sacrifice in salary that he was making. She told him that he would never find that level of income in a general practice firm unless someone was doing him a very great and unusual favor.

"I am aware of that, Chris. I have been thinking of opening my own firm. I have accumulated a fair amount of cash to hold me over while I develop my business and I was also considering bringing some of my collection work with me but promoting only my general practice and not the collection work. That does not involve the general public anyway. You just purchase bulk debt and then farm it for recoveries. I would not want to be known as a collection firm and I think I could keep that a bit undercover. I would not be pulling the scum ball tricks that I have seen pulled. I am done with that but I am not so naïve as to think I could get good collection files and totally avoid the questionable ones. Still, I will try to be careful in which ones I work with. Anyway, those are issues that have been buzzing around my head and I wanted your thoughts on them. You are in a defense firm but most likely have a pretty good handle on law firm operations."

"Trey, a defense firm does not rely on cash flow from people who will not be coming back after they have received their services like from a general practice firm. We have continuing clients that we have represented for years and they pay well. I have heard many of the attorneys in the GP firms complaining about the lack of funds. Many of them live off lines of credit from the banks, provided they can occasionally pay them back. It is a tough grind in a GP firm but then maybe your collection work could support the firm. I don't know that you could keep it a secret, though. Word would get out. It is just the type of practice that gets talked about.

"Now, I should also mention that not all aspects of defense work are totally clean either. I have learned that we defense lawyers are under the thumbs of our insurance company employers, who tell us what to do and when to do it. It is not exactly a totally ethical business. Most large insurers have their own training programs that they want their lawyers to attend. It is sort of a 'dirty trick school.' That is what we call it. We go there once a year for a week or two. Life in a defense firm is not that clean, happy place we all thought it was when we were sophomores in law school. You get out in the world and you learn it is different out there."

"Yes, Chris. I suppose so. I just can't deal with some of the bottom dweller aspects of it. I may find out that I have to. I hope not. Maybe I should go into sales but then I would learn there that I have to let the air out of the tires of my competitors. Or worse, I remember one time when I was a kid, Chris, I saw a movie of a guy that lived in a small palm-covered hut on the beach, somewhere out in the Bahamas. Beautiful scene—sunny, warm, no neighbors, just this guy and he was a writer. I thought that would be great. No, it wouldn't. Where would he get his materials, food, and everything else he would need to actually write a book. Just one more naïve thought that reality eventually destroyed. They ought to have a course in college called 'real life,' where you learn what really goes on. Maybe I am making it sound worse than it is."

"Trey, I think everyone goes through the same thing. We all learn it is not a snowy, white, vanilla-colored world out there and you just have to learn to deal with it as honestly as you can. Like I said, my practice presents issues for me all the time. Sending interrogatory answers back to a plaintiff that I know are B.S. If I went to the house attorney for my client and complained, he would ask me if I was on the plaintiff's payroll because if I wasn't, I was going to be off of theirs."

"Chris, maybe I should open my own firm, bring in the collection work and see what happens. I don't think I could go to work for another firm, have some kid telling me what to do. No, thanks. That just would not work. I've developed a collection software program that does most of the work, anyway. Just feed the files in, make a few telephone calls, all pleadings are automated as are the collection letters, feed it some ink and take in the cash. Anyway, enough of that. Are you married yet or about to be or anything like that?"

"Hell no, Trey. What ever gave you that idea?"

"I thought Macy would have convinced you by now to partner up with him. You two were a lovely couple."

"Not my type, Trey. Besides, he has a steady, anyway."

"That is news to me. Who is the lucky lady?"

"Himself, Trey. Don Macy has had a crush on himself ever since he saw himself in the mirror."

Trey laughed and said, "I knew he was crazy about himself but we all suffer from that. I can hardly criticize him when I have been accused of the same thing myself." Trey glanced down at his diamond ring that he always said he had received from the one he loves.

"Yes, Trey, but you are not quite as smitten as Macy. I'm not talking behind his back. I tell him the same thing. Trey, this is quite the story about this kid that shot the black kid on Lake Street. The media is having him for lunch. I feel sorry for the shooter."

"Yes, the media needs something to blab about and they love to build up stories that have the potential to create race riots. I understand the very Reverend Shamile whatever is coming to town to get everyone to hate each other. Best we stay out of downtown while he is here."

"You've got that right."

"Chris, I'd better drive you back to work. I have kept you well beyond your normal lunch break. Give me a call if you want to sneak out some time and we can go have a drink and continue this conversation. I look at you as a fountain of wisdom and I do appreciate your comments. Let's get going."

When Trey dropped Chris off at her office, she told him to stay in touch. Trey had every intention of doing just that. He had also firmly resolved to proceed with opening his own office but getting into general practice was sounding less attractive all the time. Trey knew it was a very rough grind and he also knew that there was not that much money in it. Furthermore, he was very proficient and successful in the collection business. Why leave that golden goose? He knew the contacts to make from his time at Gailsworth and was not doing anything behind their backs; there was plenty to go around, particularly with the economy taking a dive.

When Trey and Walt met at the diner that evening, Trey told him that he had made the decision and had quit his job at Gailsworth. He also told Walt about his lunch with Chris and how she spoke as though Macy was not in the picture at all. Trey commented that he would pursue that one when he had his new office set up or maybe even before then. Why waste time.

By the time Trey had completed his final week of work at Gailsworth, he had located office space in the south suburbs of Minneapolis and was laying out the personnel and equipment that he was going to need. He would hire one collector hopefully with experience and a clerical to handle the phone, typing and taking care of the office. He knew of a number of former employees of Gailsworth that he had been impressed with that he thought would welcome a job offer from him. He gave one of them that he had the most confidence in a call, and the fellow gladly accepted. He had been working for a competitor of Gailsworth but did not appreciate being micromanaged. That was just more proof to Trey that he was a good man for the job. The following week, Trey put the finishing touches on his office. The partitions were built to his specifications, computer and phone equipment installed, stationary purchased, business cards bought with the name of the new firm printed thereon, Minnesota Business Services, Inc., for the collection business and personal cards for his personal injury work. Each area had its own telephone line and there was no indication that they were in any way associated other than the fact the address for both was the same.

Trey was aiming at the retail collection area and was already searching the bulk debt sellers for decent inventory. Trey knew the companies that sold debt that were considered the best from his years at Gailsworth and purchased most of his debt inventory from them. The brokers knew Trey and they liked him from prior dealings. They were not giving him anything free of charge but they did see to it that what they were selling him was worth what he was paying for it.

Trey's new collector and the first shipment of debt arrived at his firm at about the same time. Trey already had his computer system installed in all office computers and within days the office was humming under Trey's knowledgeable supervision. Trey spent his time in his office, which was comfortably set up so that he could study the market and be aware of any new trends in the debt or collection market. He also communicated with other collectors both in Minnesota and elsewhere to get their take on what was happening in collection practice.

Trey's collector was doing very well right from the get-go and Trey decided to fill the second cubicle in the office that was already set up and awaiting a person to fill the vacancy. Trey listed an ad in a collection website and immediately had four applicants calling for appointments. They were all experienced and looking for new opportunities. Three weeks after opening his office, the second collector was busy working the files. Trey offered a bonus system to his collectors, which had them working overtime on their own to get into the 'real money.' Getting them into the 'real money' also got Trey into the 'real money,' and within two months of being in business, Trey was making the same money he had been making at Gailsworth. The real key to the success of Trey's collection firm was the software program that he had developed. This cut down the time invested in files to about 10% of what it would have been without his program. He had cautioned his collectors to maintain secrecy as to his software and had them sign confidentiality agreements with additional compensation for doing so. They both seemed quite pleased to be working for Trey and assured him of their loyalty.

Chapter 8

As the months passed by for Trey in his new business there were only a few bumps in the road. These mostly involved embarrassing overreaches by his staff pursuing their collection activities. Trey had a standard policy of not getting into serious arguments with clients over debt. Yes, push them to the wall but if they began to shout lawsuit or Ethics Committee, do the reverse rhumba and settle the matter at any cost. It was not worth it to spend the next six months answering letters or attending hearings. There was no money in that.

Trey did speak with Chris a number of times and their relationship was developing. Don Macy was no longer in the picture but Trey kept everything on a friendly basis. He did not like complications and wanted to get his business safely up and operating.

Trey had set his office up with two distinct sections. One handled the work and communications relating to Minnesota Business Services, Inc., and the other related to Trey Stark, Attorney at Law. One receptionist answered the phones for both entities, which was not a problem as the phones were not ringing that often and the receptionist knew exactly how to answer each line. The one that rang on only isolated occasions was the line for Trey Stark, Attorney at Law. On those occasions it was usually a call from Walt or Trey's mother, but never a potential client.

After one full year of operating with his new office setup, Trey evaluated his situation. His collection business was doing very well and handled the financial needs of the entire office and then some. His private practice efforts yielded minimal funds. He was doing some drunken driving defense work, some auto fender bender cases and other general practice cases but was kept afloat by the collection practice. Nevertheless, he did enjoy the litigation cases and did fairly well at them. He would have liked to get into the more com-

plex litigation cases where the big money was but in order to do
that he would need a runner and he was just not ready to make that
leap. Maybe sometime in the future, he was well aware that the good
cases did not just drop into his office by chance. They ended up in
law firms that either had runners or on line referrals such as chiro-
practors, physicians or medical workers. Such was life.

One afternoon as he sat in his office going over the financials, the
receptionist buzzed him and said there was a Mrs. Brandt wishing to
see him. The name did not ring a bell and he asked the receptionist
what was involved. She did not know but the woman said she would
discuss it with Trey. "She called you by your first name. You must
know her."

Trey said, "Send her in. I have no idea who this is."

As the door opened and the woman walked into his office, He
saw who it was and said, "Maud, I apologize, I did not know your
last name. If I had known it was you, I would have run out there and
ushered you in. I'm sure you told it to me before but I must have
missed it. How are you and what brings you to my humble offices?"

Maud surveyed Trey's office and complimented him on the layout
and furnishings. She asked how he was doing and Trey told her he
was doing quite well. No complaints. She then commented on her
last name. "I thought you would recognize the name from the news."

Trey thought a moment and could not make the connection. "No,
drawing a blank. What news are you referring to?"

"My god, Trey, where have you been?"

"I was in San Francisco about a year ago but otherwise right here.
What are you referring to, Maud?"

"Trey, my son Terry Brandt is the boy involved in the shooting
death of that so-called poor news victim, the so-called student Tyrone Palmer, on June 20. It's been all over the news."

"Maud, yes it has. That is a terrible deal. The media is not making
it easy for your son. I had no idea that was your son. We speak about
it quite often. It is a case that gets attention, as the media loves this
sort of thing. What is your son's status now? There seems to be a
delay in charging him with anything and I'm not sure if he is in jail
at this time or out on bail."

"Trey, they have not charged him yet on the shooting but they have him in jail on some gun charge, which is obviously hokey but the media is demanding he be in jail. At first I didn't think they were going to charge him at all—it obviously was self-defense—but with them not finding the carjacker's gun and the racial hullabaloo that has developed, I am sure they are going to charge him. It is just a matter of time."

"Does he have an attorney, Maud?"

"No, and that is what I wanted to talk to you about."

"I'd be glad to help, Maud, in any way I can. Do you want me to find an attorney for you?"

"Trey, we have been down that road. We have very limited funds, just what I make at the diner. Terry has no money. He is a senior in high school and is also taking some of his college courses. He is a helluva good kid. I have some savings but that is peanuts. Anyone we have spoken to wants big money. As for the public defenders, they want him to take a plea. They want him to plead guilty to manslaughter or murder two, both of which carry a lot of time. Terry says no way in hell is he guilty of anything."

"Maud, if you had a public defender, he would be paid by the government."

"I know, Trey. We know how it works. Terry has talked to two or three of them already. They are all willing to take on the case but they all insist that Terry cop a plea. Terry says he will not do that as he saw Palmer's gun and it was pointed right at him and the bullet damn near hit him."

"Maud, what are you going to do?"

"I've told Terry about you and we want you to take the case but I don't have much money to pay you."

"Maud, I am not experienced in criminal law cases. I studied it in law school and have handled some misdemeanor cases but it sounds like they want to make this a felony one or two case. That is serious stuff; many years involved in the sentence. You want someone who knows that stuff, big time."

"Trey, we are coming up with zip. I have spoken to attorneys who are highly recommended and they also say they would get him to cop a plea; otherwise, he is going to do serious jail time. I tell you, Trey, when we have spoken to any attorney that works in the criminal area, both Terry and I have had the same impression. They act as though the media is going to land big time on them and Terry, and there is no way we will get a fair trial. Our best bet is to go in there and negotiate for the best plea we can get. Terry says no way. He will not plead guilty to anything and then that cools off the interest anyone has had to take on his case. Terry tells me, 'Get Trey Stark. You always said he was a sharp young lawyer.' Terry is afraid these other guys will just send him to prison."

"Trey, you have to take the case. Terry will defend himself rather than get sold down the river when he knows he is innocent."

"Maud, where did Terry get the gun?"

"It's my gun. I had left it in the car. Terry had fired it a few times before. It was just there and he used it. It was my car, my gun. Terry didn't fire the gun until this Palmer shot at him when he opened the door. It's a wonder Terry is alive. Terry had taken a gun safety course, which I insisted he take, and was working on his gun carry permit. He may even have that now, I don't know. He's a good kid, Trey, and right now we're looking at you. You're the only attorney I know of that I have confidence in. What do you think?"

"I'm still thinking. When this Palmer fired at your son, where did the bullet go?"

"Into the seat cushion. The cops found it and it was a nine-millimeter slug but they never found the gun and the media says the cops cannot tell how long the slug had been in the car. The media is implying the slug was fired into the cushion long before this Palmer was shot. The police can tell it was not from my gun which is a .38, but that is all."

"Maud, this is a bit overwhelming. Let me think about this and I will get back to you tomorrow. I'll be frank, this is way over my head, but if I am the only answer for your son, I would not run away. Can you come by tomorrow and we can talk more about this? I want to think about how to deal with this one. Is that okay?"

"I'll be by at the same time tomorrow. Is that okay with you?"

"Fine. See you then, Maud. Take care, and we will come up with something."

When Maud had left the office, Trey sat back in his chair trying to get his thoughts in order. The thought of taking on a murder defense case was appealing to him as it was challenging to say the least, and could lead to more interesting cases. Yet, he had a responsibility to Maud's son to get the message across that Trey was not experienced in this area. He could take the case, but Maud's son needed a heavy hitter. When in doubt, he knew who to call. He dialed Chris Sutton's work number and asked her if she could come by his office as he had an important matter he wanted to discuss with her. He needed someone to talk with and he would appreciate her assistance. It was important. She said she would be there in half an hour.

As Trey waited for Chris to arrive, he sat pondering the situation. The case was receiving very heavy publicity, not only in Minnesota but also across the nation. The print and television media was focused on the case and were all describing Terry Brandt as a vicious killer of a poor black child who was hitchhiking to school when he was murdered. The only mention of any prior records of the two youths involved was that Terry Brandt had been on probation for fighting at one time when he was in elementary school. How the hell they had found that one item on Terry Brandt amazed Trey. Trey was also thinking about what the media would say if he took the case. He could see the headline now. Inexperienced debt collector fresh out of law school will be defending the killer of the child hitchhiking to school. He was also starting to realize why no attorney who knew criminal law was stepping forward to do the case pro-bono. They knew they would be slaughtered by the media just as he would be. Nevertheless, Trey was torn between wanting to take the case as he was by nature a rebel but he also was aware of his severe limitations to provide adequate legal services to Terry Brandt. Just because he was a lawyer did not mean he was a proficient criminal lawyer. That was a big jump up from his level of proficiency. He would see what Chris thought about it.

As Trey sat pondering the potential problems of handling the Terry Brandt case, the receptionist buzzed him and said, "Chris Sutton is here."

"Send her in."

The door opened and Chris walked in. She looked at Trey and asked, "What is the major issue that has you all steamed up?"

"Have a chair, Chris. You want a cup of coffee while we talk?"

After the receptionist had brought Chris a cup of coffee, Trey sat back in his chair and began explaining why he had called her for assistance. "Chris, you won't believe what I am about to tell you but I am sure you will be interested in hearing it." Trey told Chris about the visit to his office by a Mrs. Brandt and that he had no idea who she was until she entered his office and he recognized his favorite waitress from the diner. Chris sat locked into what Trey was saying and wondered what his favorite waitress from the diner could possibly have to tell him of such great importance.

"Chris, you are familiar with my visitor's name, Brandt, right?"

"No, Trey. Can't say as I am."

"I wasn't either. Chris, she is the mother of Terry Brandt, the vicious killer of the black kid that the media has been ramping up."

Trey now had Chris's attention. "What the hell did she want to talk to you about?"

"Get this, Chris. She wants me to defend the kid. He is facing a murder one or two charge at least. What do you think I should do about her request?"

"You should tell her to get a very experienced criminal attorney for openers."

"Yes. I did that. I will make a long story short. They have talked to private criminal defense attorneys and public defenders and apparently they all read the papers and watch TV. They don't want the case if the kid won't take a plea on murder two or manslaughter. The kid won't agree to anything that says he is guilty."

Trey explained to Chris what he knew about the case. The black kid walked up to his car, displayed a weapon and told him to get out of the car. Terry Brandt assumed he was being carjacked. Terry had fired a gun at the carjacker only after the carjacker had fired his weapon at him. When he saw a gun pointed at him and a bullet coming his way he pulled the trigger on his own weapon. He told

Chris the gun, as well as the car, was his mother's. "He was not hit but the bullet went into one of the seat cushions. It was retrieved but the police could not find a gun on the carjacker or at the scene. The carjacker was killed by the one shot the kid had fired. Witnesses do not confirm that a gun was fired at Terry so that is not a given. Terry Brandt is currently in jail on a gun charge and the prosecutors are still mulling over the charge for killing the kid. Terry says he was facing a carjacking situation and the kid tried to kill him. There is little if any support for that and the area where the incident took place was in the hood, so guess what that says."

Chris sat silent, mulling over what Trey had told her. "Wow. What the hell are you going to do?"

"I don't know. I would like to take the case but it's way out of my league. I have to give this some thought. What do you think?"

"Trey, the media would barbecue you if you took the case. The Bar Association might throw some coals on the fire as well."

"Chris, I think anyone who defends Terry Brandt is in for a very uncomfortable ride. The media will second-guess everything he or she does. You could search the country for a fair jury on this one and not find one after months of media hype. Good luck on that. Furthermore, where could you even move the case on a change of venue? Good luck on that one.

"Chris, you have always been the brains of our class. What is your advice? Keep in mind, I do not believe I can tell this kid's mother that we can't do anything for him. What the hell did we go to law school for if not to help people like her and her son?"

"Trey I don't think you could handle the case by yourself. There is just too much to learn and do. You would need help. Now, you could possibly get a public defender to monitor the progress on the case to see that you did not haul your client over a cliff at some point in time. Possibly the court would support that cost. The court would want the public defender to take over the entire case but if the kid balked at any attorney working the case that did not support his not guilty of anything position the court might let you have the case. I don't know. I would suggest for openers that you enlist the aid of someone right now who could give you assistance. Someone who would be glad to work on this case."

"Just who the hell is that?"

"Me."

Trey was silent for a moment. He could not imagine Chris wanting to leave her top drawer Minneapolis law firm to work with him on this case. "You are already employed. This could take months or even years. What about your job?"

"Trey, my job bores me. This is exciting. You and I could handle this. We are both smart and dedicated."

"Chris, I have some money but I couldn't pay you much at all. My collection department is profitable but it is not producing big money by a long shot. I take very little out of the firm as it is but if you could get along on the same peanuts I live on, I am willing to work something out."

"If we did a credible job, Trey, we could be paid as public defenders. We are smart. We can figure out how the game is played. We buy the books, sit in on a few trials, work the internet, get some advice from some pros and use some common sense. Voila, we win. Trey, think of what would happen if we did win. The media already has this Terry Brandt hung, quartered and thrown in the garbage. Let's do it, Trey. I can start tomorrow but you'd better first line the kid up so that he is aware of the risks he faces with us at the helm. I would get that on paper. I don't want to resign my job and have the kid bolt to someone else or cop a plea. My firm would never take me back. They would hang me out to dry."

"His mother tells me that the kid is insisting I take the case. Now if you work the case as well, do you want your name on the letterhead or would you prefer to be a silent partner?"

"Don't kid yourself, Trey. I want to be front and center. Stark and Sutton, Attorneys at law. You can be the head attorney but I am right next to you. Second chair—almost first chair. Get those business cards and stationary printed up. I have some money as well so I can starve right along with you. I will give word at my law firm tomorrow but first get this kid signed up on some sort of contract so that I don't commit hari-kari with my firm and then the kid decides he wants to cop a plea. This is the most exciting damn thing I've done in years! My parents will disown me. This is great. Where the hell is my office? I need my own office. I can't work out of a closet; I need some space. Cut this one in half. You could play a basketball game in here. When is Maud coming back to firm up this deal?"

"Should be tomorrow around one or so."

"Good, I will be here then. Are we in agreement, Trey?"

"Absolutely. If you are willing to share the pain, I will split the gain. Whatever the hell that might be. I will cut up the office after we meet with her and get signatures and so forth. We are going to need a real secretary as well. We can get some ads out tomorrow. This evening, think of what else we will need in the office. We also need Lexis or some internet search service. We will obviously be doing a lot of research. Draw up a list—computer equipment, desk, whatever you need. We should get all the gear as soon as the case is in this office."

After Chris left, Trey stayed in the office thinking about the case and making notes. They would need to be on speed on criminal procedure immediately. They both had taken 'crim law' but that did not make them criminal lawyers. They were legal but that was about it. The case was overwhelming and Trey's thoughts constantly drifted back to his initial view of the case as being way over his head. Chris's enthusiasm to proceed on the case had given him confidence that he lacked. He respected Chris's legal ability but wondered if she wasn't a bit overboard on this one. The first task to accomplish was to get their client out of jail on bond just as soon as they figured out how that was done. *This is stupid*, thought Chris. *We don't even know how to bond him out of jail.* The gun charge could not be too complex, though, so they figured they should be able to handle that. Quite possibly Terry was being improperly held on a misdemeanor, not even a felony, on the gun charge. If that was the case they should have him out in a day or two.

They were going to need extensive discovery on the carjacker. All prior records, especially carjacking, depositions on witnesses to the event, depos on school discipline problems, anything that would show that he was not just an honest kid hitchhiking to school. Another question involved how much of that crap they would be able to get into evidence. It was also going to be difficult to talk to Terry until they could get him out on bond and in the privacy of Trey's office. Speaking of the office, Trey took a look at his office space and figured out where the new walls would have to be placed. They were also going to have to invade the debt collection area for space; just putting walls into Trey's office was not going to do it. He would try for a little extra space from the building manager but Trey doubted anything was available there. As Trey thought over everything that had to be done, he realized that his little nest egg was not going to be able to handle all of the bills. They were going to have to convince the court to allow them public defender fees. That was going to be a hard sell with their experience level.

Chapter 9

The following morning after a restless night's sleep, Trey was confident that Maud was going to bring the case to his office and he had to start preparing the office to handle the work. He changed the letterhead, ordered stationary and firm cards for both himself and Chris. He had the sign changed on the exterior of the building to reflect the new name of the law firm. He also had lined up a painter to put the firm name on the door. He contacted the Lexis sales office and signed up the research program for one year. He would extend it later as more than likely this case was going to take two or more years before it was closed out. He contacted the building owner and made arrangements for a carpenter to come in as soon as possible to make the necessary changes to the offices, including telephone and electrical connections to handle computer needs. He called the telephone company and had two more phone lines set up. Trey figured that he could go to the office store and pick up all of the office materials that he and Chris would be needing including legal pads, pens, markers, staplers, as well as Chris' desk, chair, filing cabinet, computer stand and whatever else she would need. He also called Walt and told him what was going on.

"You what? You are going to take a murder case? That murder case? That is not the one to start on. I question the court will even allow you to take the case. Who did you say is coming to work there? No way in hell! What the hell did you promise her? I can't believe this. Wait till the guys at the Rooster hear this."

"No, it's true, Walt. Actually, Chris begged me to take her on here. She looks at this as the great challenge that life sometimes, if ever, presents to people. I guess I sort of see it the same way."

Walt was silent for a moment and then said, "Actually, I can see that as well. If you need any more help, give me a shout. I could be talked into this but I would need some money. Not much, just rent, food, gas and maybe a beer now and then."

"Walt, I will keep that in mind. I'm sure we will want some help. Possibly we can get some public defender funds and that would help us out quite a bit. I will let you know but we are really short of cash. You would have to quit your job, though."

"Like I give a damn about my job. They will have to find someone else to haul mail to the post office if I am not there. What a joke. You know, Trey, we could get Walker to organize an intern program at the school focused on this case to provide research that the case is going to need. I could staff that operation on behalf of the defense team. I'm sure Walker would love to be directly involved in a major murder case. This is hot stuff. Wait until the boys at the Rooster's Nest hear about this. They will be green with envy but not many of them have the balls to take on this mother. Takes a real debt collector to grab for the gold ring."

"The gold ring may not be what we end up with, Walt. I expect the media to really give us a hard time for assuming we can handle this case. If you want in on the case, let me know. I'm sure I could use you big time. One area that we need to cover thoroughly is criminal procedure. At Walker, we have not been thinking in those terms and we have to know what we are doing there."

Chris called and suggested she and Trey have lunch before meeting with Maud. They met at Friday's and when they were seated Chris began the conversation. "I told a couple of my fellow associates in the firm that I was most likely going to join you in the defense of the Terry Brandt case. I have to confess they thought I was completely out of my mind and out of my league. I assured them that I looked at it quite differently. I had told my parents what was going on last night and they about fainted. My mother absolutely refused to permit me to leave 'fags and bags' and get involved with this murder case. I just told her that I had to do what I had to do. Actually, I think Dad was quite proud of me although he didn't say anything— just the look on his face. Hell, I can't say that I was surprised by any of this. The point is that we are going to take a ton of crap taking on this case. I hope you are ready for that. I am."

"Chris, I have been all over that and am ready for the grief. It is also going to cost us a fair amount of money for equipment and research services and whatever. Hopefully we can get public defender status so that we can recover some of our costs. I doubt we will recover all of them. Walt also offered to come on board and if need be, we can take him. He also suggested that we get Walker to set up an intern team to help us with research. He said he would supervise that if the school sets up the program. We will take abuse, Chris. From our associates, family, Bar Association—you name it. We just have to hit them hard and let them know that we intend to take the case and we intend to win. This is definitely a winnable case from what I know of it. The biggest problem we have with it is the damage being done by the media. They are doing their best to trash our client and canonize the carjacker. That will continue until the case is completed. You can count on that. The wonderful fourth estate—like they have any principles. What they are really good at is creating race riots."

After lunch they returned to Trey's office and Maud was already there waiting to meet with Trey. Trey had her come into his office and he introduced her to Chris. He told Maud that Chris would also be working on the case jointly with Trey being the lead attorney. He then asked Maud if she had talked with Terry. She had and he was totally agreeable to having Trey handle the case. Trey told Maud that they had to meet with Terry as soon as possible to ensure that he knew all the circumstances and was in total agreement with what was taking place. Trey also had prepared a letter of agreement stating his qualifications and those of Chris Sutton to be the attorneys acting on behalf of Terry Brandt defending him for any and all charges arising from the incident of June 9, 2009. Both Maud as the guardian and mother of the minor as well as the minor had to sign the document. Maud immediately signed.

The three of them then left Trey's office and drove to the Hennepin County Jail where Terry was being kept. Trey asked if there had been any court appearances by Terry since being arrested. Apparently there were none that Maud was aware of. She also did not know of the charges, if any, that he was being held under.

When they arrived at the jail, Trey introduced himself at the office to the deputy and told him that he was the attorney for Terry Brandt. He asked what the charges were against his client. The jailer responded that he believed he was being held on violation of firearms statutes and was also under investigation in a murder case. "Beyond that," he said, "You will have to talk to the prosecutor on the case and that is Fred Jackson, who heads up the criminal division of the County Attorney's Office."

The jailer took Trey, Chris and Maud to a hearing room and then brought Terry back with him. When he entered the room, Trey saw that he was a decent-appearing young man that would present well in front of a jury. His mother gave him a hug and then she introduced Trey and Chris as his new attorneys. Trey asked him if he had made any court appearances since being arrested and Terry said he had not. He was being held on a possession of a gun charge according to the deputy that had arrested him. That was about two weeks ago and since then he had heard nothing. Trey told him that they would be taking steps immediately to get him released from jail. Terry brightened up upon hearing that. Trey then told him that he wanted to get all the details of what took place but he would do that when Terry was released on bond and they could meet in Trey's office.

Terry signed the retainer agreement after Trey explained the experience level that he and his partner, Chris, possessed. Terry did not seem concerned and said that he had great confidence that both of them would serve him well. As they were about to leave, Trey advised Terry that he was to say nothing about the case to anyone either verbally in conversation, on the telephone or in writing.

"Say absolutely nothing. I don't want to hear at trial what you told someone that you spoke to in your cell. You can trust no one in the jail. Not the guards and not your cellmates. Keep in mind that cellmates tend to cooperate with the detectives hoping to work deals with them. Most of them would turn in their best friend for a few months off their sentence, not to mention somebody they didn't even know. You got that? Nothing. Say nothing about the case to anyone unless I am there telling you it is okay to do so. You've got a decent case. Let's not blow it."

When they left the jail, Trey wrote down the name of the prosecutor that was handling Terry's case. He would contact him when he returned to his office regarding getting Terry released from the jail.

Trey dropped Maud off at the diner and then he and Chris returned to the office. When they were back in Trey's office they lined up the tasks they had to get involved with immediately. Trey was going to work on getting Terry released from jail either under bond or by order of the court. Chris was going to start working on lining up the discovery depositions that they would need but first getting a secretary hired for all the typing that they would need to have done. Chris mentioned they would need an experienced legal secretary familiar with criminal procedure and not a beginner as a knowledgeable secretary could provide a great deal of assistance to two neophytes.

Trey called the prosecutor Jackson and soon had him on the phone. Trey identified himself as the attorney for Terry Brandt and Jackson said that he was not familiar with Trey's name as an attorney working in the criminal field in Minneapolis. Trey explained that he had just been practicing in the city for a little over a year and had been contacted by the family to represent Terry. Jackson did not comment on this information but asked Trey what the purpose of the call was. Trey replied that he wanted information on the charges against his client and what court appearances had taken place or were on the calendar.

Jackson replied, "There have been no court appearances yet. He has only been in jail a few weeks."

"What are the charges against Terry Brandt at this time?"

"Unlawful possession of a weapon, a misdemeanor."

"You've held him for three weeks on a misdemeanor?"

"Yes, but we are also investigating a murder one charge on him."

"When is he appearing before a judge?"

"He is presently under the jurisdiction of the Juvenile Court due to his age of seventeen. We have just filed a motion with the Juvenile Court for certification allowing us to proceed with adult charges and we will be sending you notice of that hearing. That is a 260B hearing, in case you are not familiar with it."

"Can't say I am."

"The hearing will be in two weeks in Juvenile Court. Due to the seriousness of the crime, we are anticipating that we will be allowed to proceed with a murder one charge and the hearing after that will most likely be in another week or so when the clerk will schedule an arraignment on the weapons charge."

"Has Terry Brandt been offered release on bail?"

"No, he hasn't. Keep in mind, no bail in Juvenile Court."

"Yes, of course."

"Meanwhile, we are still investigating the shooting of the hitch-hiker."

"You mean the carjacker, right?"

Jackson ignored the comment by Trey and said he had business to take care of and had to hang up.

Trey was annoyed at the casual treatment of his client by the public official. "Look, charge him or release him. This is unconscionable."

Jackson said he had to leave and would talk to him later.

Trey sat back in his chair and made some notes of the call to Jackson. He also added a note, "Bail on juvenile defendants." He called Chris into his office and told her what the prosecutor had said regarding bail for juveniles and the 260B hearing. "I assume the certification hearing is to determine if this is a proper case for certification of the defendant as an adult chargeable with the felony of murder one."

"I'm sure it is," Chris said, "but I will check that out right now. Being seventeen and a half on a murder charge would bring him into court as an adult unless his perfectly clean record prevents that."

Trey received the notice for the certification hearing two days later and it was to be held in Juvenile Court at two p.m. the following Wednesday.

He passed it on to Chris and told her and Alice Bentley, the new legal secretary, to prepare the necessary papers for the hearing.

Trey visited Terry Brandt in jail later that day and informed him that in view of the fact he was being held pursuant to the Juvenile Court rules, he did not have access to bail but the hearing would be in the following week and Trey would see what they could do at that time to get him released.

On the day of the hearing, Trey sat in the courtroom awaiting the call of his case. When it was called, another attorney stood up and approached the table reserved for motion attorneys. Trey assumed he was Jackson or one of the attorneys on his staff. Trey sat down across from his opponent and introduced himself. The other fellow was not overly interested but did introduce himself as Fred Jackson, prosecutor. The judge who had been inspecting the file nodded to Jackson and asked who was appearing on behalf of the juvenile. Trey introduced himself as the attorney for Terry Brandt and provided the clerk the name of his firm, the address and phone number.

The judge commented that the charges pending against the juvenile in this case were quite serious and in view of his age, which was almost at the legal age level, did not bode well for the juvenile. He asked what the defendant's attorney had to say on behalf of his client with respect to granting or denying certification.

Trey stood and addressed the court. "Your Honor, this young man, Terry Brandt, is a first year college student, recently graduated from high school with honors, and has a perfectly clear record devoid of any convictions, juvenile or otherwise. He is a fine young man who was defending himself from an attempted carjacking and had been shot at by the decedent before he used a gun to defend himself."

"Mr. Stark, as I am sure you are aware, the presumptions that apply in certification cases are all basically against your client. His age being over seventeen and the gravity of the crimes charged against him presume certification as an adult in the absence of clear and convincing evidence to the contrary. What do you have to say that is clear and convincing that would cause me to deny certification as an adult in this case?"

"Your Honor, the facts of this case clearly show that the defendant was acting in self-defense. He was also licensed to have and to operate a weapon in his own self-defense."

"Mr. Stark, I am certifying Mr. Brandt as an adult with respect to the charges pending from this matter. Is there anything else?"

Trey had nothing else to add at this point. He would have liked to discuss bail but that would not be set until Terry was turned over to criminal court procedures.

When Trey left the courtroom, he returned to his office and stopped at Chris's office to discuss the hearing. Trey sat down in the chair in front of Chris's desk while she asked him how it had gone.

"Well, it sure as hell didn't go in my favor. He is being tried as an adult and the little arguments that we had discussed to stop that from happening were just not too impressive as far as the court was concerned. The 260B presumptions wiped out any argument we had; can't say that I was surprised by that. Anyway, we are now back where we were when we weren't aware that Terry was being held as a juvenile. Next stop is the arraignment and the bail hearing. We should do okay there, I would think."

The following day charges were filed against Terry Brandt, including murder in the first degree for the intentional killing of Tyrone Palmer. There was also a companion charge of illegal possession of a loaded firearm.

Trey inquired as to the bail assigned to the case and was told it was set at five hundred thousand dollars, which was the standard murder one bail figure. Trey asked Alice Bentley if she was familiar with the motion papers for release on bail and for release on non-financial bail. She said that she was and she said she would have the papers roughed out for his review within an hour. When Trey reviewed Alice's product, the motion papers were virtually completed with the exception of the particulars from Terry's case that Trey or Chris would need to insert.

Trey called the Clerk of Court and inquired how he was going to get his client on the calendar for a bail hearing. The Clerk added Terry Brandt's name to the motion practice list for the following week. He was to be arraigned at the same time. Trey had his work cut out for him right from the get go—how to get his client released on bail. This would probably be one of the simpler issues he would face and he was already stymied as to what to do. Trey researched the matter on Lexis and finally came up with motion verbiage that seemed to fit the case. Trey had his motion advanced for hearing on the grounds it was an emergency measure to get his client released when there were no grounds for holding him and there had been no probable cause hearing on charges against him, whatever they were.

Chapter 10

The following Monday morning Trey was in court with his client to argue his motion and the first matter to be called was the arraignment. The court advised Trey and his client that the defendant was charged with first degree murder and unlawful possession of a weapon. When asked how he was going to plead, Terry Brandt spoke up and said, "Not guilty."

When the motion cases were called and the Brandt motion came up, Trey again stepped forward as the moving party representing his client, Terry Brandt. An Attorney for the State stepped forward and Trey saw it was Fred Jackson. As the moving party on the motion, Trey introduced himself to the judge hearing the motions. Trey stated that his client had been held in the Hennepin County Jail for the past three weeks without being charged with a crime other than a misdemeanor gun charge, possession of a weapon with a permit. He had in the last few days been charged with murder in the first degree. Up until this week there had been no indictment by information or otherwise, and no bail set. From everything Trey knew about the case, "Terry Brandt should be released immediately."

Fred Jackson then stood up and introduced himself as the prosecutor on the case. He said that Terry Brandt was the highly publicized person who shot the hitchhiker to death on June 9, 2009. He was being held for unlawful possession of a firearm since then and the prosecutor had still been awaiting a detailed investigation report on the shooting. He expected the report in the next few days and would be filing an Information at that time. In the meantime, there had been a certification hearing which had held up the process for a period of time and that had been finally adjudicated to allow prosecution of the defendant as an adult. The prosecutor stated that a formal charge of murder one was now filed with the Clerk of Court and bail was set at the standard amount for that charge at five hundred thousand dollars.

Trey stood up and said that he had a motion on file for this hearing calling for bail to be reduced to a non-financial bail in view of the fact that the defendant had no prior criminal record, was a young man aged seventeen who had been attending college until the decedent in this matter attempted to carjack him while he was on his way to school. The defendant had utilized a weapon for which he had a license to carry and fired it at the decedent only after the decedent had attempted to kill him with his own weapon.

Fred Jackson angrily stated that no weapon was found in the vicinity of where Tyrone Palmer had fallen after being shot and a number of witnesses would testify that they only heard one gunshot, from the weapon fired by Mr. Brandt. Apparently Mr. Brandt took the life of Tyrone Palmer in a premeditated violent manner. Jackson requested that the defendant be held in jail pending and during trial, not subject to bail.

Further arguments both for and against bail were raised by the two attorneys. Finally the judge spoke. He said he agreed with the defense counsel that in view of the lack of any criminal record on the part of the defendant and in view of the defendant's contention that the killing was done in self-defense, the defendant could be released from jail immediately pending further order of the court and that should he not appear at any subsequent hearings or court appearances, he would then be subject to custody in the county jail without bail. The judge said that he would issue an order that afternoon.

As Trey walked out of the courtroom all of the defense counsel in the room were staring at him. He had no doubt that many of the newer ones were envious. This was a case that could put them on the map. They had not considered the time involved or the money it would take to handle this case, much less the abuse from the media. The older attorneys were most likely wondering who the hell did Trey think he was. This was way over his head and he was just too stupid to realize it in their opinion. *Such is life,* Trey thought as he made his way out of the courtroom. A group of men who appeared to be reporters accompanied him out. When he was in the hallway, he was bombarded with questions while TV cameras were whirring and camera flashes were lighting up the lobby. A reporter shoved a microphone in his face and asked him why his client had killed the child "when he was just hitchhiking to school?" Trey responded, "There was no child hitchhiking. The young man that had been killed was a carjacker who had fired a weapon at Terry Brandt and Brandt had returned fire in an attempt to save his own life."

Other reporters were shouting questions at him dealing with the incident and one reporter asked Trey what he was doing handling the case when he had no experience. Finally Trey refused to talk with them and made his way to the jail in order to retrieve Terry Brandt. It was clear that he was going to have to sprint Brandt out of the jail or the reporters would land on him en masse. Trey called Chris on his cell phone and told her to have a car parked outside the jail exit so that he and Terry could get out of the government building without reporters joining them.

A short time later, Trey made his way to the jail office and presented his copy of the order calling for the release of Terry Brandt. The deputy looked it over and then called to have Brandt sent to the office with all clothing and personal items the deputies had taken from him. Some of the reporters had tried to gain entrance to the jail office but the deputies restrained them and told them to stay out in the hall. Trey told the deputies he was going to need some help to leave the jail exit safely and requested that they keep the reporters inside the building and away from the exit. About that time Terry appeared with a big smile on his face and greeted Trey. He wondered what the crowd of reporters were doing out in the hallway. Trey said he would explain later. Trey placed a call to Chris to find out where she was. She had left the office immediately upon getting his call and was pulling up to the jail exit as she spoke. Trey grabbed Terry and the two of them made their way out the exit and spotting Chris's car were soon inside and being driven away.

They had made their escape successfully and within minutes they were seated in Trey's office interviewing their client. The phone was ringing constantly and Trey had instructed the receptionist to advise all callers that Mr. Stark and Miss Sutton were not in the office. Fortunately Alice Bentley, the new secretary, was on duty in the office organizing her desk and equipment. She was also busy handling the

phone calls and was obviously wondering what she had gotten herself into. Actually, she was excited to be involved in what was the
most interesting case in the twin cities. She had worked for a criminal law firm in Minneapolis for a number of years until the principals had retired and she was very knowledgeable on procedure,
which was what her new employers needed the most assistance on.
She was proving to be invaluable assistance and had explained to
Chris the timeline for handling a felony murder case and the documents that would be required to process the case. She had her own
form file, which was a fortunate find for the firm as they were very
much in the dark when it came to the documents they would need.

Trey and Chris questioned Terry for three hours on absolutely everything that occurred on the day of the incident. Where was Tyrone
when Terry first observed him? When he approached Terry's car,
what was his demeanor? Terry said he was just smiling and did not
consider him a threat until he pulled the gun out when he was right
next to the car. Then Terry knew he had a serious problem. Terry
said he played it cool and smiled up at Tyrone who was looking
down at him seated in the driver's seat. Terry asked Tyrone what he
wanted and Tyrone responded that he wanted the car. He then told
Terry to "get the hell out." Terry said no problem, unfastened his
seat belt and pretended to be getting out of the car. In the process, he
grabbed his gun but not fast enough as Tyrone then fired the gun he
had. Fortunately the bullet missed. Terry then reacted quickly and
fired his gun. That was the sum total of events. After questioning
Terry at length, they discussed what to do with him as his home was
undoubtedly being watched by the media; Maud confirmed that. She
suggested that he stay with a friend of his who had his own apartment and that was agreeable with everyone so they sent Terry down
to the garage below their offices and he got into the trunk of the collection attorney's car and departed for his friend's apartment. Terry
called from the apartment and said that he was there and there was
no sign of any reporters around the building. He was instructed to
stay inside at all times and to let Trey's receptionist know what food,
books, or other items he would need and they would be delivered
to him.

While Terry seemed secure in his friend's apartment, it was obvious that Trey and Chris would be bombarded by the media who

were assembled outside of their office building. Television trucks were parked on the street and RVs being used for housing reporters were parked as close to the building exits as they could get. Trey and Chris realized they were observing their new closest friends awaiting their exit from the building. They also realized this would be the situation until the case was closed.

When Trey and Chris had a moment to sit back and relax, Trey told Chris what had transpired in the courtroom. Chris was quite impressed as Trey's entry into the world of criminal law appeared to have been quite successful. Hopefully it would keep the wolves away from challenging his qualifications at least to this point. Trey likewise congratulated Chris on finding such a well-qualified secretary. Chris had followed up on a tip from a friend who was aware that Alice Bentley was looking for work having been recently laid off as the firm where she worked had dissolved. She was exactly what Trey and Chris needed in the office to ensure that criminal court documents were prepared accurately and in accord with their time constraints.

The work arrangement that Trey and Chris had worked out seemed to be functioning satisfactorily. Trey would be the front man for presenting the case in court although Chris would be functioning there as needed. Chris's primary function was to prepare arguments and pleadings needed for the court appearances by Trey. In this function she was very ably assisted by Alice Bentley. Chris would preview all documents with Alice before they were actually printed up. Chris was also locating and arranging witnesses for all depositions. Again she was discussing the deposition schedule with Trey to ensure that all important witnesses were included.

As they talked, it was clear to both that their lives in future months or maybe even years were going to be covered in the newspapers and in the media. Hopefully they would still be able to relax in restaurants and at the Rooster's Nest with their friends. They laughed as they pondered the need to buy disguises so that they could slip out of the building undetected. Chris hoped that her home was not being monitored. If it was, her parents were going to suggest she live elsewhere. She said she was only joking but they would not enjoy living in a fishbowl. Trey suggested that possibly they could make an arrangement with the media for periodic press conferences to avoid the impromptu swarms of reporters that they had already observed. Chris added that the court would most likely be placing limits on whatever they had to say to the press and they would most likely hear about that quite soon.

Trey had thought about the bullet fired by Palmer that must have come close to Terry Brandt. Very likely there would be trace elements of the bullet, associated powder and chemicals on the clothing that Terry was wearing at the time. In view of the fact that according to the media there was no gun found at the scene that would support the argument that the carjacker had fired a gun at Terry Brandt. Trey was going to need all the evidence available to prove that a gun was fired at or near Terry Brandt. That raised the further issue of was there a bullet casing from the ejected shell lying on the ground. The hijacker's gun was most likely a nine-millimeter semi-automatic and would have ejected a shell somewhat forcefully from the right side of the weapon. That casing should have been lying somewhere near the automobile aft of the rear passenger door. Unfortunately a sufficient amount of time had elapsed since the shooting for the casing to have disappeared. The police normally look for this at all scenes where a shooting had taken place. Trey told Chris to include that in her discovery questions. Trey placed a call to Terry and told him not to wash those clothes. If he was still wearing them, they had to be secured in plastic bags for further exam.

Terry told Trey that he would then need another pair of jeans, t-shirts, shorts and a shirt to take their place. Trey got his sizes and made a note to have the receptionist find replacement clothing in the morning and deliver it to Terry. She was also to pick up the clothing Terry wore at the time of the shooting. Apparently that clothing had been temporarily taken from him when he was placed in the county jail and he was given the usual inmate uniform. Trey wondered if Terry's clothing had been examined by the prosecutor or if it had been washed by anyone. He would have to pursue that later. He also suggested that Chris come up with someone to examine Terry's clothing for indications of a gun having been fired in the direction of the clothing and if so, was it possible to determine how close the bullet had passed by the clothing. He also suggested that Chris inform the examiner that the person wearing the clothing had also fired a thirty-eight-caliber weapon but that should have been in a direction away from the clothing. Another thought that had come to Trey—security video—but it was most likely too late to take advantage of that. Did any of the stores or other places of business along the street where the incident occurred have video of the event? Trey doubted that such video even if it once existed would still be available. Too much time had passed but it was still something that should be checked out. Possibly the police had pursued that, but he doubted it. He would have Chris check it out. If there was video and the police had not pursued it, they could use that as well.

The following few days were devoted to getting the offices constructed and equipped to handle the work. It was still quite crowded as Trey was not able to expand his office space beyond the limits that he already had. He solved his space needs by invading the collection area depriving it of about a third of the space they previously had. He had managed to create a work room for the criminal case with a large work table where they could lay out their research materials, pleadings, court documents and forms that would be needed as discovery progressed. They had also increased their library with the purchase of criminal law procedure and practice books as well as court rules, evidence manuals, and other related materials. Trey and Chris had a lot to learn and fortunately they were young, smart and eager. They had all of the necessary qualifications and they were planning on working long hours learning the proper procedures, the forms needed, the law involved in the hearings they would be involved with as well as the law involved in the death of Tyrone Palmer.

A few days later, Trey received notice of the Preliminary Hearing and it was scheduled for the following week. He called the new legal secretary into his office as well as Chris to discuss how they were going to handle the hearing. As they were all seated, Trey explained that they had received notice and they had to decide what they were going to do about it. Trey was aware that they could participate in the hearing or could refuse to participate. It was an opportunity to know more about the State's case and to cross-examine some of the witnesses but Trey questioned that they would learn anything from that and would possibly be giving away valuable information on their case. Alice said that her firm seldom became involved in the prelim but sometimes they did. In this case, there was little doubt as to what case the prosecution would be putting on. It was pretty much an open and shut case as far as the prosecution was involved. The real questions dealt with what the defendant's case was going to look like. The purpose of the hearing was to determine the existence of probable cause. There was no doubt the defense attorneys would not be negating probable cause in this instance. There was also little expectation that the prosecution would be unveiling their entire case. All they had to do was to show that there was probable cause for the charges. There was also no admission of guilt on the defendant's part if he waived the prelim. Trey said that he was for waiving the prelim and if others thought they should pursue it, they should speak up. Both Chris and Alice said that at this time they had no opinion either way. Chris suggested giving her another day or two to do some research and then she would give her opinion. That was fine with Trey.

Trey and Chris divided up the work that needed to be done so that they were prepared for upcoming events. Chris was assigned the task of preparing papers and the law on requesting their appointment as public defenders. Their new secretary, Alice, was familiar with the process as well as the layout of the motion papers that would be required. There appeared to be no negative media attention on Tyrone Palmer. Trey had an investigator digging up whatever he could find on Palmer and apparently he was coming up with quite a bit, none of it complimentary to Palmer.

In view of the fact that when the matter went to trial the judge could allow the jury to find the defendant guilty of murder one or of a lesser offense such as manslaughter, they had to be prepared to defend on those charges as well.

Trey had the receptionist pick up copies of local newspapers and some national papers. In all of the papers, there was news of the release of the killer of the student hitchhiking to college. One paper admitted the fact that the carjacker was not registered at any college or university but stated that he undoubtedly was on his way to register at the county community college, which was somewhat in the direction Terry was driving when accosted. When asked, Tyrone's mother backed up the story that her son was indeed on his way to register at the college. One of the local newspapers commented that the defense attorney made remarks in court that the decedent was a criminal and the defendant Brandt had killed him when the unarmed boy was merely seeking a ride to his school. Trey's investigator learned that Tyrone Palmer had never graduated from high school, which would render his intent to register for college highly unlikely. There was no mention of that fact in any of the papers. One of the papers even had a comment that Tyrone Palmer was doing excellent work as a student in his college courses.

The very Reverend Shamille Armstrong had arrived in Minneapolis and was already busy setting up a protest march down Hennepin Avenue condemning the intentional killing of this unarmed boy and calling for a quick sentencing of the killer putting him away for life. According to the Reverend, it was unfortunate that Minnesota did not have a death penalty in first degree murder cases because this was a case that clearly called for a death penalty. Shamille Armstrong had printed a slogan below a graphic of a black child nailed to a cross. The slogan said, "One down. How many to go?" The poster was liberally displayed throughout the city.

The Reverend was prominently and frequently presented on all local television stations and on the front pages of all newspapers, local and national. Clearly the publicity on this case was causing great concern for Trey and Chris as well as for their client, Terry Brandt. Trey was becoming very concerned that some aroused citizen would take it upon himself to serve a death sentence on Terry Brandt and possibly even on his attorneys.

Chapter 11

As the publicity for the Hennepin Avenue March built up, the media began to refer to it as a million-man march protesting the kid glove treatment of Terry Brandt who even now was not in jail. The county attorney's office was receiving a barrage of petitions, phone calls and accusations of being in the pocket of the defense firm of Stark and Sutton. There were pickets surrounding the courthouse day and night demanding justice for Tyrone Palmer. His photograph taken at least five years or more prior to the incident depicting him as a young boy was used in all media on television or in the newspapers. Pictures of him taken in recent times that were beginning to surface on the internet showed a very mature and somewhat angry appearing man. The pictures certainly did not appear to resemble a young child on his way to school.

In the morning as Trey drank his coffee and searched the morning paper for any articles relating to the Terry Brandt case, he noted that there was an editorial dealing with the qualifications of the attorneys handling the Palmer murder case which immediately caught his attention. The article commenced with a paragraph that read as follows:

It seems the defense attorneys handling the case of the killer of Tyrone Jackson are the principals in the debt collection firm of Minnesota Business Services, Inc., namely Trey Stark and Christine Sutton. Both are relative newcomers in the Minneapolis legal community, having only recently passed the Minnesota Bar Exam for admission to the profession. Neither one has any experience in criminal defense work, so the public may be exposed to even lower levels of performance than we have heretofore had the opportunity to view from other stalwarts from the legal world. Hopefully the judges handling this case will have the foresight to spare us further embarrassment by removing these two from the case and replacing the debt collection company, Minnesota Business Services, Inc., with a real law firm. It is our fond hope that more responsible attorneys will be placed in charge of this case, which has important implications for the stability of our community.

Trey was infuriated by the insulting tone of the editorial. He called Chris into his office and showed her the article. She said her parents had just called her about it and again asked her what she was doing working on that case. Her parents said they could hardly go out to dinner without someone bringing up the Palmer case and asking why their daughter was involved in it. Trey said that he was going to respond to the article and demand that the newspaper print his response. Chris was not sure that was a good idea but Trey was of the opinion that they could not just let the article sit out there and smolder. The criticism of them was not going to go away so they may as well let the public know what they think of the editorial. Furthermore at the moment there was no restriction upon them with respect to comments on the case. So they had best respond now before the court placed controls on them prohibiting them from giving opinions relative to the case.

Later in the morning, Trey prepared his response to the editorial in the Minneapolis newspaper. He stated that:

Both attorneys working on the case were duly licensed, fully authorized and are competent to pursue a very active defense on behalf of their client, Terry Brandt. The evidence accumulated as a result of the unfortunate loss of life of Tyrone Palmer clearly showed that their client, Terry

Brandt, acted in self-defense after being fired
upon by the carjacker and deserved to be acquitted
of all charges in connection with the incident.
Furthermore, the Stark and Sutton Law Firm
is totally organized, equipped and prepared to
provide a thorough and complete defense for their
client. The entire staff of the firm, comprised of
six individuals, are working full-time in preparing
the case for trial and fully expect to receive an
acquittal on behalf of Mr. Brandt. There is no
need to disrupt this smooth operating defense
team from pursuing its goal unless the purpose
was to deny Terry Brandt the defense that he was
entitled to as an innocent man.

Trey had the collection attorney deliver the letter to the editorial
department of the Minneapolis newspaper with the request that it
be printed on the editorial page as soon as practicable. Trey's response was in fact printed less than two days later and prominently
displayed on the editorial page of the paper. It was captioned, "Collection Firm attorneys respond to criticism of their handling of the
Terry Brandt Case."

The following morning, Trey had not heard from the prosecutor or the clerk of court as to when the motion appointing Trey and
Chris as Special Counsel would be held, so he placed a call to the
clerk. Trey was told the matter was on the calendar for hearing the
following morning. Trey asked why he had not been notified of the
hearing and the clerk informed him that there was no record of him
as being the attorney assigned to the defense of Terry Brandt. The
two discussed that for a minute or two with no satisfaction to Trey.

Chris had prepared all of the documents that they figured they
would need for the hearing. These included the request to the court
that the firm of Stark and Sutton be appointed as Special Public Defenders acting on behalf of Terry Brandt and the further request that
they be shown as the attorneys representing Terry Brandt at the request of his mother and guardian, Maud Brandt, in all court filings.

This was the area that appeared to be a problem for the firm.

Trey had been told that there was considerable discussion going on among the criminal lawyers in the community as well as in the media with respect to the limited experience of the attorneys that were handling this very important criminal matter. The pressure would be on the court to do something about it. Their best argument for staying on the case was the demand by their client and his guardian that Stark and Sutton handle the case and they were doing quite well so far.

On the morning of the hearing, Trey and Chris were both in the courtroom as the Terry Brandt case was called. Trey stood and announced to the court that he and Miss Chris Sutton, who was there as well, were the attorneys acting on behalf of Mr. Brandt. The judge studied both of them for a moment and then asked if they both realized this was a murder one case as filed by the prosecutor. "Are you aware of that?"

Trey responded that they had been aware of that for quite some time and had been preparing for it.

The judge pondered that for a moment and then suggested that both of them should meet with him in chambers after the hearing. Trey then said that he had other motions to be made in connection with the case and inquired if they were to be heard in open court or in chambers. The judge replied that they would be heard in chambers. The clerk then called the next case. After the docket was cleared, the judge returned to his chambers and Trey and Chris followed him out of the courtroom along with the prosecutor, Fred Jackson.

When they all entered the chambers of Judge Lindquist, Trey suggested that the court reporter transcribe their meeting and that the defendant also be present. The judge thought for a moment and then told his clerk to bring both the reporter and Terry Brandt to his chambers. The court reporter was located and had set up her equipment in the judge's chambers and Terry Brandt had been sitting in court awaiting the hearings. The judge said they could proceed without out Mr. Brandt on some of the issues before them unless their client preferred to be present. Terry indicated that he wished to observe. The judge then told Trey and Chris that he had serious concerns that they were not qualified to be handling a murder one charge in his courtroom. He explained that he had a responsibility to see that a defendant in such a case was represented by competent counsel and asked Trey what he had to support the proposition that he and Miss Sutton were sufficiently competent to handle the case.

Trey replied that they were both duly licensed and currently qualified members of the Bar Association and had responded to the direct requests of both the defendant and his guardian to act on behalf of their client. Both Trey and Chris Sutton had made it very clear that their experience level in criminal felony cases was limited but that they were confident they could and would provide adequate legal defense for Terry Brandt sufficient to prevent a guilty verdict on the felony charges. Since agreeing to do so, Trey and Chris had devoted every minute of every day and night to seeing to it that Terry Brandt received excellent representation. They had not stumbled yet in handling the defense of the case and had no intention of stumbling at any time. Trey added that the only area where they were challenged was in devoting all of their time, assets and staff to this case foregoing any revenue they might obtain from other legal work. Consequently, in view of the limited finances of both Mr. Brandt and his mother, Maud Brandt, they were being hindered by a severe shortage of funds to pay their staff and to support the defense of this case. They requested the court deal with them as Special Public Defenders and compensate them in similar fashion to other public defenders so that they could continue devoting the time and effort the case demanded.

Thereupon, Trey handed his motion papers to the judge for the appointments together with his affidavit and an affidavit signed by both the defendant and his guardian that specifically stated that they were fully apprised of the legal experience of both Trey Stark and Chris Sutton and were confident that the two attorneys would be providing competent legal counsel on the defendant's behalf. They further requested that the firm of Stark and Sutton be appointed as Special Public Defenders in all matters relating to Terry Brandt. Trey stated that any reasonable compensation for their services to the State normal for the defense of a case of this type would be acceptable. Terry Brandt had been present in the judge's chambers and was very interested in the issue being discussed. At the conclusion of Trey's remarks, Terry commented that he had complete confidence that his best interests were being ably represented by Trey

Stark and Chris Sutton.

The judge only commented that he would take the motion under advisement and asked about the other motions Trey wished to bring

The prosecutor was visibly upset that the court was going along with Trey's requests and said that he had a request to make as well. The court said for him to go ahead and make it. "Your Honor, the defendant's attorney has been arguing his case in the press and that is most improper. We have avoided all public commentary and have tried our best to stay above the fray even though we, too, have been bombarded by the media. I request an order gagging the defendants and those they represent from making any more arguments, allegations, outlandish claims of mysterious disappearing guns or whatever in connection with this case. Their action in this matter is most likely due to their inexperience in criminal matters and has been shameful. It has to stop."

When the prosecutor was silent, Trey explained that there had been a severely disparaging piece of crap in the editorial section of the Minneapolis paper insulting and slamming both he and Chris Sutton without any substantiation and it was necessary to call it out for the piece of trash that it was. That was the only comment he or Miss Sutton had made, even though the media was frothing at the mouth and cutting down his client constantly. Trey commented, "Someone ought to gag them."

The judge responded to Trey's comments. "We have all suffered from them, Mr. Stark. Unfortunately they have all the freedom and power to do virtually whatever they want with some limitations. If they continue publishing comments that affect the defendant's right to a fair trial they can be restricted. Gag orders have been issued by this court in the past but they are very seldom granted. As for you and the prosecutor, no more comments not approved by this court."

Trey nodded and said, "Very well, Your Honor."

Before Trey left the judge's chambers, he handed Jackson a copy of the Notice of Discovery, which was required under the court rules to initiate the discovery process and required the prosecutor to serve a written discovery exhibit on the defendant within fifteen days listing all material evidence including documents and statements permitting the defendant to examine and copy virtually all information in the possession of the prosecutor. The defendant was under similar obligations pursuant to court rules to divulge documents and materials supporting their client's case. In the event the defendants relied upon an alibi for the charges specified, they were subject to provisions of the court rules whereby the prosecutor could demand all evidence supporting the alibi. In this case, Trey was relying heavily on the issue of self-defense. Trey and Chris discussed if this came under the alibi rule but both concluded it did not as the alibi rule related primarily to the question of the defendant's presence at the scene of the alleged crime.

The day following the hearing the Minneapolis newspaper had an editorial criticizing Judge Lindquist for releasing the killer, Terry Brandt, with absolutely no bail, this after murdering the unarmed student, Tyrone Palmer, with no warning. According to witnesses at the scene who were neighbors of Mr. Palmer, he was merely requesting a ride from the defendant so that he could attend school at the community college. Judge Samuel Lindquist would not respond to reporters' questions for the reasons supporting his release of the killer.

In the days following the hearing, Trey and Chris were busy gathering all facts relating to the incident and preparing for the depositions of all witnesses they could identify and all witnesses the prosecutor's office listed, all parties shown on the police report, persons who had known Tyrone Palmer, including neighbors, custodians of records relating to Tyrone Power's incarceration in juvenile or adult facilities. A separate list of john does was prepared for all investigation officers who had performed any tests of any nature on evidentiary materials collected at the scene or who in any way related to the death of Tyrone Palmer or to the defendant Terry Brandt.

Trey had been informed by his investigator that Palmer had been incarcerated as a juvenile on a number of occasions. He doubted that he would be able to obtain this information in the juvenile court records without objection as they were normally considered privileged documents but he would give it a try. If any of the charges related to any of the facts of this case, Trey could possibly defeat the privilege. He served a subpoena on the juvenile court clerk for release of these records and was shortly thereafter informed by the juvenile court that the records had all been sent to Judge Lindquist for determination of the issue of further release to the attorneys.

As Trey was aware, Tyrone Palmer had an extensive juvenile court record and in view of the fact that he was no longer alive, the juvenile court had questioned the continued existence of the privilege and that was the main issue for consideration by Judge Lindquist. After two days considering the matter, Judge Lindquist took the position that the records would be released to both parties but nothing would be released to the public by either party pending further order of the court. The attorneys were warned that any leak of the documents would be met with severe penalties. The release to the attorneys was done to allow the parties to formulate their respective legal arguments for release for trial or for the continuance of the privilege on appeal. Without knowing the contents of the documents, neither party would have all of the information the documents contained that would support their separate arguments.

According to the information contained in the records, Palmer had brutally beaten fellow students when in high school on three separate occasions and had threatened another student with a knife. On all of these occasions, Tyrone Palmer had to be physically restrained from inflicting additional injury, including possibly fatal injuries to his victims. All of these incidents had occurred less than one year prior to his being fatally shot by the defendant, Terry Brandt. Clearly this evidence would be of considerable benefit for the defense of Terry Brandt.

A collateral issue involved the matter of a blood test, which had been performed on the decedent, Tyrone Palmer, shortly after his body was removed to the morgue and the results were believed to be in the possession of the investigating officers and the prosecutor. Chris prepared a discovery request for the blood test results, as well as all investigation reports relating to the search for the weapon alleged to have been used by Tyrone Palmer, including findings related to any ejected cartridges, together with copies of all statements taken from all witnesses by the police or others working on their behalf. This motion was scheduled for hearing the following week before Judge Lindquist. Memos for admission were prepared to support all requested information.

When the initial load of motion papers, supporting affidavits and memoranda had been prepared awaiting service on the prosecutor, Trey suggested to Chris that in view of the fact it was Friday evening, they should take the evening off and say hello to their classmates at the Rooster's Nest. They would send the motion papers, affidavits and supporting documents to Jackson on Monday. Chris and Trey had been working continuously for the past two months and Chris said that she was ready to kick back among friends.

As the two walked down to the Rooster's Nest, Chris said she had received a very interesting report from the chemistry expert they had retained to do the analysis of the clothing Terry Brandt was wearing at the time of the shooting. Terry had verified that the clothing had never been washed after the shooting and was returned to him in the same bag he had placed it when he was initially confined. The chemist stated that gunshot residue was composed of burnt and unburnt particles from the explosive primer, the propellant, as well as components from the bullet, the cartridge case and the firearm used. Gunshot residue may also be deposited on the hands of the shooter. The residue could be expelled out from the gun a distance of three to five feet or farther depending upon the circumstances. In this case the residue would have been all within the automobile, including the interior and exterior of the driver's side window, or on the clothing or skin of the two participants. The location and quantity of the residue found could tell a great deal as to who fired the gun, what the gun was fired at and how close the shooter was to the location where the residue was found. A considerable amount of residue was found on the sweater that Terry was wearing, particularly along the left front side of the chest with less residue spread across the right side of his chest and some on the cushion in the vicinity of the bullet hole. The residue conformed to that in nine-millimeter shells, the size of the cartridge retrieved from the seat cushion. The chemist was prepared to testify that the bullet found had been fired from a point in very close proximity to where Terry Brandt was sitting in the car.

As for the gun fired by Terry Brandt, a thirty-eight-caliber revolver, there was very little residue found other than at the cuff of the right arm of the sweater Terry was wearing. Expelled residue would have generally been away from Terry and towards Tyrone Palmer. The thirty-eight fired cartridge remained in the revolving chamber of the weapon and was not subject to being ejected. There was a considerable amount of residue found on the interior window of the car from the thirty-eight-caliber bullet as there was on the exterior of the window from the nine-millimeter bullet.

Trey was excited to hear this and said they would be obligated to provide the prosecutor with a copy of the report pursuant to the discovery rules. "This can make our case. This may support a motion to dismiss on the grounds of self-defense. This is great, Chris. You did a great job on this. Where the hell did you find the expert?"

"I cruised the internet and spoke to a number of criminal attorneys regarding chemical findings relating to gunshots and a number of them recommended this fellow. He has testified a number of times. He is located in Phoenix. He may be rather expensive but we have to have him."

"Chris, this raises the question, did the prosecutor or anyone check Palmer's hands for gunshot residue? I have heard nothing from anyone on that. Frankly, I doubt they did. Obviously it is a bit late to request that now but possibly not. If that evidence was found, that would be the clincher for sure. If they did not, we can certainly argue that they should have in view of the reports that Palmer did fire a gun. Show me that report tomorrow. This is great. Well, here we are. Let's say hello to the troops."

Chapter 12

When Trey and Chris entered the Rooster's Nest it was filled with the usual Friday evening collection of attorneys and law students. There was a momentary pause in the noise as the crowd observed who it was that had just entered. After a very brief moment of silence, a crescendo of cheers and clapping filled the room. It was apparent that aside from all the snide remarks in the print media and television news reporting both in Minneapolis and the nation, Trey Stark and Chris Sutton were revered, respected and given a resounding cheer by their friends and associates in the legal profession. They had stepped forward in a gutsy move to represent an individual who was being crucified by the nationwide media for defending himself. The legal community knew where the chips lay in social issue cases and this was certainly one of those. Many of those present were, unbeknownst to Trey and Chris, assisting with research on the case including evidentiary issues at Walker College of Law. They were being directed and assisted by Walt Clark and others, including Don Macy. Their view of the case was that it would be a tough one for Trey and Chris to win but they were, of course, unaware of the most recent findings relating to the gunshot residue. That would be another hotly contested issue for them to research when they became aware of the opinion of the chemist.

Trey and Chris joined Walt and others sitting at a large table in the bar and ordered a beer from the waitress, who had come over to serve them. There was no chance for Trey or Chris to pay for their own beers as the others at the table were all insisting that they would pay the tab. Chris commented that they appreciated it as they had still not heard from the court if they were to be compensated under the umbrella of the public defender status. It would help greatly if the court came through on that, as the costs alone in defending the case would come close to one or two hundred thousand dollars, including all deposition and expert costs. Neither Trey nor Chris had access to funds in those numbers.

The questions from their cohorts were all related to the case and how they were dealing with a murder one defense case so soon out of law school. Trey told them that they had been working day and night on the case and that Chris was tremendous in preparing arguments on all issues that they were facing. Others were also providing greatly needed assistance. He thanked Walt, Macy, and the others involved in the Walker legal research efforts. Trey said that having access to the research reports on evidentiary issues just added a great deal to his confidence level in arguing the issues before the court. So far he had been rather successful in arguing disputed issues and the prosecutor was not as arrogant and overbearing as he had been at the start of the case. He was beginning to realize that he was dealing with people that knew what they were doing. "I thank every one of you for that."

A number of those present asked about the gun that Palmer was said to have fired at Terry. "Did they ever find that?"

Trey smiled and said, "No, undoubtedly it was picked up at the scene and taken by one of the locals. Others obviously saw that but so far no one has admitted even seeing it. Fortunately, a couple of witnesses coming out of a store heard two shots, not just the one fired by Terry. They were very adamant that there were two shots." Trey added, "We also have some other arguments to prove there were two shots aside from our client's statement that Palmer shot at him and barely missed."

Chris said, "Our biggest problem is the media. We need an unbiased jury here and God knows what we will have when the media gets done telling everyone that this innocent child on his way to school was slaughtered by our client. By the way, do not quote us on anything. We are not to be talking to the media at all and I don't see any here but there are a couple of faces I do not recognize. So for the record, I said nothing."

They were asked about a change of venue. Trey responded, "We have pondered that and still are considering it, but the problem is, change to where? The media has been heavy on the side of the prosecution all across the state and out of the state. We may as well fight the case right here.

"Enough of the case. We have been living this case day and night forever. I do have to praise Chris, though. Talk about brains, attitude, personality, humor, and knowledge; I would have bailed on this case long ago if it was not for her. She has kept me going."

Chris smiled and said, "Look who's talking. Trey does all the arguing in court and he hasn't lost an issue yet. He knows his stuff. He has common sense and that precedes any legal argument ever made. He is the best damn debt collector to ever handle a murder trial." This broke up the group and everyone cheered again for both of them.

A number of them were curious as to how they were handling the bills. Both Trey and Chris laughed that off and explained there was nothing they could do about that problem other than to hope that the court made both of them special defenders. They both thought the court would do so as they had already handled a number of difficult criminal issues without looking like fools. Trey added, "The issue of granting us special defender status presents an interesting question for the prosecutor to deal with. At the start of this case when this first came up, he was totally silent. I know he was hoping we were not replaced as at that time he viewed us as two neophytes who had no idea what we were doing and it would be an easy challenge for him to topple us. He did not know we had this megalopolis support group behind us or that we were going to be working our tails off on this case. But now, he is starting to think, 'if these two neophytes whip my ass, I will be pilloried in my next election.' He has modified his comments to say little things like 'it would benefit the justice system if more experienced attorneys were involved.' While he is changing his view of our presence, I also believe the judge is changing his opinion as well. I know he was against us taking the case initially but I don't get that impression any longer. We will see what happens."

Chris spoke up. "Okay, what have you guys been up to? Where are the wild parties these days? Who has run off and gotten married?"

With the last question, the group all laughed loudly and pointed at Don Macy. Macy shook his head, waving away the allegations and

said, "Chris, there was talk but no action. I had a friendly relationship going and this bunch just misinterpreted what was going on. I
have always been loyal to you, Chris."

This brought more laughter, including from Chris. She commented, "I sure hope so, Don. It's good to know that when I have been
working 24/7 that you have been sitting home reading law books
and working seven days a week for your firm."

"Chris, that's me to a T."

Chris and Trey both laughed and Trey said, "When this case is all
over, it is going to be good to get back to leading a normal life. I am
looking forward to that. I should say that I know Don has also been
working on our case providing some great research with opinions on
how to handle some of the evidentiary issues. We appreciate it, Don,
and there is nothing wrong with having a little fun on the side." The
group broke out in laughter again as it was obvious that Macy had
been very active in the social scene.

Trey and Chris stayed until the late hours and then walked back
to their office to get their cars. When they arrived, they found that
Trey's car's tires were slashed. They had been afraid of this sort of
vandalism occurring, as the media was quite willing to publish the
location of their office in Minneapolis along with articles on their
racist defense of Terry Brandt. As they surveyed the damage, Trey
said, "In the future, we are going to have to have secured parking for
our cars. What a wonderful world we live in, Chris, I hope you don't
mind giving me a lift to my apartment. Better check your tires first,
though." Chris's tires were fine. Trey's name was the one used most
often in the media and that explains his selection for the vandalism
that evening.

In the morning, Trey called the police station and identified himself as the attorney for Terry Brandt. He then described the damage
to his automobile and requested, as he had done previously, that
his office be subjected to more frequent patrols in the evening and
throughout the night. He said that he was very concerned that one
of these nights the culprits responsible were going to burn down
his offices. Hopefully, more frequent patrols would prevent further
damage or even personal injury to the men or women working in
Trey's offices.

The media continued their acerbic remarks regarding Trey or Chris, referring to them constantly as the debt collection attorneys defending the killer of the student, Tyrone Palmer. From time to time small groups of demonstrators would congregate outside of Trey's office holding up placards denouncing Terry Brandt and demanding he be found guilty of murder. Apparently the continued assaults on the defendant by the media were taking their toll on the public perception of the innocence of Terry Brandt; a recent poll showed that over half of the persons polled were of the opinion that Terry Brandt was guilty of murder. Trey was still of the opinion that it would not help to change the venue of the case to an outlying court in the State of Minnesota. The Minneapolis paper and Twin Cities television stations were the main sources of news throughout the state.

The workload handling the Brandt case changed from day to day. At times, there was a crisis brought about by having to draw together information and action plans in a minimal amount of time. At other times, Trey and Chris were able to work normal hours with evenings to themselves to handle day-to-day chores. That was the status for a while following their evening at the Rooster's Nest. Trey was able to have dinner with Walt and even a beer at one of the many smaller beer joints in Saint Paul, such as the Fairview Palms that the two enjoyed visiting from time to time. Walt was always asking about Chris and how the two of them were getting along. Trey stated that they had both been so damn busy they were two ships passing in the night. There was no relationship to speak of. They both had their hands so full of challenges that they had no time to consider their status with one another, yet there was no question the two were growing closer together as they devoted all of their time to a common goal. Trey said he had been very impressed with Chris as he mentioned to the group the night they were at the Rooster's Nest.

Walt said that the word among the attorneys at the Rooster's Nest was that Trey and Chris were obviously very involved as a couple. "That's what they say, Trey."

"Walt, you may not believe this but we've never really had a personal talk about anything. I don't know that I even want that. We have a great working relationship—why the hell ruin that now? We have a client that needs serious representation by two attorneys that have a lot to learn. Maybe down the road when we are more confident of what we are doing, I will tell Chris that I have enjoyed working with her. I do like Chris a lot. She is an outstanding person. She does an awful lot and demands very little. Other than that, we will just have to see what happens. She has indicated that when this case is done, if the situation works out, she would be interested in joining me in private practice. That will take more funds than I presently have so I don't know. Have to wait and see. She is a real asset for me. I am well aware of that."

The following weekend, the Minneapolis Star had a lengthy section of their editorial page devoted to letters to the editor responding to Trey's reply to the editorial criticizing the attorneys representing Terry Brandt. The letters were generally very critical of Trey and Chris as being inexperienced and not sufficiently competent to be defending anyone on a charge of murder in the first degree. The letters supporting Trey and Chris were for the most part written by young attorneys who knew both Trey and Chris. They strongly defended the work done by the two attorneys up to this point and had the definite impression that the quality of their work was very good and constantly improving. What bothered Trey and Chris the most about the letters was that most of the critical letter writers were of the opinion that Terry Brandt was guilty.

It was Chris who finally broke the ice on getting somewhat personal with Trey. One morning as they sat drinking their coffee in Trey's office, Chris commented that they had been working together on the case now for some six months and to her knowledge, Trey had never had a date with any girl. Chris commented, "I'm getting worried about you, Trey. I had always thought you were sort of a wild guy, but boy, I was really wrong about that one, right?"

Trey smiled and thought for a moment. "Wow. Where did that come from? I haven't had time to even think of dating some girl, much less how to afford it. I'd have to invite her out to dinner at Subway and even that might stretch my budget. Besides, I'd rather spend my time with my co-counsel—she's prettier, smarter, more fun, and apparently suffers from the same malady. Haven't seen any boxes of flowers come to the office lately for Miss Sutton, unless I've just missed it. I think we both are workaholics."

Chris laughed. "You are right, Trey. We are getting awfully bor-ing. Even my parents mentioned it to me last week. They wondered who this Trey Stark guy was or even if there was a Trey Stark. You know, you have never been to my house. Now that is almost anti-social behavior. We work together 24/7 and you have never met my parents. I'll tell you what, I am going to talk to them about the four of us going out to dinner or having dinner at my house. Do you think you could deal with that?"

"God, I don't know if I could. I would have to get a book and learn how to act. What would you do if your parents went along with that and then said, 'that guy is a slob.' Could you deal with that?"

"Trust me, Trey. They would not say that. I have told them all about you and obviously they would very much like to meet you. They are of the opinion that you are more important to me than they or anyone else is. At first they were angry with me for leaving the prestigious law firm but as time passed, they concluded this Trey guy must be real. I will set up a date sometime for dinner with them, either out or at my home. Is that okay?"

"Chris, you know that anything you do is always all right with me. Sure, I would enjoy meeting the people that brought you into my office. That would be a very interesting experience. Just let me know when. You also know that then I will have to reciprocate. You have never met my parents. They thought I was crazy to take on this case and are still a bit put out about it as they catch a lot of flak from their friends and associates." Trey told Chris about his parents, his father's job in the retail clothing store taking care of inventory and his stay at home mother taking care of the house. "Both hard work-ing, very principled people, Catholic to the max. Their social life revolves around church activities so be sure to tell them that I'm in church every Sunday, and don't be surprised if my mother says she wants me to serve mass next Sunday. I hear that quite often."

"I will not lie on your behalf. I'm not a good liar anyway. I would screw that up. My parents are Catholic as well, Trey, so at least they have that in common."

"That is surprising. I don't believe I've seen you in church."

"No, Trey, you probably haven't. You have to be there to see me."

"Okay, smarty pants. Here's one you can't top. I really was an altar boy for a number of years. My mother thinks I still am."

"If that is true, I am going to have to have a talk with the Pope."

"It is very true, but I am not going to dazzle you with my Latin responses. Okay, you set up the first dinner with your parents, and assuming we are still talking to each other after that I will set up my family dinner. They will like you, though, so I have nothing to worry about there."

"Okay altar boy, I will do that. This may make our parents nervous, Trey. They will think we are engaged or something."

"I thought we were, Chris. That's why I haven't had any dates with all the girls I know."

"I walked into that one, didn't I?"

After Trey was alone in his office, he thought, *I sure as hell could do a lot worse.* The more he thought about it, the better it sounded. He had always been crazy about her and she must be aware of that. He would apply himself a bit more diligently to making her aware of that fact before someone else stumbled into the picture and hauled her away.

Trey had been giving a great deal of thought to proceeding with discovery in the Brandt case. This was a new experience for him and it was a fairly complex challenge that he very much wanted to do correctly. The law on discovery in a criminal case was not as liberal as it was in a civil action. Furthermore, some judges applied even more restrictions to discovery than were called for. Trey assumed that Judge Lindquist would be fairly liberal in interpreting the rules compared to others. He hoped so anyway.

Trey had inquired of Terry Brandt a number of times regarding any and all statements that he had made to the police, all documents that he had signed, any statements or comments he had made to other prisoners while in prison. Terry had spoken with two prisoners at length about the death of Tyrone Palmer and how it occurred. Terry insisted that the comments he made all supported the argument that he shot Palmer in self-defense.

Terry did not know the names of the two prisoners he had spoken with while in jail. He had mentioned the shooting to them but only to deny having fired the gun first. He also denied having a prior criminal record of any kind, including traffic violations.

Trey wanted to obtain any photographs that the police may have taken of the scene of the shootings. He prepared discovery requests that all of the materials relating to these areas of inquiry be made available to him. Trey requested all test results related to the charges against Terry, whether the police intended to use them at trial or not. Trey also requested all scientific reports and tests in the possession of the prosecutors or others acting on their behalf relating to drug tests, autopsy reports on Tyrone Palmer, fingerprint analysis, DNA tests, ballistic tests, cartridges found at the scene, gunshot residue on the decedent's hands, and all tests on the clothing worn by the decedent or by the defendant.

Alice, their legal secretary, had all discovery documents prepared in draft form for further review by both Chris and Trey. Alice added some suggestions of her own and Trey adopted them without question. He was very impressed by Alice's knowledge involving proper processing of a criminal case. Chris commented that her boss at her old firm frequently said that an experienced legal secretary frequently knows more about the law involved than the attorney handling the case. Alice was demonstrating that daily to Trey and Chris.

A week after the discovery drafts were prepared, a discovery request was served on the office by the prosecutors demanding much the same information that Trey had sought. Trey told Alice to rough out a response and then advised her that they needed to admit the gun residue testing and results on Terry Brandt's clothing, and the findings relating to Tyrone Palmer's prior problems with the law and his failure to graduate from high school.

As discovery requests were served on the prosecutor's office and answers were then forthcoming, the responses to Trey's discovery requests produced more questions and additional discovery directed at the prosecutor's office. This sequence of events worked both ways with further discovery originating from Trey and Chris and also coming from the prosecutor. This back and forth discovery process spanned four or more months and then it became time to take witness and expert depositions.

There were approximately twenty witness depositions that Trey and Chris were aware of that needed to be scheduled. Again, these depositions would in turn generate additional depositions. The prosecutor's office was likewise serving deposition notices on Trey's office of all persons with any knowledge of Terry Brandt's prior life, employment, schooling, or facts relating to the shooting. The discovery requests such as relating to production of documents or interrogatories did not particularly involve great cost but the depositions were costly as the transcribed and printed deposition could be expensive, on up to a thousand dollars for an original copy, depending upon how voluminous the product was. This was becoming an insurmountable burden for Trey, who was already short of funds. He finally inquired of Judge Lindquist by phone as to the order regarding Trey and Chris's status as special public defenders in the Brandt case. The judge said that he would have the order out shortly and for Trey and Chris to begin accumulating all invoices for their costs. That was an indication to Trey that the judge was going to allow them special public defender status.

That was good news for both Trey and Chris as they were looking at a brick wall for further financing of the Terry Brandt case. Neither Trey's family nor Chris's were in a position to finance further handling of the case and Trey had no idea as to where he could turn should the court deny his request. Trey's collection business was operating at a profit but not sufficiently large as to accommodate the litigation staff and expenses. A few days after having spoken to Judge Lindquist, his order finally came in the mail and both Trey and Chris were placed on Public Defender status, which allowed them reasonable repayment for all expenses incurred in defending the case and payment for reasonable counsel fees. Trey immediately had Alice begin compiling statements of costs incurred for all filings, service of process fees, deposition copies, expert witness fees and miscellaneous costs incurred in connection with the case. The total of the first statement of costs incurred came to fifty five thousand dollars, payment of which would take the pressure off of the two attorneys and all members of the staff who wondered if they were going to be able to keep their jobs. Trey also looked at the order as confirmation that the Judge viewed their separate performances as at least acceptable for criminal defense attorney status in a murder one case. He passed that on to Chris and she said she had come to the same conclusion. Trey suggested to Chris that she review court rules and statutes for all restrictions and responsibilities of their new status as special public defenders. "Best we not be discovered coming up short on meeting our new obligations."

Chris smiled and said, "I have already done that. Alice is preparing a memo for the file dealing with our new status. Nothing we cannot handle. You should have a copy of the memo by this afternoon."

"You are always ahead of me, Chris."

Chapter 13

Finally the day arrived and Chris told Trey that she was making a reservation at Friday's for Trey, herself and her parents this coming Friday at six if that was agreeable to Trey. Trey was not looking forward to meeting Chris's parents. He had nothing against them and certainly nothing against Chris but it was one of those life events that he just did not enjoy. He would have to be on his good behavior, not say the wrong thing, be courteous and look somewhat intelligent so her parents would not think their daughter had really screwed up. Some guys were good at performing at such events. Trey usually did just fine but he had to be up for it. He finally responded and said that he would plan on Friday's at six on Friday. "I will have to go home and clean up a bit. Are you going to return home and come with your parents or do you want me to pick you up?"

"I suppose it would look best if we came together. Pick me up at the office at five-thirty. Is that okay?"

Friday evening arrived and Trey was wearing his one and only best suit, freshly shaved and shoes even shined. He and Chris sat at the reserved table awaiting Chris's parents. The restaurant was filled and they had already become objects of attention for the other customers. By this time in the proceedings of the Brandt case, there were very few people in the twin cities that did not know who they were. Most of the curious seemed to be friendly without any animosity to the two attorneys. There were always one or two that could be counted on to make a comment that could be taken as an insult. Trey had learned early on not to pay any attention to those people.

At six p.m., Chris's parents arrived. They appeared very well dressed, were in their fifties or thereabouts and both were smiling as they approached the booth where Trey and Chris were seated. Chris introduced Trey to her parents and Trey had the definite impression that they were studying him but doing so in a friendly manner. Trey apologized for not having introduced himself before this but explained that both he and Chris had been working 24/7 on the Brandt case to the exclusion of all other social events. It had been challenging but was moving along quite well. He added that Chris had been a great addition to the team working on the case and Trey was very impressed with her abilities. He knew she was smart from hearing her recitations in class for four years and observing her class standing in the top five from day one. He had been surprised and very pleased when she indicated an interest in joining the defense team. Chris's parents did not comment on her interest in joining the team. Her father was smiling but her mother looked more serious.

Jack and Margaret Sutton said they both understood the great amount of work that had to be involved and were well aware that Chris was very much tied down to the case. The four ordered drinks. Trey and Chris each ordered a beer while the Suttons had mixed drinks. Jack Sutton was very curious about the case and how it was progressing. It was obvious that he had been keeping up with it in the newspapers and commented that the media was not helping out the defendant at all. He commented as to how the media criticized the judge for awarding Trey and Chris public defender status. Trey replied that he and Chris had anticipated how the media would deal with the so-called victim and the defense attorneys. "Actually, Terry Brandt is really a very fine young man. You certainly don't get that picture from TV or the media and that is unfortunate."

The Suttons were interested in Terry Brandt's background and Trey described Terry as the fine young man that he was—absolutely no criminal record of any kind, a very studious young man, intent on completing his education. Trey mentioned that Terry had been a student at De La Salle High School, which obviously made points with the Suttons. He achieved even higher approval when Trey said that Terry had been awarded Eagle Scout status with the Boy Scouts of America. Apparently, Jack Sutton had spent a fair amount of time in the Scouts but had never achieved Eagle Scout status. He said he had considered putting in the effort to achieve that rank but other interests intervened. Trey said that he had some scouting experience but certainly not on that level. Chris smiled as Trey had told her about his scouting days with Troop 22, which were not exactly exemplary.

Jack Sutton inquired as to the gun. "What do you suppose happened to the gun that your client says Palmer fired at him?"

Trey smiled and said, "Not for publication, but the incident took place in the hood and I am assuming that as soon as Palmer was shot by Terry and dropped the gun that one of the residents immediately took possession of it. I think we can convincingly prove that he did have a gun and did fire it at Terry so I think we have that covered. We have some good evidence in the case but our primary problem is a number of prosecution witnesses who were there. They are saying things that Terry says are blatantly untrue. All we can do is refute those statements, but they are there and they may hurt our case."

Mrs. Sutton added what obviously was a thorn in her side. "What about the comments in the media directed at your debt collection practice. Wouldn't you be better off dropping that from your practice?"

"Mrs. Sutton, that is what has kept us afloat ever since we took on this case. We now have the benefit of defender status and some payback on our bills but that still does not cover all of our trial expenses by a long shot. The collection business should handle the future costs not covered by the defender payments so I will keep it around for the time being. Neither Chris nor I work in that area. I supervise the attorneys a bit but that is all. We have avoided troublesome cases that lead to bad publicity; I know the media is watching all the time hoping to trip us up. In any of our collection cases, if there is any dispute involving payment of a bill, we generally work out a very generous settlement of the claim so that nothing gets to the media. On top of that, I personally go over the collection files and if there is one in there that is potentially embarrassing, I remove it. We have had a few of those. Also, the collection work is operated under a totally separate name and staff. Some of the staff working collection do assist us when we need someone for a particular task but that is it." To change the topic, Trey asked Jack how the dental profession was working out. That occupied the discussion for the next fifteen minutes as Jack mentioned the many advances in dental work that were taking place with implants, dental equipment, procedures, and new methods of reducing discomfort for the patient. Then Jack inquired as to what Trey's plans were for the future after they finished the Brandt case.

"That is a good question, Jack. Chris and I have not spoken much about that as we are assuming another year or more defending Terry and hopefully not appealing his case. If we win the case, which I am hopeful of doing, I would assume the publicity would bring an influx of criminal cases. I would rather work on the civil side but a good criminal practice can be very rewarding as well. I would hope that any future criminal cases would provide us with as clean-cut a defendant as Terry Brandt. There is no doubt that affects our view of criminal practice."

Margaret Sutton added a comment to the conversation. "Trey, Jack and I were disappointed when we learned that Chris was going to be involved in a highly publicized murder case. Frankly, we did not consider that to be a positive statement on her resume. I have trouble referring to Chris as a criminal lawyer. It sort of leaves a bad image."

Chris joined in on the issue. "Mother, the responses that I have received have been all positive. All of my classmates are very impressed and people that I have known for years wish me well and say they are following the case with great interest. I am very proud of the work we have done on behalf of Terry Brandt and I know his mother is quite confident that she and her son made the right decision in hiring us to defend Terry."

Margaret only replied with, "Well, I only hope that when this case is over, you two can find less controversial cases to work on."

Chris laughed and said, "You mean more boring cases to work on. I think this case is just about perfect—clean-cut defendant who looks like the all-American boy charged with a crime he did not commit. Give me those cases every day."

Mrs. Sutton asked Trey what his father did and Trey responded that he handled inventory for a small retail store on Lake Street. Mrs. Sutton asked if he had gone to college and Trey laughed and said, "My father had gone no further than the fourth grade but he had read just about every book, primarily historical fiction novels, ever published. He also enjoyed westerns. He was an avid reader and very knowledgeable about the world and the people in it. If he ever saw me sitting around doing nothing, he would say, 'get a book and read it. Don't waste time.' I learned a lot from my father, who I hold in great respect. He was a great fan of Louie L'Amour. I am sure he read every book L'Amour ever wrote, and he wrote a lot of books. There is not an American classic that he has not read. It was my Dad that got me started on Jack London."

Jack Sutton added that his father was much the same except he had gone on to the eighth grade before leaving school.

Trey added that our culture was not as focused on formal education then as it is today. "At times, I think we are too focused on that."

The four of them had an enjoyable dinner with most of the remaining conversation dealing with a cruise the Suttons were planning on taking and the happenings of Chris's many friends that she had grown up with and had missed talking with since taking part in the Brandt case. Mrs. Sutton also inquired about Don Macy, who she apparently held in high regard.

Trey replied that they saw quite a bit of Macy, as he was assisting them on evidentiary issues and had contributed quite a bit to the progress of the case. Don was still working for the Taylor Caldwell Firm and was doing quite well in his practice. "Don is a very sharp young attorney and he will do well wherever he is."

Mrs. Sutton only replied, "Yes, he is an impressive young man." She glanced over at Chris as she said this.

When the four finished dinner Chris rode back home with her parents and Trey headed for his apartment. He went over the events of the evening and thought that the meeting had gone about as well as could be expected. He had no doubt that the Suttons would prefer that their daughter had stayed with the blue chip firm she had first joined and that Mrs. Sutton would much rather have preferred having Don Macy sitting with them instead of Trey Stark. Trey rather enjoyed Jack Sutton and hoped he would stop by the office as he had indicated when they departed. Mrs. Sutton had not commented on the visit to Trey's office but she was sufficiently polite the entire evening. Trey had never been a hit for any girl's mother that he could remember so he was quite familiar with not having to deal with praise from Mrs. Sutton. That was just the way it was; mothers just did not take to Trey when their daughters were involved. No matter how hard Trey tried to change that result, he never succeeded. Now he would have to set up a dinner with his own parents. He would enjoy that. His parents played no games. They went directly to the point at hand but they would enjoy Chris—he had no doubt about that.

The following week both Trey and Chris were busy preparing motions dealing with discovery issues. The prosecutor had provided minimal responses to a number of questions and failed completely to respond to a number of other requests. They included a request for compensation for their time in preparing the motion but were well aware that such requests were seldom granted. During the week, Trey asked Chris when would be a good time for her to have dinner with Trey's parents.

"Oh, did I agree to that? I don't recall that."

"Oh, no you don't. No way, Jose. I will just set it up at my convenience and drag you down there."

"Okay. Set it up. I have the same schedule as you do so you know what times are good."

Trey set up the dinner with his parents for Friday evening at six at Friday's. "I want to be fair and keep everything the same as you set up. Just the way I am—fair and balanced."

"I don't know about the balanced part but okay, I will be there. In fact, plan on me riding with you, so if I am not there, it is your fault."

During the following week, the receptionist buzzed Trey and said there was a Doug Wilson that wanted to speak with him. Trey thought for a moment, wondering who this was and then picked up the phone.

"Trey, how are you doing on your case? I read about you almost daily in the paper. You are becoming quite famous."

"Yes, not the popularity I was after but it is certainly out there." Trey had no idea who he was talking with.

"Trey, I was thinking you have certainly managed to make a mark for yourself in the legal field. I should have hired you. Live and learn."

Then Trey remembered Wilson from the Chesterton Billings Firm. "You are too kind, Doug. Great to hear from you. Yes, we have been burning the midnight oil but we really are enjoying our work. Contrary to what the media is saying, I am fairly confident about winning the case."

"Yes, you don't get that message from the newspaper. I see they made you both public defenders on the case so that you can get paid. The editorial section slammed the judge for doing that. He deserves an 'attaboy' for doing what was right."

"I haven't seen that yet. I will have to check for that when I return home, probably around midnight. You know my co-counsel on the case is one of my classmates, Chris Sutton. She left a great job with Fuller and Brown to come in with me. She is an outstanding lawyer. We work very well together and I cannot give her enough praise."

"The media aims most of their criticism at you and they enjoy using the term, 'the debt collector.' It is almost humorous the way they try to put you down, yet when an issue develops, it seems you always come out ahead. Listen, Trey, if you ever need an extra body over there to do grunt work or whatever, give me a call. If I can't do it myself, I will send over one of our recruits. They can always file, type or stamp envelopes even if they did go to Harvard; they can go to the post office, Subway, wherever. Just let me know."

"Doug, thanks a ton. I will keep that in mind. At times we are grossly overloaded. I hope you are doing well and if everything goes south here, I may be pounding on your door again."

"Trey, you have 'winner' written all over you. Keep up the good work."

Chapter 14

That Friday evening, both Trey and Chris worked until a quarter to six when they headed over to Friday's to have dinner with Trey's parents. As they walked in the restaurant, Trey waved at some of the people that he knew and then he spotted his parents sitting in a booth up by the bar. When they approached the table, Trey introduced Chris to his parents who both gave her a very friendly handshake and greeting. Trey apologized for being a bit late but his father only said, "What's new."

Trey commented to Chris that his father was always kidding him for always being on time. Chris asked Mrs. Stark how she was handling all of the publicity on the trial.

"Chris, call me Mary. I've heard so much about you that I feel I have known you for a long time. You are as pretty as Trey said you were and you must be smart if you can deal with my son."

"Mrs...or I should say, Mary, working with Trey has been a big positive in my life. He is a working machine and gets everyone around him to produce as well. I have enjoyed it very much."

"Chris, where did you attend school? I know you went to Walker for law school, but where did you attend college?"

"I went to Princeton, which is where my father went and I did not know Trey until I went to Walker. I graduated from law school the same year as Trey and we have been pretty much together ever since."

Dan Stark spoke up and said, "We both admire education which both of you have had, as neither one of us attended college. It just was not in the cards for us. We have both tried to fill in that gap in our schooling by learning as much as we possibly can from good books and exposure to educational opportunities as they come along."

Trey added. "Dad left formal schooling after the fourth grade but he knows a hell of a lot more of our history and our country than I ever did. I don't think there is a book written that he has not read."

Dan Stark smiled and said, "Not quite that well-read, Chris. Many men my age had the same amount of schooling or even less. That is just the way things were back then. Now, let's talk about you. I suppose this court case puts a lot of stress on you with the articles in the paper and on TV. Sure would bug me. I noticed when you two walked in here that many of the customers recognized you. They seemed respectful though so you two must be making a good impression on the local citizenry."

"Surprisingly, Mister Stark, the adverse media reports only spur me on to do a better job for our client. He is a very good young man and deserves our best. So far he has received that, I am sure. I know Trey has produced above and beyond and I feel that I have as well. We do get a lot of support from our law school classmates and friends as well. Our offices are filled with volunteers working on research, mailings and whatever. I have thoroughly enjoyed working on this case and I know Trey has. We are both confident we will win when it is all over."

Mary stark commented, "I suppose it is very difficult when you come up against issues that you have never handled before. I would not know where to go to find answers to that problem."

Chris thought for a moment and then said, "That is true. That is our biggest problem, dealing with the unknown; but, we have much support. Numerous classmates are doing the research and feeding us information. The law school has a group put together to assist us with research on issues that we run into. Trey's friend, Walt Clark works with that group and provides them direction on areas that we need help on. We study what they provide and put it to work. So far that has solved the problems. We have not yet been caught short on arguing issues in court or proceeding correctly with criminal procedure issues. We have both learned a great deal. We also have an excellent legal secretary working for us and she steers us in the right direction so that motion papers go out on time, completed in accord with court rules and worded well. She is a gem and we are very thankful to have her in our office."

Trey nodded his head and added, "She was one of Chris's finds. Thank God Chris found her. That could have been a disaster."

Dan looked at Chris and asked her how her parents were dealing with all the publicity their daughter was getting. Chris thought a moment and then said, "That is difficult to answer. They are not crazy about me working on this case but I think when it is all over they may have other opinions. I hope so anyway."

Dan commented, "I think it is great. Two new attorneys stepping up to defend the innocent young man in the face of a deluge of one sided media attention. That is what good attorneys do. They step up to the plate. You two are role models for all young attorneys. No doubt about it."

Chris smiled and said, "I hope you are right, Dan. We shall see."

Mary then asked Chris what it was that got her to sign on with Trey to defend this young man.

Chris chuckled. "Well now that is a difficult question to answer. I never gave it any thought. I just immediately offered to work on the case. Now I will tell you something about your son. He did not set any records in law school yet he was very respected. Don't ask me why he was so respected. I am not sure. He just had a certain attitude that was attractive to most everyone. In his very non-business way, he was all business and that is what made me take note. I liked his style and like it even much more now. Trey is spring loaded to making the right decision and I have watched him make many difficult decisions with no moaning and groaning. You should be very proud of your son."

Trey spoke up. "Don't let her kid you. She is the brains of this team. I look at her and just ask myself, what would she do about this? That is the right answer. Chris was one of our top students at Walker. She was working for this blue chip law firm and left it like now. Everyone was shocked to hear Chris had come in with me. I was amazed and very pleased. We work together very well and the only problem is that it is all work. I hate to see her putting in ten and twelve hour days 24/7." When this is all over, we are going to enjoy life a bit. I hope we haven't forgotten how to do that."

The four sat and talked for hours after their dinner and the conversation ranged from the case to books that the four of them had read. They compared notes on various novels and Dan Stark led the discussion with perceptive comments on virtually all novels any of the four had read. Chris added that with Dan's strong interest in literature, he should write a novel. To Trey's surprise, Dan said he had been giving that some thought. Chris said she would be glad to help him in that endeavor if he pursued it further.

At the end of the evening, the four parted with assurances that they would get together more often in the future. As Trey drove Chris to her home, she said, "What enjoyable parents that Trey had."

"Yes, I agree. I do think they are both exceptional. They have always supported me in everything I have become involved with. They never blinked an eye about my taking this case. That is extraordinary." Chris only commented, "Yes, it is."

The following week Trey and Chris were busy with sending out discovery requests, admissions, interrogatories, and deposition notices. They had listed twenty people they wanted to depose whose names appeared on witness statements or in the police reports and were listed on the prosecutions discovery document. Volunteers were preparing the proper forms, notices, affidavits and mailers and putting the documents in proper order awaiting signatures from Trey or Chris. Depositions in criminal cases were not as freely allowed as in civil actions and they had to be permitted by the rules of court. The twenty people listed by Trey and Chris appeared to meet the restrictions. Trey had taken a number of depositions in his civil negligence cases but never in a criminal case. He was concerned that he handle them properly. Chris had never taken a deposition in any case but was confident she could observe a couple with Trey and then do fine on her own.

The first deposition that Trey arranged was of a witness, one LeRoy Carter, who gave a signed statement to the prosecution wherein he stated that he was standing by the side of the road and saw Tyrone Palmer approach Terry Brandt's automobile and request a ride. He stated he did not see or hear a gun other than Terry Brandt's gun. According to the statement, LeRoy Carter was on the west side of the intersection and observed Palmer approach the driver's side of Brandt's vehicle. Carter claimed that he heard Palmer ask the defendant for a ride to his school.

The deposition was held in the court house in Minneapolis in a courtroom that was not scheduled for any hearings. There were two other depositions to be taken after that of LeRoy Carter. The others had also signed statements but Trey did not observe anything of consequence in the statements. He was taking these two in order to protect himself from any surprises at trial. When it was time to take the depositions, Trey called for LeRoy Carter to come up and be sworn in. He had been subpoenaed for the deposition and Trey expected him to be present. Carter did not come forward immediately but after another request, a young black man sitting in the rear of the courtroom stood up and Trey asked him if he was LeRoy Carter. Receiving an affirmative response of sorts, Trey told him to step forward and be sworn by the court reporter. Following his swearing in, Trey motioned for him to sit in the witness box. Trey figured that Carter was about twenty years of age, give or take a year or two. He was dressed in the uniform of the hood, a hooded sweatshirt hanging loosely over jeans that were being held up by the right hand of Carter with the excess length of the trousers partially covering an expensive pair of Nike gym shoes. Carter's hair was done up in hood style with dreadlocks of the overly matted hair variety. He glared at Trey who was organizing his notes for the deposition.

After LeRoy Carter was sworn in, Trey began the deposition. Trey covered the witness's educational background wherein he testified that he had completed the seventh grade and then had dropped out so that he could get a job and make some money. Trey asked him what he had done for work. Carter replied with, "Whatever, nothing special." Trey was not able to get any definitive answer to this question. Trey had the criminal record on LeRoy Carter and proceeded to go through the relevant charges on his record dealing with honesty and also with prior carjacking charges. Carter had been charged with three carjacking allegations, which were still pending.

Trey was aware that at least two of the carjacking charges also involved Tyrone Palmer. "Mr. Carter, I have read the statement you made in connection with this case and want to cover some of your comments as I have some questions. First of all, were you personally acquainted with the decedent in this case, Tyrone Palmer?"

"Yes, we was 'quainted'. We was friends."

"How long had you known Tyrone Palmer?"

"All my life."

"How old are you now, Mr. Carter?"

"Twenty, next month."

"Mr. Carter, you say that you heard Mr. Palmer request a ride, and you were some twenty feet away from him at the time, correct?"

"Yeah, 'bout that."

"Did you hear Mr. Palmer fire his gun at Terry Brandt?"

"No, sir. He never fired a gun at Mr. Brandt."

"Did you hear a gunshot while you were standing by the road?"

"Yes, sir. I heared the shot when Mr. Brandt shot Tyrone."

"Okay, but nothing before that, right?"

"Yeah."

"Mr. Carter, you are presently out on bail on a carjacking charge, right?"

"Yeah, right."

"Are you presently negotiating with the prosecutor to get that charge reduced?"

"I don't know what that is."

"Did you tell the prosecutor that you would testify that you did not hear Tyrone fire a gun at Terry Brandt?"

"He ask me something like that. I don't remember."

"So the prosecutor was interested in how you were going to testify in the Brandt case, is that right?"

"I guess. I don't know."

"Has your carjacking felony charge now been reduced?"

"I guess so."

"Did you see a gun lying in the street after Tyrone Palmer was shot?"

"I don't know. I went home right after Tyrone got shot."

"Were you aware that Tyrone had a gun in his jacket pocket before he was killed?"

"I don't know. I don't think he had a gun with him."

"Were you aware that Tyrone owned a gun?"

"I don't know."

"Well, you were aware that he had a gun in the other carjacking cases, right?"

"No. I didn't know that."

"Well, the police charged both of you with armed robbery, right?"

"I guess so."

"Then was that your gun that they found that time?"

"No, sir."

"Then it must have been, Tyrone's, right?"

"Yes, sir. Must have been."

"Was anyone else involved with you in the carjacking that you were charged with?"

"Yes, sir."

"Who else was involved with you?"

"Just me and Tyrone."

"That would be Tyrone Palmer, the decedent in this case, right?"

"Yes, sir."

"Have you committed other carjackings other than the one the prosecutors are reducing to misdemeanors?"

"They reduced all of them."

"How many were reduced?"

"Three, I think."

"Were Tyrone's also reduced?"

"I guess so."

"Mr. Carter, where was Tyrone Palmer hitchhiking to, as you say, when he was shot by Mr. Brandt?"

"I heared him say he wanted a ride to the college so he could become a student."

"Did the prosecutor tell you that?"

"I guess so."

At this point the prosecutor objected to the question by Trey and Fred Jackson made a motion to strike the response. The judge overruled the objection and denied the motion.

At this point in the testimony, Trey requested that the deposition be temporarily continued until the following morning at nine a.m. as he had other meetings scheduled. There was no objection.

As Trey and Chris drove back to their office, they discussed the short testimony of LeRoy Carter.

"Trey, this Carter sounds like Tyrone Palmer's crime partner."

"That is what the investigator said in his report. He and Palmer were arrested together a number of times. I suspect that Carter was actually involved with Palmer in the attempted hijacking of Terry Brandt's car. Had Tyrone been able to get into Brandt's car, LeRoy would have soon joined him."

"That would not have gone well for Terry Brandt."

"Not very well at all."

"Trey, I hope LeRoy is their star witness."

"Chris, I suppose he is but my thoughts on these blacks has changed a bit. I did not consider them to be overly intelligent when this case started but now I think they are very intelligent and they are good actors. They put on the dumb guy bit and seem to just roll along but when the depo is over, they have to be chuckling to themselves. They will drop you a gumdrop every now and then, like Carter sort of admitting that the prosecutor told him to say that Palmer was asking for a ride to the college so he could become a student. Sort of builds up his credibility and doesn't hurt the prosecutor's case that much. LeRoy is not stupid. He handles himself quite well on the stand."

Chris thought a moment and then said, "Interesting."

The following morning Trey continued his deposition of LeRoy Carter, who testified that Tyrone had walked over to Terry Brandt's car and said hello to him and then asked him for a ride to the college so he could register. He later denied that Tyrone had said he was going to register, as he was unable to define what that meant. He changed his testimony to say that Tyrone said he wanted to go to the college to study.

Trey took three more depositions of witnesses, who were all black. All three were listed on defendant's discovery notice. They all claimed to have been standing on the same street corner as Le-Roy Carter. Trey thought they must have been having a convention there. None of the three could explain why they were standing on the corner. On direct by the prosecutor, in response to his leading question, they agreed that they were there to get candy at the corner store. Their testimony was amazingly similar to LeRoy's. They did not restate it as LeRoy had stated it, rather they said they heard Le-Roy say what he claimed he heard. They were not able to state the exact words that they had heard coming from Tyrone's mouth as he approached the Brandt automobile.

Chris commented to Trey when the depositions were over that it was amazing that they all heard the conversation between Tyrone and Terry Brandt, but did not hear the first gunshot from Tyrone's gun. None of them ever saw a gun lying in the street, either. Trey was also wondering what happened to the shell casing ejected from Tyrone Palmer's semi-automatic weapon. Terry Brandt said it definitely was a semi-automatic, which would eject a cartridge upon being fired. It would have thrown the cartridge out the right side of the gun towards the rear of Terry's car with sufficient force to have sent it five or more feet from the point where it was ejected. It could then have rolled an additional distance.

Even though it was some time since the event, Trey sent his investigator to check along the curb in the vicinity where the cartridge could have landed to see if by chance it was still there. Trey's investigator did find a substantially damaged cartridge lying in the gutter of the roadway some forty feet away from the location where the incident occurred. It had obviously been run over numerous times by auto and truck traffic. The cartridge was barely recognizable, however measurements indicated it was a nine-millimeter cartridge, which matched the slug removed from the cushion of Terry's car. There was no proof that the cartridge was the same one that was connected to the slug removed from Terry's car as the damage from the extended exposure to auto and truck traffic had obscured all transfer signs between the casing and the bullet in the cushion. There was no evidence as to how long the cartridge had been laying in the roadway before the investigator found it that would prove it came from Palmer's weapon. There was a fifty-fifty chance or better that it would not be admitted into evidence.

Trey and Chris worked on discovery depositions and further investigation until the pretrial conference in the spring. The judge blocked out the trial of the case for fourteen days in June. There were still motions pending made by the defense to have complete responses made to their interrogatories served on the prosecution. The judge held a follow-on hearing and told the prosecutor that if they persisted in failing to respond to the interrogatories that he would find for the defendants and suspend all charges against Terry Brandt. The prosecutor's office provided somewhat more complete responses to outstanding interrogatories, not perfect responses, but sufficient to get the court off of their back.

The media had continued their assault on the defense team and worked overtime to spin all news of the case in the prosecution's favor. They had built Tyrone Palmer up to be an excellent student at the community college and that he hoped to become a medical doctor so that he could set up a clinic to serve the poor. They had interviewed a number of his neighbors and they all said that was what he wanted to do when he completed his education. When the facts did not support the media's thirst for more material, they just made it up preceded by words such as, "according to comments from many of Tyrone's friends and associates."

The media also criticized the judge whenever the opportunity presented itself such as when the judge warned the prosecutors to abide by discovery rules or face punishing sanctions. The media said the judge was being unfairly favorable to the killer's attorneys.

Trey and Chris were both beginning to realize that some people that they had each known for years were beginning to turn against them, apparently based solely on the media assault. Trey told Chris not to let it bother her—that was the price they had to pay to handle this case.

Trey decided to pursue the issue of Tyrone's student status at the community college. The investigator told him that there was no record of Tyrone having registered at the college but Trey needed some proof of that fact that he could enter into evidence. He decided to depose the Registrar of Students at the college and served a subpoena on him to produce all documents relating to student status of a person named Tyrone Palmer. At the deposition no documents or records were produced supporting such status of Tyrone Palmer and the Registrar testified that there was no record at the college of any written or verbal application by Tyrone Palmer to become a student there. In Trey's opinion, that resolved the matter.   The following day the local newspaper discussed the issue and the deposition as an attempt to attack Tyrone's student status. Tyrone's mother told the media that Tyrone had spoken to the staff at the college and was going to submit his formal application the day that he was shot down in cold blood by Terry Brandt. His mother produced an application that was filled out showing Tyrone's personal information and requesting admission as a student. The so-called application bore no identification as an official Hennepin County Community College form, rather having all appearances of a document homemade on a personal computer. Nevertheless, the media accepted it as hard evidence.

Trey took a follow-on deposition at the college and subpoenaed their student application forms, none of which resembled that submitted by Tyrone's mother. When shown the application form submitted by Tyrone's mother, the Registrar stated it bore no resemblance to any application form ever used by the college for any student, regardless of ethnic background.

After the deposition and examination of all registration forms, Chris commented that Tyrone's mother would opine that the college used the forms Trey had examined for the wealthy white students and the others were given the forms produced on personal computers by the secretarial staff. Trey smiled and replied that Chris could well be correct and only time would tell.

In the following days and weeks, the prosecutor was sending statements provided by his experts as to the finding of gunshot residue and its implications. These tests were done in response to the findings of Trey's expert regarding the gunshot residue presumably from Tyrone's gun as well as the residue findings from Terry Brandt's gun.

According to the prosecutor's expert, all residue, wherever found, was from Terry Brandt's gun and there was no proof of a gunshot coming from the direction in which Tyrone would have been firing. Some of the conclusions in the prosecutor's report were clearly a stretch in Trey's opinion but nevertheless, they would have to be refuted clearly or they would carry some weight. As for the existence of two holes in the driver's side window of Terry's car, the witness for the State testified on cross that only one of the holes was made by a thirty-eight-caliber bullet. The other lacked the findings associated with a bullet passing through the window. This required a follow-on examination by Trey's expert with emphasis on the findings present in both holes in the window that would indicate the forces exerted on the window causing the penetrations.

In the month prior to the scheduled trial date, Trey and Chris were busy putting the finishing touches on their defense of the murder charges pending on Terry Brandt. The newspapers and television stations, both locally and nationwide, were clamoring for a guilty verdict from the jury against the killer of the student, Tyrone Palmer. There were odds placed on the outcome of the trial by the major odds makers in the country and all of them were predicting a guilty verdict by a substantial margin. Trey and Chris were concerned, no doubt, but still held to the firm belief that they would be able to successfully defend their client.

Trey had decided that he would give his opening statement immediately following the prosecutor's, rather than after the prosecutor had put in his case before the jury. Trey did not want the prosecutor's evidence to fester for that long a period without being refuted. Consequently, he was working on his opening statement at least a month prior to the anticipated trial date. Both Trey and Chris assumed the jury selection was going to take a considerable amount of time.

Due to the extensive publicity the case had engendered and the need for standby jurors, the judge was going to allow the parties twelve peremptory strikes of jury members. These are strikes of potential jurors that did not require justification by the striking attorney. The attorneys were also allowed unlimited strikes for cause or for justifiable reasons that would prevent them from being fair and unbiased jurors on the case. In most jury trials, strikes for cause were usually granted in somewhat limited numbers.

Trey and Chris had continued to discuss the issue of a change of venue for the trial. The problem was that there was no safe venue anywhere in the state that would be free from the reach of television or newspapers that were strongly in support of the victim of the killing, Tyrone Palmer.

Chapter 15

The tension for both Trey and Chris was rising daily as the trial date grew near. The criticism of their handling of the case had never disappeared and appeared to be increasing with the proximity of trial. Two weeks before the scheduled first day of trial, Trey suggested to Chris that they take the weekend off and just take it easy. On Saturday night they could go out to dinner at a good restaurant. Chris could pick it out and they would let loose a bit, maybe have Walt or whoever join them for dinner. Trey left that up to Chris. She was all for the idea. They had been 24/7 for so long that they had forgotten how to relax. They had been going from one crisis to the next without pause. Chris said she would work on the schedule and talk to whoever was going to dine with them. She raised the name of Don Macy and Trey was not sure if that was to get his attention or if she was serious. He told her whoever she wanted was fine with him and Don would be a good dinner-mate. He added a minor qualifier, 'as long as he brings Sue Tompkins,' who was a very attractive classmate of Trey and Chris and Macy had dated her at one time. Chris raised an eyebrow at that suggestion but only replied with, "Whoever you would like to have there." Trey let that one ride.

When the evening of the dinner arrived, Chris told Trey where she had made the reservation and that their partners would be Walt and his date, who neither one of them knew. Trey was glad to hear that Walt was joining them and asked, "What happened to Don Macy?"

Chris smiled and said, "He just could not make it."

Trey only said, "That's too bad."

When Trey and Chris arrived at Charley's Restaurant, Walt and a very attractive young woman were sitting at their table awaiting them. Walt introduced his date as Kate Jackson. After they were seated, Trey had to ask, "I am assuming your father or brother is not the prosecutor in the Brandt trial, right?"

"As a matter of fact, Trey, he is my older brother. I hope that is not a problem for us."

Trey had to think for a moment if there was some conflict issue involved, but he could not come up with one other than the fact it would hinder conversation between him and Walt, who most likely had twenty questions that he wanted answers to. *Well,* Trey thought, *Walt should have considered that when he asked Kate to join them for dinner. It might be a better selection for someone that would not inhibit Walt's questions at all as this was.* On the plus side, they could discuss non-trial matters, which would be much more relaxing for both Trey and Chris. He finally responded, "Kate, that is no problem at all. We won't be discussing the case, anyway. Both Chris and I have been working on nothing besides this case and we could both use a break."

Walt told Trey that he had recently changed jobs over to another law firm but would continue working on the side for the defense of Terry Brandt. Trey said he appreciated that as Walt had contributed quite a bit to the case. That was the end of discussion of the Brandt case. Trey directed his attention to Kate Jackson and asked her if she was employed or in college.

"In college, Trey. Not heading for law school. I just don't see the future there. Too many attorneys already."

"How smart of you, Kate. I totally agree. I may become a nurse."

"A what...you must be kidding. Are you?"

"I am. Both Walt and I always said we should have become nurses. That way we would have had a job. Sort of an inside joke. Sorry."

Kate laughed and said, "Yes, Trey, you would have always had a job. That is for sure. Well, not to mention your present case but if everything there went south, you could still become a nurse."

"Righto."

Walt called it a night after the dinner had been taken care of. He had to take some depositions the next morning and still needed to review the file. He apologized for the early go but said, "Work calls."

"No problem, Walt. Chris and I will have a drink and then take off."

After the others had left, Trey and Chris ordered a drink and continued talking. Chris looked at Trey and commented, "Well, Mr. Excitement, what happens now?"

"Good question. I'm having trouble dealing with trying to relax. Hopefully when this case is over, I can get into my real life. I have never worked so hard on anything in my entire life. Really, Chris, this has been an experience for me. I want to finish this trial and then get the hell out of Dodge for a week or two. What do you think?"

"What do I think about what? I think that is a great idea, provided I am going with you. Are you asking me to go with you or are you asking me what I will do when you are gone?"

"I prefer it the other way, Chris. We should both take off. How about a trip to Frisco? I think you would like that a lot."

"Sounds good to me. What do I tell my mother?"

"Probably better tell her you are going to Frisco with Don Macy."

"Oh, you picked up on that, did you?"

"Hard not to, Chris."

"I hope it didn't bother you, right?"

"No, it didn't. Actually, I found it a little humorous."

"Okay, I will go to Frisco with you if you will tell me what you are going to do after you return."

"I think I will become the debt collector who takes only good cases. It worked out quite well this time and debt collection brings in the bucks. Hate to ignore that fact."

"And where do you see me in that picture?"

"Chris, I see you standing right alongside of me. Just the two of us. Both smiling and working on interesting cases that we enjoy. How's that?"

"I like that picture. I have to admit, Trey, I have enjoyed working with you and furthermore, I will say I have enjoyed being with you."

"My attitude as well, Chris. Maybe we should make the big leap and formalize the relationship."

"Trey, I think that is a very good idea. Should I discuss that with my mother?"

"I would not suggest that. I would suggest that we could make that very formal move when we are in Frisco. If that is too complicated for Frisco, we could always run over to Reno, which is right next door. You could always tell your mother, 'He got me drunk and the next thing I knew we were married.'"

"Trey, my mother might surprise you. You may find that she is one of your staunchest allies."

"Maybe. I learned long ago not to presume how people will react."

"Okay. Are you going to make all the resies for both of us or do I have to get myself out to California on my own?"

"Chris, I will take care of everything. Now, if you change your mind, be sure and let me know. I would hate to find myself in Frisco looking at the ocean and wharf wondering what to do on my own. There is a bar that has a great piano player that you will really enjoy. He asked me why you were not with me when I was there the last time and I told him you were coming with me on my next trip."

"You are pulling my leg."

"No, that is a fact. His name is Sam and he plays 'As Time Goes By' the way it should be played. Now, let me know if you are not going to make the trip.

"Don't worry about me."

As they left Charley's the maître d' thanked Trey by addressing him as "Mr. Stark." Trey asked him how he knew his name. The maître d' replied that everyone in the restaurant that evening was aware as to who he was. "You and Miss Sutton are well-known persons now, Mr. Stark. You might as well enjoy it."

Trey only replied, "I wish I could."

That night when Trey drove Chris home for the first time in their relationship, he kissed Chris at the door. When they parted, Chris thanked him and said, "I will be there, Trey." As he drove back to his apartment, he thought about their conversation and thought, *Finally, things are working out.*

Back in his apartment, Trey thought of all the things he would have to do before he returned to Frisco. The trial would demand well over a hundred percent of the time he had available for preparation and then the outcome could go in a number of different ways. He decided that none of the potential avenues available to the trial outcome would interfere with his trip to California. Trey assumed that the trial would start as scheduled by the judge and would last no longer than two weeks. He added another week just in case. Then the jury could take a week or two in making their decision. He added in another week for unforeseen circumstances and marked out the following ten days on his calendar with a line and wrote, "San Fran." He then decided to make the reservations for the trip for both Chris and himself. Win, lose or draw, there would be a period of time after the trial for he and Chris to take some time off and get back to a somewhat normal life. The following morning, Trey made reservations to San Francisco on the airlines for both of them. The reservations were eight weeks out and they should be safe from trial conflicts with that time span. He also reserved a room at the Mark Hopkins Hotel for seven days. That would give them plenty of time to tour the city and get their feet back on the ground after the exhausting work the trial would produce.

In the morning, Trey was organizing the work he had to do in the coming two weeks. The phone rang and it was Walt. "Enjoyed it last night, Trey, but what did you think of my date? Kate is a great gal. A little young but quality, don't you think?"

"Yes, I thought she was quite sharp. Too bad her brother is a real jerk ass."

"I didn't think he was too bad when I met him but I can sympathize with your position. Most attorneys on 'the other side' are jerks. Just the way it goes."

"I suppose, Walt. Let's hit the diner for some breakfast."

"Be there in ten."

When they walked in Maud Brandt was on duty and ushered them to a vacant booth. She asked Trey how everything was going and he said, "Well as could be expected, Maud."

"Yeah, Trey. I suppose the media gets you down a bit now and then."

"You might say that. I am confident though, Maud, so don't get the wrong impression." A couple of the other waitresses came over and wished Trey good luck on his case and commented that the trial was drawing near.

When they were seated, Walt commented about how great Chris looked last night. "She is a good-looking gal, Trey."

"Like I don't know that."

"When are you two going to tie the rope? That is the question I am asked all the time, Trey. The old gang figures you two are a unit for sure."

"Well, maybe we will do that but don't tell anyone. We are talking about it now, Walt. Her parents would faint as they have already picked out Don Macy as the acceptable one. They are not big on the credit collection aspect of my business. Don't know why that is. Her old man is a pretty good guy, but Mom? Well, that is another story."

"The old mom issue, eh? Yep, we have all been there. Fortunately for you, Chris seems to have a mind of her own so I don't think Mom is calling the shots."

"No, I don't think she is at all."

The two talked for another hour as Trey laid out issues that he needed further research on. He also told Walt that his opening statement was basically ready to go and he was going to give it right after the prosecutor's opening. He was also going to put Terry Brandt on the stand. Many defense attorneys had advised against that, but they did not know Terry Brandt. In Trey's opinion, he would be a very good defense witness—personable, smart, nice appearing and very convincing as the innocent defendant.

"You know, Walt, I have never agreed with the theory that you don't put your client on the stand. There are times when that is a smart move but many times I have seen cases that were winnable with the defendant's testimony and the jury never hears it. I think you can be so careful that you lose the case. Terry is a smart kid and he listens to advice. He is not going to sit there and shoot his mouth off."

The coming week was the beginning of jury selection. The jury venire listing of potential jurors for the Brandt trial was provided to both attorneys. The information was turned over to Trey's investigator who was assigned the task of finding out who these people were. The information available on such short notice would not be extensive but it would provide some basic information that would assist Trey in jury selection. He was not using a psychologist to provide advice during jury selection as he could not afford the expense nor could his client. He had chosen juries before but most of them were in civil cases where the consequences were not as serious. He had tried a number of DUI cases with six-man juries and he had won three of them. They were considered losers by most attorneys who handled DUI cases, so Trey assumed he had done a fairly decent job in winning half of those he tried.

In a criminal case as this was, the jury would consist of twelve members with maybe four alternates, and the jury decision to convict would have to be unanimous. Some courts did not require unanimity and the unanimous requirement was definitely favorable to the defendants. A hung jury, where the jury could not arrive at a decision, could frequently result in a negotiated plea by the defendant to a lesser charge. Trey did not believe that Terry Brandt would agree to anything other than innocent of all charges. That could mean that a hung jury would most likely result in a retrial. That was not something Trey wanted to happen.

In general, Trey had decided that he would prefer successful or semi-successful college-educated white men, but he had to be careful about that as well. He would accept a black man or two who were well integrated into the business world of Minneapolis to give the appearance of fair mindedness on his part. When dealing with an ethnic group that voted 95% of the time in favor of candidates of their same ethnic group, he figured they would most likely side with the black victim in this case. Ignoring that simple fact was just plain foolish.

Trey discussed the issue of racial bias among the jurors with Chris and how they should handle the issue. Walt had provided material for thought on racial issues among the jury and how to deal with them. Both Trey and Chris had reviewed what Walt had submitted. While his material was interesting and did give some guidelines it really left them with more questions than answers. Trey concluded, and Chris agreed, that they would have to attack the issue directly and ferret out any jurors who were going to find Terry Brandt guilty because he was white or because Tyrone Palmer was black. They had to ask racially specific questions to the jury and trust that the court would not prevent them from doing so. Trey made up a list of general questions to the entire jury and would then get specific depending upon the responses. The first was as follows: *You will be told that the person that died in this incident was black and that the person who shot him was white. Does the fact of skin color alone have any significance to you with respect to the guilt or innocence of any crime charged?* The next question: *The defendant in this case, Terry Brandt, will testify that Tyrone Palmer approached his car and told Terry to get out of the car as he was taking possession of it. As he did so, Terry Brandt will testify that Tyrone Palmer was hold-ing a gun on him and fired the gun narrowly missing Terry Brandt, who then fired a gun at Palmer, killing him. Does the fact that Terry Brandt is white and that Tyrone Palmer was black affect whether you believe Terry Brandt's testimony or not?* Trey assumed that the prosecutor would make some objections to the racial line of ques-tioning in voir dire, but he would just have to deal with that when it happened. He did request Walt to prepare some research to counter-act that with the judge.

He would try to stay away from women who were primarily housekeepers with children. His thinking there was that they were more likely to have been home being bombarded by local radio and TV with propaganda about the poor black victim trying to hitchhike to school. College-educated women who worked in the downtown areas of Minneapolis or worked late into the evening in the suburbs would be preferable. The reasoning there was that they would be more concerned with their personal safety in the city and didn't have time to listen to the radio or watch television. He would also try to avoid people who were involved in the caring ministries such as so-cial work, religious charities, and teachers in the inner city.

He did not want to have anyone on the jury that would use their vote just to send a message. He wanted a jury that would listen to the judge's instructions and then cast their ballot accordingly. He also wanted Chris involved in jury selection to get the female opinion in the mix. She had a good handle on how certain women and men might view the case after the overwhelming one-sided propaganda campaign of the media. Trey valued Chris's input very highly. She was very perceptive.

Trey had been very busy getting his case ready for trial and working closely with Chris. His relationship with her had taken on a new tack becoming more of a personal relationship than it ever had been before. Both Chris and Trey were realizing that they were a pair with many things in common. They both respected one another and enjoyed life and the challenges that it presented. After they had decided to make the California trip, they were more involved in their relationship as they each realized the step that they were taking. They had both indicated a strong desire to make their relationship permanent and as time passed, this intention to do so only grew stronger. Trey had thought that he would have great difficulty thinking of any one woman as his partner for life but Chris was assuming that role in his thinking more every day. Trey found Chris more attractive and exciting than ever before but he held back from going beyond limits that he considered permissible. He wanted to be very careful not to screw up what he considered a very good deal. He had decided that he would not cross any lines until they were married and they could do that as soon as they arrived in California. He would discuss this with Chris on down the road when they were about to leave on their trip.

By the time jury selection began, Trey had a fairly large amount of information dealing with all the names on the jury venire list. There were a few that the investigator was not able to find any information on at all. In all cases, a residence address was given in the venire list for each name. In the case of little or no other information, the residential address was quite informative on its own. A woman living in Edina would be a better gamble in this case for the defendant than one living on Portland Avenue in the city but again, Trey could easily see an opposing view to that test. What type of work they did was also quite informative. In his civil cases, working on the plaintiff side, Trey had avoided people employed by the insurance industry when he was representing a plaintiff. In this case, representing a criminal defendant, that would be a reason to select them for the jury.

There were a number of boilerplate questions that Trey had avail-

able to assist him in his selection of the jurors when the investigator's report did not provide many clues as to who he was dealing
with. In these cases, in the Voir Dire questioning of the jury by the
attorneys when it was his turn, Trey would ask the clue-giving questions and Chris would record the responses. If he or she had additional questions, he would ask them and then Chris would record her
vote. If Trey agreed with that, he annotated the listing to indicate his
agreement and they would move on to the next candidate. Trey had
Walt sitting out in the audience in the courtroom making his own
notes, and at the end of the day they would compare their notes.
Usually they were in agreement but on occasion they were not. Walt
commented on those occasions that he would remind Trey and Chris
after the trial when the jurors had voted where Trey or Chris had
gone wrong.

The time finally arrived for Trey to stand in front of the jury and
commence his voir dire. He introduced himself and gave a very brief
statement as to the parties in the case and the facts that gave rise to
the charges against Terry Brandt. He specifically stated that his client, the defendant Terry Brandt, was a young white man attending
college and that the person he shot and killed, Tyrone Palmer, was
a young black man. He said that Terry Brandt would explain that he
was driving his mother's car, a 1995 gray Ford Fairlane, to attend
school at Hennepin Community College when Tyrone Palmer approached him while he was stopped at the traffic light. Palmer then
showed him that he had a gun and told Terry to get out of the car.
Terry assumed he was being carjacked and acted as though he was
getting out of the car. Instead, he grabbed a gun sitting on the passenger seat and when he did so, Palmer fired his gun at Terry Brandt
but missed. The bullet buried itself in the passenger seat cushion
next to Terry Brandt. Terry then fired his revolver and fatally injured
Tyrone Palmer. Trey went on to say, "The prosecutor has stated facts
not in accord with what I have told you the evidence will show. I
ask you now, is there anyone here that believes that because Tyrone
Palmer was black and Terry Brandt is white that has any bearing or
effect on whether or not Terry Brandt is guilty of a crime? Raise your
hand if you think that it does." No one raised their hand. He asked a
follow-up question: "Are all of you able to ignore the racial issues in
this case and decide the question of guilt or innocence solely on the

instructions that the court will issue at the conclusion of the trial? If so, please raise your hand indicating that is how you will decide." All of the jurors raised their hands indicating they would be fair and impartial. Trey had his doubts but he figured that he had gone about as far as he could to dampen the racial issues in the case. Trey added that this was a very important case for everyone involved and it was essential that they have a fair and impartial jury to decide the guilt or innocence of the charges against the defendant, Terry Brandt.

By the end of the week, They had four jurors dismissed for cause either due to obvious prejudice against a white person who had killed a black person or others who admitted that they had followed the case carefully in the newspapers and the media and their minds were already made up. There were also a number still on the jury, three black women in particular, that Trey had his doubts about but he did not consider it wise to strike them as jurors using his peremptory challenges as that would leave a jury with no black jurors and that could end up after an appeal as a retrial, which Trey did not want to experience.

Trey had used all of his peremptory challenges and could not remove the three jurors without cause. He knew you could think you knew what was going on in their minds but then maybe you were reading the wrong signs. If someone was against private ownership of guns, did that mean that he would find Terry Brandt guilty of shooting someone even if it was in self-defense. Trey had his doubts about such people but then, on the other hand...

After the jury was selected, Trey was fairly confident they had kept the least desirable candidates from being selected. He would find out at the conclusion of the trial if he was correct or not. At the end of jury selection, the prosecutor requested a sidebar conference with the judge. He agreed and both attorneys approached the judge. The prosecutor, speaking out of the hearing of the jury, questioned the propriety of Trey's questions to the jury on the racial issues but did not want to present himself as in favor or against either one. He thought the court should add some definition to Trey's questions. The judge disagreed and suggested that the prosecutor was free to add whatever he believed was lacking in Trey's questions. The prosecutor decided to let the matter drop rather than appear favoring one side over the other.

The rest of the week was devoted to arguing motions that were still outstanding, most of which involved failure to respond properly to discovery interrogatories or requests to produce.

Chapter 16

On Wednesday afternoon of that week when Trey and Chris were back in the office after arguing motions, Jack Sutton came in the office for a quick tour. He gave Trey a big smile and apologized if he was interrupting anything. Trey assured him that he was not but Jack said he would keep it very brief. He just wanted to see the offices and he said that he could tell this was a working office as everyone was obviously deeply involved in some task. Chris told her father to come in and see the plush office that Trey had arranged for her. Trey quickly commented that it was almost as plush as his own bare-boned operation. Jack spent about twenty minutes touring the premises, including the collection area, and Trey explained the tasks various people in the office were busily engaged in. When the staff was told that Jack was Chris's father, two of the secretaries commented on what a competent intelligent daughter he had. They said it in such a way that it was obvious they were very sincere in their comments. Jack was clearly touched not only by their words but also by the look of complete interest and pride Chris's face showed as she took her father around the office. When she introduced him to Alice Bentley, Jack said, "You don't have to tell me what you do here, Alice, Chris speaks about your great contributions to this case all the time. She has been very impressed with your work."

Alice responded, "We all just believe in this case so very much, Mr. Sutton. I have been involved in criminal defense work my entire life and I have never worked in any office that was so dedicated to winning the case as this one is. You should be very proud of your daughter and Trey. They really are dedicated people."

Jack Sutton was very impressed by what Alice had to say. He thanked her for her kind words and then said, "I have enjoyed this. I will get out of here so you can all do your thing. Thanks, Trey, and thanks, Chris, I will see you this evening." He was soon out the door and heading for his car.

On Monday morning the jurors were all sworn in by the court followed by a brief statement by the judge as to their duties and how the trial would be conducted. The judge also advised the jury as to the charges against the defendant and provided a very brief overview of the facts that gave rise to the charges. He then inquired as to whether or not the prosecutor would be delivering an opening statement. Receiving an affirmative response, the judge told the prosecutor to proceed.

The prosecutor commenced his opening by introducing himself again to the jury. He then restated what the charges were in the case and the allegations that pertained to the actions of Terry Brandt, who was seated at the table with his attorney, Mr. Stark. According to the prosecutor, the killing of Tyrone Palmer was the basis for the charge of murder in the first degree of an unarmed student hitch-hiking to his college. He stated that proof of that would be provided by the testimony of three witnesses who were all standing in close proximity to where Terry Brandt was sitting in his automobile when he fired the gun that killed Tyrone Palmer. The prosecutor stated all three witnesses distinctly heard Tyrone Palmer request a ride to the college and that was followed by the loud blast of the gun fired by Terry Brandt that extinguished the life of Tyrone Palmer. Jackson stated that there would be allegations that Palmer had fired a gun at the defendant but no gun was ever found at the scene of the crime and the defendant was not struck by a bullet. He further stated that experts would discuss the finding of gunshot residue, which examination would show came from the defendant's weapon and not from any weapon fired by the decedent. He said that, "Smoke and mirrors cannot fire a non-existent gun. The only gun found at the scene of the crime was fired by Terry Brandt and that gun will be introduced in evidence during this trial." He concluded his statement by saying that at the end of all of the evidence in the case the jury would be asked to find the defendant, Terry Brandt, guilty of murder in the first degree, which was defined as taking another's life with deliberation and premeditation.

When the prosecutor had completed his opening, the judge asked Trey if he was going to deliver his opening at this time. Trey indicated that he was and he stepped up to the rostrum with his notes for his opening, directing his attention at the judge awaiting his go-ahead to proceed.

The prosecutor had taken thirty minutes to deliver his opening and Trey assumed that his would take about the same amount of time. Trey had worked on his opening daily for the past month, adding a little here, deleting there. He was under a great deal of pressure to deliver a good opening as he wanted to dampen the effect of the prosecutor's opening remarks and raise doubt as to the strength of the State's case.

The local newspaper on the streets the following morning described the opening statements. They emphasized the complete absence of any witness that would be testifying as to a gun in Tyrone Palmer's hand, other than the gun in the possession of the defendant. "And thus far, no gun has been found bearing Tyrone Palmer's fingerprints."

Trey knew he would have to hit that issue hard when he presented his case to the jury. He had good evidence that Palmer did fire a gun that narrowly missed Terry Brandt, but there were a number of witnesses that were saying otherwise. He also covered the fact that a nine-millimeter slug was extracted from the seat cushion to the right of where Terry Brandt was seated. Trey spent a fair amount of time describing the finding of gunshot residue both on the inside surface of the driver's window glass and on the outside surface, indicating two separate gunshots. He mentioned the finding of a nine-millimeter cartridge on the curb by the scene where the incident had taken place. In his opening, Trey did bring out the decedent's problems with the law, including prior carjacking charges, to show the propensity the so-called victim in this case had to act in the way the defendant alleged he acted. The prosecutor objected to the use of the term 'so-called victim,' but the court overruled the objection on the grounds that he had used the victim term himself in his opening.

After the opening statements, the prosecutor began presenting his witnesses. His first witness was Tyrone Palmer's mother who testified to her son's intention to register for college that day and hitch-hiking to the community college for that purpose. She said that he was going alone to the college and carried his application with him.

She stated that she had the application that had been retrieved from Tyrone's jacket pocket. This was the original of the copy that Trey had seen and she pulled it out of her purse. Her copy of the application was crumpled up and torn, which according to her was the result of the violence that her son had experienced as the fatal bullet struck him and he fell to the ground.

The application had what appeared to be dried bloodstains on it, giving graphic testimony to the death of Tyrone Palmer. Tyrone's mother testified that her son wanted to study social work so that he could someday help the poor that lived in the hood. Trey seriously questioned that the apparent bloodstains were in fact bloodstains or were bloodstains from the decedent in this case, Tyrone Palmer. He knew that blood had been withdrawn from the decedent that was presumably available for DNA comparison with the stains on the paper, but a full-blown DNA comparison test would take more time than was available prior to trial. Tyrone's mother had not come out with the stained form until two weeks prior to trial.

After Tyrone's mother completed her testimony, a teacher that had taught Tyrone when he was in the second grade testified that he had been a very nice child in the classroom and had told her then that he wanted to go to school so that he could help all the children when he was an adult. She said that Tyrone always got along very well with the other students. On cross-examination, the teacher admitted that she had no contact with Tyrone for about the last ten years and had no idea how he was getting along with his fellow classmates in later years. Trey asked her if she would be surprised to learn that he had been suspended from school fourteen times over the ten-year period and had been arrested five times for assault committed on his fellow students. The teacher said she would be surprised to learn of this.

At the conclusion of her testimony, Trey requested that he be allowed to approach the bench. When he was standing in front of the judge and out of the hearing of the jury, he stated that he wished to make a motion striking this witness's testimony as irrelevant to any issue in the case by reason of its lack of timeliness. The judge looked at the prosecutor for a response who stated that the witness testified she was very familiar with the child and testified accordingly. The judge would not strike the testimony and said the jury was free to value her testimony as they saw fit. Trey made a note to be sure to cover her testimony in his closing argument.

The next witness was the Reverend Jamal Paradise of the Freedom Baptist Church of Minneapolis who testified that Tyrone and his mother were regular attendees at his Sunday service. He testified that he had many long talks with Tyrone and knew him to be an honest young man intent on acquiring a good education so that he could help those most in need. Reverend Paradise was aware that Tyrone had some problems with the law over the years but that in recent years he had made a great effort to avoid jail and become a model citizen.

In his cross-examination, Trey again brought out the criminal records of Tyrone and asked the Reverend point by point if he was aware of the list of charges, all of which were no more than three years old against Tyrone. The Reverend said he was but Tyrone explained to him that most of those were alleged to involve him but in fact he was totally innocent of most of the charges. Trey asked him if he was aware that three of the charges involved attempted carjacking by Tyrone Palmer and were still awaiting trial. Reverend Paradise stated that he was certain the charges would have been dropped before going to trial in view of the lack of evidence existing against Tyrone. There was some truth to that statement as in all three of those cases the victims had been warned that if they testified they would regret it and all three of them were vacillating on giving their testimony, which was the main reason the cases had not yet proceeded to trial. At the conclusion of Reverend Paradise's testimony, the Reverend Shamile Armstrong, who had been seated in the courtroom, approached him and loudly congratulated him on standing up for this fine young man. The judge admonished him for speaking so loudly in the courtroom and told him to leave the courtroom immediately. He then instructed the jury to ignore anything they had heard him say.

The following three witnesses were all associates of Tyrone Palmer and clearly heard him request that Terry Brandt give him a ride to the community college. The next thing they heard was Terry Brandt's gun being fired point blank at their friend and associate. All three testified using virtually identical words. Trey was unable to attack the testimony of any of the three witnesses other than to bring out that each one had criminal charges brought against him for theft and fraud. Two of the witnesses had also been convicted of carjacking, one of whom was a co-defendant with Tyrone Palmer.

There were three other character witnesses testifying on behalf of the prosecution. Their testimony was so fanciful that Trey did not devote a great deal of time to their cross-examination. There were four blacks on the jury of twelve jurors and Trey could only hope that they rejected the testimony that they had just heard. He was somewhat confident that the one black juror, a sixty-five-year-old manager of a small appliance repair shop, appeared to have followed the evidence in the case and had answered Trey's questions on voir dire in a fairly acceptable manner.

During the prosecution's case, Trey would occasionally study the jury to try to determine whether they were absorbing the evidence the prosecutor was presenting or if they were not accepting it as credible. Most of the prosecution witnesses had direct ties to the decedent and would appear to most jurors as being quite willing to see that the defendant was convicted. Trey could only rely upon the pledge all jurors made before evidence was entered in the case to be fair and impartial and abide by the court instructions. During a break, Trey asked Terry Brandt what he thought of the case that was being presented against him. Terry smiled and said, "I don't think many jurors are going to believe this stuff. It just doesn't make a hell of a lot of sense." Terry then asked Trey what he thought. Trey told him that he agreed with what he had said but they'd have to wait and see who would believe what. Trey had been surprised by juries before this one.

The prosecutor's case was not completed by the end of the first week, which told Trey that it could possibly extend the trial beyond the two weeks that the judge had allocated to it on his calendar. His case was going to take less than a week but it all depended upon how much more time the prosecutor was going to take. Fortunately, he presented his last witness Monday afternoon. This witness was the gunshot residue expert, who proceeded to explain all findings of residue anywhere as having been expelled from Terry Brandt's revolver. Trey pointed out on cross-examination of the expert that for his testimony to be correct, Terry Brandt would have to have fired his gun from the passenger seat of his car rather than from the driver's seat, where he was seated wearing his seat belt. Furthermore, the expert had no opinion regarding the finding of a nine-millimeter slug buried in the cushion of the passenger seat and no opinion as to how long the slug had been buried there. He was forced to agree that finding the slug in the cushion would comply with the theory that Tyrone Palmer had fired a shot at Terry Brandt and missed.

Trey was advised to proceed with his case in the morning.

The following morning, Trey opened his defense case by putting Maud Brandt, Terry's mother, on the stand. Maud explained that she was a waitress at a diner and that she had raised her son, Terry, on her own after the death of her husband when Terry was five years old. He was now seventeen years old. Trey had Maud explain that she owned the gun that was in the car and she had it there for her protection as she frequently worked evenings. The gun was normally loaded at all times and kept out of sight except at the time of the incident involving the death of Tyrone Palmer. On this occasion she had left it on the passenger seat and told Terry to be sure and secure it when he parked the car. She also testified that she had insisted that Terry received gun training and that he have a concealed weapons license as she did. Terry had received the training and had just been awarded his license. She testified that Terry was very responsible when handling a gun and she had witnessed this at the gun range where they both trained.

Maud testified that she had Terry drop her off at the diner where she worked and that Terry was then going to proceed to his college classes at Hennepin Community College. Terry was completing his high school education at the same time that he was taking some college courses at the community college. Terry was hoping to complete his requirements for a degree in three years instead of the normal four years. Maud testified that Terry was a very responsible and upright young man. He had never been in trouble with the law and his school record was unblemished other than one suspension a number of years ago for getting involved in a fight with a bully in one of his classes. She had learned of the shooting of Tyrone Palmer the day it occurred when Terry explained it to her. She was very thankful that she had forgotten to put the gun in the trunk of the car when she turned the car over to Terry. "If I had put the gun away, Terry would not be with us anymore." The prosecutor chose not to cross-examine Terry's mother.

Trey's next witness was Terry's scoutmaster, who testified that Terry had been an outstanding scout and had achieved Eagle Scout status just the previous year. Terry had continued his participation as an assistant to the scoutmaster in conducting weekly meetings with the young scouts. He testified that Terry was highly respected by all of the scouts in the troop and by other scoutmasters in the Minneapolis area who had witnessed his scouting activities. Terry had also achieved marksmanship honors firing the very gun involved in the case at hand and had qualified for a scout merit badge in shooting competition. Again, the prosecutor chose not to cross-examine the scoutmaster. He apparently saw nothing to gain in hearing about further accomplishments of the Eagle Scout.

The next witness was a professor from the community college who had taught Terry a course in American History and he testified as to the quality of work that Terry was performing at the college. He testified that Terry appeared to have the ability and the drive to be well on his way to graduating with honors from the college.

Trey's next witness was the registration supervisor at the college who testified about the process required for a student to register at the community college. He laid out the qualifications for acceptance and the papers that would be required to prove that an applicant was duly qualified. He said there was no record that Tyrone Palmer had ever applied for admission nor had he ever submitted the paperwork that would be required to support his application. Trey showed the witness the application the prosecution claimed had been prepared by Tyrone Palmer for registration at the college. The witness denied the document bore any resemblance to the form the college used for registration application. Trey inquired of the witness if graduation from high school was a prerequisite to admission and he said it was. There were some exceptions to that rule but they always involved very high grades for the applicant for the years of attendance in high school. Trey asked him if a grade average of less than 2.00 or below a C average would suffice and the witness said, "Absolutely not."

The prosecutor did cross-examine the registration supervisor, who was involved at the college strictly working in administration. The prosecutor brought out that he did not get involved in teaching any courses and had no direct contact with Terry Brandt other than seeing his name on lists of students. The prosecutor brought out that there were a total of six people working in the registration office and it was not unusual for others in the office to discuss registration matters with applicants that never did come in direct contact with the supervisor. While the supervisor agreed that did happen on occasion, he denied that any person with marginal performance high school records would be admitted without his involvement and agreement. That was a very strict policy of the institution and to his knowledge it was a practice that had never been violated. He did admit that preliminary conversations could have involved other staff members in registration that had not developed to the point where he would be brought into the discussion.

On redirect, the supervisor stated that without exception, it was his understanding that the college had never admitted a high school student with grades similar to those of Tyrone Palmer. They had admitted some students who had not graduated from high school due to illness and had missed no more than part of their last semester. In those cases, the involved students had grades of at least a B or 3.0 average throughout their high school years up to the portion of the year that they had missed due to illness or other excused absence. His final statement was that, "There is no way Mr. Palmer would have been admitted to Hennepin Community College with the grades he possessed. We occasionally make exceptions for minority students but his grades precluded admission under any policy exception."

Trey's last non-party witness was the gunshot residue expert. Trey spent two hours qualifying this witness to impress upon the jury the fact that the witness knew what he was talking about. He possessed a doctorate degree both in physics and in chemistry. He was considered to be an expert by the State Crime Lab and had also testified over one hundred times around the country in cases involving gunshot residue on behalf of the Federal Bureau of Investigation, various State Crime Laboratories and numerous city, county and state prosecutors. He had also testified over two hundred times on behalf of persons charged in shooting cases. He said that with careful examination of gunshot residue, he was able to testify accurately as to the exact location of the shooter, the general location of the target and the exact location of any other shooter involved in a shooting. He further testified that he had a complete laboratory equipped with the latest equipment available for studying gunshot residue, including scanning electron microscopy and associated testing equipment.

Trey then had the witness describe what the evidence in this case showed. He said there were clearly two shots fired and the first appeared to be from outside of the car with the bullet passing through the driver's window and following a trajectory down to the point in the cushion where it was eventually located. He said there was considerable gunshot and window glass residue sprayed across the sweater worn by Terry Brandt that indicated the gun that fired the bullet was positioned approximately six inches from the driver's car window with the bullet smashing through the safety glass of the car window before entering the interior of the automobile.

A second bullet fired from inside the car, presumably by the driver, Terry Brandt, was fired from his right hand towards the driver's side window when the gun was level with Terry's chest, the position being proved by the residue found on the upper chest and left arm of Terry's sweater. Most of the gunshot residue from Terry Brandt's gunshot was found on the door and the driver's side window inside of the car, with minor traces found on the clothing of the decedent. He explained that the minor traces on the defendant were due to the fact the bullet penetrated the safety glass of the window leaving a hole approximately the size of the thirty-eight-caliber slug, and consequently most of the residue was captured on the interior of the car rather than the exterior side of the window. The expert testified that the evidence available in the case was conclusive that one gun was fired from inside the car and the other gun was fired from outside the car. He explained in graphic detail the evidence of the bullet holes in the driver's side window that showed exactly where the bullet first penetrated the window glass. The holes were classical examples showing point of origin. He used blow-up photographs of the damage to the window, which clearly showed the difference between the area of original penetration compared to the exit area. The expert was on the stand for over five hours of direct examination by Trey Stark.

The prosecutor spent over an hour cross-examining the expert and getting him to admit that the best evidence of what took place in the shooting was still just his opinion. He did agree that other experts had disagreed with him in prior cases and could possibly disagree with him in this case were they present. It was only his opinion as to what exactly happened based upon the evidentiary findings. He questioned if it was possible that it could have happened quite differently, and the expert testified that was possible but not likely. The expert was quite adept at protecting the integrity of his testimony. He would admit the obvious but would not impeach his own opinions.

Trey requested a sidebar conference at the bench and the judge allowed that. The court reporter positioned her recording equipment to record what was about to be said and when that was accomplished, Trey proceeded with the purpose of the sidebar.

"Your Honor, I have one more witness that is not on our pre-trial statement, but that is because he was unknown to us until yesterday. This witness, I am told, is prepared to testify that he heard two separate gunshots and was standing in the same general area as were the other witnesses who have testified. I have not spoken with this witness but my investigator has. He is an electrician who had been repairing the traffic semaphore at the intersection where the events that gave rise to this case took place. His testimony should take no longer than ten minutes at the most as I am only interested in what he heard. I am told he was not observing what was taking place in the immediate vicinity of Terry Brandt's car so does not have anything to add to that. He heard two separate shots and that is his testimony."

The judge looked over at the prosecutor and asked him for his comments. Jackson just shook his head and said, "Here we go again, Your Honor. I object to this witness being allowed to testify without prior notice and after the prosecution has put their case into evidence. This is very prejudicial and I object on those grounds."

The judge thought for a moment and said, "We have made other exceptions, and again," addressing the prosecutor, "I think this is something you can address in your closing. The proposed testimony will be permitted and I will permit it only to the extent that the defense counsel has indicated. Two shots. Nothing else. Your objection is noted, Mr. Jackson."

Trey called Mr. Larkin to the stand. A white man, approximately fifty years of age, a little on the heavy side, approached the witness chair and was sworn in by the clerk. When he was seated, Trey had him state his name and address for the record. Trey then stated that he and the witness had never spoken prior to this moment and the witness agreed. Trey then told the witness that he had some questions for him relating to his whereabouts on June 20, 2009, that related to a shooting on that date at the intersection of Portland Avenue and 45th Street in Minneapolis. "Were you in the vicinity of that intersection at that time?"

"Yes, I was. I was repairing the signal light at that intersection at that time." Trey had the witness specifically describe the location of the light signal, which was the red light that had Terry Brandt's car stopped at the intersection.

"At any time that you were working at that intersection, did you hear any unusual sounds that caught your attention?"

"Yes, I heard what sounded like gunshots. One was quite loud and the second one was sort of muffled but also loud."

"Were you able to tell where the shots had come from?"

"It seemed to me that they had come from the street where the car involved was parked."

"What car was that—can you describe it?"

"Well, it was a gray-colored car, but I was out there for quite some time and it was the one that was involved in the shooting of the black kid."

"Did you observe any activity around the gray-colored car prior to the time you heard the shots fired?'

"No, I had my back to that. I was focused on the problem with the light. When I heard the shots, I turned around to look and traffic was moving but the gray car was not. Then the driver stepped out and apparently was bent down. I assume he was helping out the boy that was shot. I don't know."

"Very well, Mr. Larkin. Can you give us some idea of the time span between the shots that you say you heard?"

"They were almost together. It was 'bam, bam'—about like that, except the first one was louder."

Trey said he had no other questions. The prosecutor said he did have some and the judge told him to proceed.

"Mr. Larkin, is it possible that one of the sounds you heard was a car back firing?"

"I don't know. That is possible, but now knowing that there had been a shooting, it sure sounded to me as though there were two shots. They were both loud but the first was very loud and I clearly associated it with a gunshot. Then and now."

"But you do agree that possibly you heard a backfire as well? Would you say that possibly one sound was a backfire and the other was a gunshot?"

Larkin thought for a moment and said, "Possible, yes. But I think it was two gunshots."

The prosecutor apparently concluded that he should stop while ahead so he said he had no more questions.

Trey thought for a moment and then decided to go with the testimony as it had gone into the record. He told the judge he had no other questions and dismissed the witness.

Chapter 17

Trey's next and final witness was the defendant, Terry Brandt. Terry was wearing one of the two suits that Trey had purchased for him to wear at trial. He was a nice looking young man and Trey had spent considerable time in telling Terry how to act at trial and to appear confident of his innocence but in no way arrogantly so. He advised him to be courteous towards the prosecutor and not to become irritated or argue with him on anything, but not to be overly cooperative either. "Just answer the questions and keep in mind, we can always clean up afterwards. Be concerned, but don't make any outward signs of disagreement with evidence or comments by witnesses. We don't want to challenge the jury to find you guilty."

Trey proceeded with the questioning and went through Terry's home life, his participation with the Boy Scouts of America and his schooling. He also brought out that Terry had been an altar boy when he had attended De La Salle High School. Terry had graduated Salutatorian of his high school class and thus far in college had attained an A minus average in his classes. Terry enjoyed his college classes and hoped someday to attend law school. Trey discussed the gun training that Terry had and the fact that the only gun that he had ever fired in training or elsewhere was the very gun that had been involved in the shooting of Tyrone Palmer.

Trey asked Terry if he had known Tyrone Palmer prior to the incident that gave rise to this trial. Terry said he had known who he was but the two were not friends and had never or very seldom spoken before. Trey asked if there was any reason that Terry had not spoken with Tyrone and Terry responded that Tyrone had a reputation for being "A bit of a tough guy." Terry just, more or less, stayed away from him and that was the way it went. He said further that he had never had any problems with Tyrone, which made him somewhat question his reputation. The prosecutor was about to object to this line of questioning but as it ended he apparently decided to let it be. He knew if he made headway with an objection at this point in time, Trey had all sorts of data to bring before the jury that was far worse than what they were hearing from Terry Brandt. Trey was purposely avoiding an all-out attack on Tyrone's reputation, as he did not want the jury to think this was just a way to get them to favor the defendant.

Trey then went into the details of the shooting. At the intersection, Terry saw LeRoy Carter standing on the right side of the intersection and Tyrone was over on the left side beginning to walk across on the green light. Terry did not see the other witnesses who had testified that they were standing in the vicinity of LeRoy Carter. He also testified that he did not know the other two witnesses and consequently would not have recognized them were they present at the intersection. When Terry saw both Tyrone and LeRoy standing on opposite sides of the street, he hit the door lock, which locked all four doors of the car. Trey had not known this before and asked Terry why he did this. He said that he knew that both Tyrone and LeRoy Carter had been charged with carjacking and he just took the precaution. At that point in time, the thirty-eight-caliber pistol was loaded and sitting in the passenger seat of his car. He intended to secure it in the trunk when he arrived at the college. He had his license to carry a firearm in his wallet.

As Tyrone was walking across the street, he turned and angled towards Terry's car, which was the first car at the red light in the slow lane of traffic next to the right side curb. As he approached the car he was smiling but as he came up to the driver's window he pulled a gun out of his jacket chest pocket and held it up so Terry could see the nine-millimeter automatic. He said, "Open the window, Brandt, and get out of the car. Now!"

Terry said he hesitated for a moment and acted as though he was going to get out of the car. He placed his left hand on the left door handle and rotated his body as if to get out of the car while reaching for the thirty-eight with his right hand. When he did so, Tyrone fired his weapon and that was followed immediately by Terry firing his thirty-eight-caliber revolver through the driver's side window with the bullet striking Tyrone in the chest and killing him instantly. Tyrone fell to the ground and Terry said he was out of the car then and spun around to see where LeRoy was—he wasn't sure what he was going to do. He saw LeRoy still standing on the corner and apparently he was not going to do anything.

Terry then checked Tyrone to see if he was injured seriously. He saw that Tyrone was not breathing and he could not feel a pulse. He did attempt to resuscitate Tyrone but was not successful.

Within minutes the police arrived and Terry explained to them that Tyrone had tried to carjack him and that Tyrone had then fired a gun at him but had missed. The officer found the hole in the cushion and after examining Terry's license to carry a firearm let him go. Terry stayed there until Tyrone's body was removed from the scene and then departed for the college.

Trey asked Terry if after the shooting he saw the gun that Tyrone Palmer had used to shoot at him. Terry replied, "It was laying right next to the body and I assumed the police were going to take it. I never saw them or anyone pick up the gun. When the body was removed, the gun was no longer there. I did not mention the gun to the police, as it was not hard to see. I understand they now say they did not see it. I don't know how that could be. Now, there were a lot of people around the car and looking at Tyrone and possibly one of them took the gun. Security was not tight at all; at first there were only two or three cops around and they were trying to control car traffic more than the people walking around." Terry testified that he was not arrested on the case until about two weeks after the incident occurred when the press began demanding his arrest, and then that was on a gun violation charge. Terry was not sure as to what the grounds were for the gun violation as he had a concealed carry permit, and to his knowledge everything was in order permitting him to possess a weapon.

Trey had Terry on the stand for three hours; he wanted the jury to get a good look at him and see him as the nice young man that he was. He had about completed his direct testimony of the defendant and noted that the courtroom clock was getting close to the usual closing time. Trey stated that he had no further questions of this witness and the prosecutor informed the judge that he would be having a rather lengthy cross examination of Mr. Brandt and suggested they continue that the following morning. The judge agreed and dismissed the jury for the day.

Before they parted for the day, Trey met with Terry Brandt to give him some extra advice on how to handle his forthcoming cross-examination by Jackson. They were seated in the jury room when everyone had left the courthouse and Trey told Terry that he had confidence in him that he would carefully listen to the question before answering it.

"If there is any part of the question that you do not agree with or you do not understand, then do not answer it. Tell Jackson to explain what he means. Do not let the prosecutor lead you along the primrose path right into the brick wall. We are doing quite well in the case so far so let's not lose it on cross-examination.

"He is going to hit you hard on the scene where the shooting took place. Who was there? Where were they standing? What were they doing? Who said what, and so forth. He will do all of that with leading questions. Again, if all parts of the leading question are not clearly factual, do not agree with them. You do that and we win. Do not let Jackson take over what you have to say about the shooting. He is allowed to ask leading questions in his cross-examination, so expect it in spades.

"I am expecting him to lay a trap for you in this cross-exam. I do not know what it may be but one area that bothers me is the time you spent in custody and who you may have spoken with. I believe you told me you had spoken with two fellows while you were in jail but that you do not believe anything was said by you that could be a problem. Now, a common trick some prosecutors use is to get a con to snitch on another con. He may try to lay a trap by referring to one of the fellows you spoke with and have you give opinions on that person's truthfulness or opportunity to know your experiences. If his leading questions contain anything of that nature, beware. You may be looking at the next witness in this case who is coming in to testify about what you told him when you were both in the cell. Do not vouch for anyone's truthfulness or ability to know the facts of this case that has not yet testified. A simple 'I don't know' would suffice there. It is not unheard of to offer a fellow con a shorter time in jail for his testimony, if you know what I mean. Do you know what I am talking about?"

"Yes, Mr. Stark, I do, and I will watch out for it."

The following morning, the judge began the proceedings promptly at nine a.m. He told Terry to resume his seat in the witness box
and asked Jackson if he was ready to proceed with his cross-examination of Mr. Brandt. Jackson indicated he was and the judge merely
said, "Your witness."

Jackson began his cross of Terry with non-controversial questions
relating to his education, when he had began study at the Hennepin
Community College and what his intended course of study was. His
purpose clearly was to get the witness to relax and freely expound.
As time progressed the questioning became more targeted on the
shooting and the principals involved.

"Mr. Brandt, you attended the same high school at the same time
as Tyrone Palmer, isn't that correct?"

"Yes, sir. We were there at the same time."

"Did you associate with Mr. Palmer at any time when you were
both students at De La Salle High School?"

"No, sir. I had seen him in the halls and in the cafeteria but I don't
believe I ever spoke to him. He was one of the students there that
was involved in sort of a tutored student program that the school
operated. It was a program for students who needed some extra help
on getting through the academics at De La Salle. I knew he was in
the program as their classes were in a certain part of the academic
building and I saw him entering or leaving those classrooms."

"If Mr. Palmer said that you and he had spoken on a number of
occasions, would you say he was mistaken?"

"No. I just don't recall that we ever actually spoke to one another,
but we may have."

"Did you ever have any problems in your time at De La Salle with
Mr. Palmer?"

"No, sir. Not that I recall."

"But, I believe you said you considered Mr. Palmer as being a bit
of a 'tough guy.' I believe that is what you said. Did you consider
him a 'tough guy,' and if so what did you mean by that?"

"I may have said that, and I did consider him a bit on the tough side. What I meant is that he hung with a rougher crowd than I would have associated with, and he dressed in the 'tough guy' manner—baggy trousers hanging down, shirt unbuttoned, that sort of thing. I never did witness Mr. Palmer involved in fighting or anything like that, but I did hear that he was quite disruptive in his classes. I did not witness that myself. He had the general reputation in the school as being someone to avoid."

"Yet, you yourself never had any problems with Mr. Palmer, correct?"

"Yes, I guess that is correct."

"Well, is that correct or not?"

"Yes, sir, I never did have any problems with Tyrone Palmer that I can think of."

"Mr. Brandt, you knew a Mr. Simmons, Robert Simmons, while you were in custody in the Hennepin County Jail, correct?"

"I think that is the name of the fellow that was in the same cell I was in following my arrest. Yes, sir. I can't remember his name but I think that is the fellow."

"Very well, Mr. Brandt, let us assume that is his name. Now, how long were you in the same cell as Mr. Simmons?"

"I believe we were together for about two weeks. He was being held on some other charge and I don't right now recall what it was."

"Now, Mr. Simmons seemed like a normal, regular sort of guy, correct?"

"I guess so, Mr. Jackson, He seemed okay to me other than the fact we were both in the county jail."

"You talked about many different things, didn't you?"

"Yes, sir. That is true."

"Did you think he was being truthful to you in your conversations?"

"Yes, sir. I didn't have any reason to think he was lying about anything."

"So, you thought he was a regular, normal, honest young man, correct?"

"From what little I knew about him, yes. I had no reason to disbelieve him."

"Did you talk to him about why he was in jail?"

"Yes, I believe I did and right now I can't remember why he was there."

"And he asked you why you were there, right?"

"Yes, sir. We talked about that as well."

"Did you relate to him the facts related to the shooting as you have related them here in court?"

"Yes, sir. I believe I told him how the shooting had occurred and that Tyrone Palmer had fired his gun at me and I immediately fired at him as I feared for my life."

"And you considered him to be a fairly normal, truthful person aside from the fact that you were both in the Hennepin County Jail, correct?" Jackson framed this question in a jocular fashion as with a bit of a humorous smile on his face.

"Yes. I had no reason to distrust him. I was aware of many things that the two of us talked about and he seemed to discuss them factually. I had no reason to disbelieve anything he said but keep in mind I had never met him before we met in the county jail."

"Did the two of you discuss getting together again when you were both out of custody—out of jail, that is?"

"Yes. We did discuss that."

"And it was your intention to continue the relationship in the future when you were both free again to live your lives as you saw fit, right?"

"Yes, if our paths crossed again. There were no specific plans to get together again when we were out of jail but there was a general agreement that we might do that."

"Because he seemed like a decent, honest fellow that you would be glad to associate with in the future, correct?"

"From everything I knew at the time, yes."

Jackson then went into the shooting sequence and in particular discussed the placement of the gun on the passenger seat of Terry's car. Jackson quizzed Terry on whether or not he had moved the gun to a more accessible spot on the passenger seat so that he had better access to it. Terry denied that he had ever touched the gun prior to the time he actually used it in the shooting but he was aware of the exact position of the gun at all times.

Jackson had Terry describe every movement he went through in taking the gun and firing it at Tyrone Palmer. First of all, the time interval between Terry seeing Palmer showing him his gun and Terry firing his weapon was minimal. When Tyrone held up his weapon and it was visible through the driver's side window, Terry immediately put his right hand on his weapon and as he was swinging it around to aim at Tyrone, that was when Tyrone fired at Terry. Terry immediately fired his weapon at Tyrone and that was the end of the shooting.

Jackson asked Terry if he didn't find it strange that only one person heard two gunshots. The others only heard one shot that Terry fired at Tyrone Palmer.

Terry immediately replied that he had given that a great deal of thought and he concluded that he fired his gun at almost the same time as Tyrone fired at him. "Mr. Jackson, the gunshots may have been in such close sequence that most people were under the impression there was only one gunshot."

"Then how do you account for the fact that the police could never find the gun that Tyrone Palmer supposedly had fired?"

"Mr. Jackson, I believe someone picked up the weapon on the street and never turned it in to the police. This incident occurred in the hood and we know there is a market for weapons in the hood. The police did not show at the shooting site for, I would say, about fifteen minutes after I had called, and there were a number of people around my car and checking Tyrone to see if there was something that could be done for him. Any of them could have picked up the gun and kept it for their own purposes. Also, I know when I tried to resuscitate Tyrone that the gun was laying fairly close to his body. With all the traffic next to Tyrone's body, the gun may have been pushed some distance away. I just don't know."

"Mr. Brandt, is it your testimony that when you picked up your pistol and turned it on Mr. Palmer it was your intention to shoot Tyrone Palmer at that point in time?"

"When I pointed the gun in his direction, I was hoping that he would see the gun pointed at him and he would put his weapon away. That was when he fired and I fired. He fired first and I fired just a second or two after he did."

"So, Mr. Palmer saw you swinging your weapon around to aim at him when he fired his weapon, correct?"

"Yes. I would say that was about the way it happened."

"Mr. Brandt, is it not reasonable to assume that Tyrone Palmer fired his weapon at you in self-defense, believing that you were about to shoot him?"

Terry thought for a moment and then replied. "He may have thought that, but that was not my intention."

"Mr. Brandt, is it not possible that had you not turned your weapon on Tyrone Palmer that he and you would both be alive today?"

Again, Terry paused for a few seconds before responding. "I don't know the answer to that."

"But it would be possible, isn't that true?"

"Maybe. I don't know."

The prosecutor terminated his cross-examination of Terry Brandt at this point and requested a sidebar conference with the judge and Trey. The judge granted the sidebar and motioned for the attorneys and the court reporter to step forward. When they were all settled in position before the judge and the reporter was ready to record the testimony, the judge motioned for the prosecutor to proceed with his comments.

"Your Honor, I have another witness that I wish to present but he is not on our submitted witness list. I wish to present him for impeachment purposes with respect to the defendant's testimony just given. I had just learned of this witness within the past week or two and did not know if I would ever use his testimony until it became apparent this morning in my cross of the defendant, Terry Brandt."

The judge leaned forward and asked the prosecutor, "What is it that you expect this witness to testify to that will impeach testimony of Mr. Brandt?"

"Your Honor, he will testify to admissions made by the defendant that contradict his testimony on direct and on cross-examination."

The judge looked at Trey and asked him, "Do you have any comment to make, Mr. Stark?"

"Yes, Your Honor. The surprise witness that so frequently comes up in these cases is always the fellow that was in jail with the client who amazingly gets a reduced sentence shortly thereafter. We have made numerous inquiries of the jail supervisors, the prosecutor's office, and anyone in a position of authority who could give us the name of anyone that was ever jailed with Terry Brandt following this incident. We received nothing. I would suggest, Your Honor, that before this witness is allowed to testify before the jury we have the opportunity to voir dire the witness concerning how and when he was contacted to testify, what he has been examined about by the prosecution and what he intends to testify about with respect to counteracting testimony from Mr. Brandt. I would also request the court to inquire of the prosecutor under oath regarding any offers to this witness with respect to diminution of charges of pending sentences, and if any are found that this witness not be allowed to testify in this case."

The judge looked over at the prosecutor and said, "I think Mr. Stark's request is reasonable, Mr. Jackson. Let me ask you, are you aware of any deals made or to be made with this witness that would affect any sentence he has been given or will be given?"

Jackson shook his head. "Your Honor, I have never spoken directly to the witness. My staff has and I am not aware of any negotiations with the witness to reduce any prison time he may be facing in return for his taking the stand and testifying today."

The judge responded. "Let me just say this, Mister Jackson, if it turns up today or anytime following this hearing that the witness surprisingly has his sentence reduced and there exists no clearly reasonable basis for the reduction, I will grant the defendant an immediate re-trial in the event he loses this one. Is that understood?"

"Your Honor, I don't have any reason to assume that will or may happen. I also don't have any ready objection to make so I will just pass on that for the time being."

The Judge smiled and said, "That is fine, Mister Jackson. We will temporarily dismiss the Jury and permit Mister Stark to proceed with his voir dire of the witness. I assume he is present and available, correct?"

Trey interjected, "Your Honor, for the record, I object to this witness being permitted to testify when he was not listed on the prosecutor's pre-trial statement."

The Judge merely replied, "Overruled" and nodded to Trey Stark to commence his voir dire when the witness was presented. The Judge then sent the Jury back to the Jury Room so that they did not hear the testimony.

Chapter 18

The prosecutor indicated the witness was present and available for the voir dire. Jackson signaled one of his staff to bring the witness into the courtroom and to have him take the witness stand.

The witness entered the courtroom and Trey noticed that he was a nice appearing young white man, about the same age as Terry Brandt and reasonably well dressed for his court appearance. Trey had him sworn in and had him state his full name and address clearly for the court reporter.

Trey commenced his voir dire with preliminary identification questions and then got to the point. "You were confined in the same cell at the Hennepin County Jail as was Terry Brandt, correct?"

"Yes, sir. I was."

"And during that confinement with Terry Brandt, the two of you discussed what each of you had done in order to result in your confinement, correct?"

"Yes, sir."

"Do you recall what Terry Brandt said to you that resulted in his confinement?"

"He told me that he had shot and killed a fellow and he was charged with murder."

"Did he tell how the shooting occurred?"

"Yes. He told me that the fellow approached his car and Terry assumed he was going to try to carjack him."

"Then what happened?"

"The fellow that he shot seemed to be reaching into his pocket to get something and Terry thought he was going for a gun and that was when he shot the guy. Turned out he did not have a gun. Just as the guy was shot he said something about 'hitchhiking.' Terry felt pretty bad about the shooting as he figured out that the kid was only hitchhiking and wanted a ride."

"As you testify here today, do you recall that Terry Brandt said he did not ever see Mr. Palmer pull out a gun?"

"I don't recall Terry's exact words but that was the impression that I had regarding our conversation. That is what I remember being said."

"Mr. Simmons, what were you being charged with that put you in the Hennepin County Jail?"

"I was initially charged with armed robbery but due to the amount involved, it was dropped to petty theft, a misdemeanor."

"Did you serve any jail time for the charge of petty theft?"

"I did serve one year, which I thought was excessive for the charge."

"Were you aware of the time you could have served for armed robbery?"

"I was told anywhere from ten to twenty years or even more, depending on the circumstances."

"When was the charge reduced?"

"Just when I was going to trial."

"At any time did you have any discussions with the prosecutors about the charge of murder against Terry Brandt?"

"They did ask me about that and if I had any discussions with him when we were together in jail. I told them just what I told you."

"And after that your charges were reduced to petty theft, is that right?"

"Yes. About that time."

"Was it your understanding that the charges were being reduced in exchange for your testimony against Terry Brandt?"

"Possibly, but I don't know. It was never put into those words."

Trey then requested a sidebar. The two attorneys and the reporter approached the bench and when the reporter indicated that she was ready to transcribe, Trey began talking. "Your Honor, I move that this witness not be allowed to testify as a witness for the prosecution. I think it is apparent that he was given an unusually good deal dropping the charge from armed robbery to petty theft, supposedly due to the amount involved in the theft. There is a sharp conflict between the witness's recollection of what Terry Brandt told him and the testimony from Terry Brandt and the suspicion that a quid pro quo was involved is certainly present."

The judge looked at Jackson and said, "Mr. Jackson, do you have anything to say?"

"I should first say, Your Honor, that I have never spoken with this witness before today. I am not aware of any negotiations between him and others from the Attorney General's office but I am aware that there was an issue regarding the charges against Robert Simmons with respect to the amount of funds allegedly stolen, which were minimal, and that a charge of armed robbery for the theft was excessive. I should add that there was no weapon involved in the theft other than a stick of wood I am told. It was not a solid armed robbery case in any event, and furthermore, Mr. Simmons had no prior criminal record whatsoever. That is all I can say with respect to the matter, Your Honor, other than the fact that I suggest that the allegations suggested by Mr. Stark do not arise to the level sufficient to strike this witness's testimony in this case."

The judge looked at both attorneys and said, "This is a difficult question. Charges were reduced and his proposed testimony is completely contradictory to what the present defendant has to say. That does raise the question of whether the reduction was given in return for the testimony. It may have been or may not have been. I will ask the witness some questions regarding the charges that were against him and then decide. You may be seated and I will rule later on the admissibility of his testimony."

The judge then proceeded to cover all aspects of the original charges that were filed against Robert Simmons. He cautioned him a number of times to be aware of the fact that his testimony was under oath and that penalties of perjury would apply if he was not telling the truth. The witness stated he was well aware of that fact.

When the judge had completed examining what Simmons had

done, who the victims were, what weapon was used and how much was stolen or taken from them, he commented that Mr. Jackson's explanation of the case was reasonably accurate. He then asked the two attorneys if they had any further questions for the witness and they indicated that they did not. He told the witness to leave the witness box but to remain in the courtroom as he was still under subpoena and would possibly be taking the stand when the jury returned.

The judge then announced a fifteen-minute break and departed the courtroom. He obviously was going to decide the issue in the privacy of his chambers. Trey commented to Chris that it appeared he was going to allow the witness to testify regarding his conversation with Terry Brandt and that was going to be very damaging.

When the judge returned to the courtroom, he confirmed Trey's suspicions and announced that he would allow the witness to testify and he would also allow the defendant's attorney to cross-examine the witness and to argue in his closing argument the possibility of a quid pro quo arrangement between Robert Simmons and the prosecutor's office with respect to his testimony against Terry Brandt provided that Trey laid out the foundation for the possible arrangement in his cross-examination of Robert Simmons.

Trey objected to the admission of Robert Simmons's testimony for the record and the Judge promptly overruled it.

When the jury was reseated, the judge announced to the jury that the prosecutor had an additional witness whereupon Robert Simmons was sworn in and Jackson began his direct examination of Simmons, concentrating on his arrest on the charge of armed robbery. He spent considerable time covering the events that led up to Simmons being charged with armed robbery including the particulars on the weapon used to intimidate the victims, the victims involved, the amount of funds involved in the robbery and the criminal record of Simmons at the time of the robbery. At that time he had no criminal record whatsoever. Jackson's direct examination of Simmons was clearly for the purpose of minimizing the gravity of the events and the instrumentalities that led up to the armed robbery charge.

The prosecutor then covered the time span between the filing of charges and the reduction of charges to petty theft. The time span was a little less than one year and the reduction of charges occurred as the case against Simmons was being prepared for trial. The arrangement was being brokered primarily by the attorney representing Robert Simmons. The exchange called for Simmons to take a guilty plea to a misdemeanor of petty theft with the understanding that he would be serving a one-year term in the county jail for the crime. It was also agreed at that time that Mr. Simmons would be appearing as a prosecution witness in the murder case against Terry Brandt to testify concerning their conversations while both were incarcerated. Neither Simmons nor his attorney objected to the one-year sentence, which was excessive for a misdemeanor charge as their understanding apparently was that Simmons was coming out very well in the bargain.

When the prosecutor had completed his direct examination of Robert Simmons, Trey began his cross-examination and covered in detail all negotiations involved in the exchange, whereby the charge against him was reduced to petty theft and in return he agreed to testify against Terry Brandt with respect to the conversations he had concerning the details of the shooting of Tyrone Palmer. Trey concentrated his cross to connect the quid pro quo aspects of the trade-off of petty theft for the incriminating evidence against Terry Brandt. Trey was successful in showing that the charge was reduced at virtually the same time as Simmons agreed to testify against Terry.

After the witness was excused, the prosecutor rested his case and Trey followed suit. Trey then announced to the judge that he wished to make an additional motion to dismiss. The judge then excused the jury until 9:00 the following morning and when they had left the courtroom, the judge said he would take a ten-minute break and the parties could join him in his chambers to go over the jury instructions and the defendant's attorney could make his motion at that time. When the judge's clerk announced that the judge was ready for the attorneys, they filed into his chambers along with the court reporter.

When they were seated, the judge looked at Trey and told him to proceed with his motion. Trey said that the motion was one to dismiss the charge of murder in the first degree as the evidence was lacking that supported the requirement in the definition for murder in the first degree in Minnesota: that it be deliberate and premeditated. All of the evidence adduced by the defense attorney and by the prosecutor indicated that it was absolutely devoid of premeditation and was not a deliberate act, one done with care and purpose. Trey pointed out, "The defendant testified that he had pulled the trigger that fired the fatal shot, but it was not done with any intentional thought to inflict injury or death. It was done in response to a perceived threat that became real when Tyrone Palmer pulled the trigger on his weapon. It was purely a defensive action on the part of Terry Brandt.

"It is also arguable, Your Honor, that the actions of Mr. Brandt do not meet the requirements of second degree murder in that the act of pulling the trigger by Mr. Brandt does not appear to be the result of any intentional act. It was a spontaneous defensive reaction resulting from being fired upon by Tyrone Palmer. As he testified on direct, at no time did he intend to injure or kill Mr. Palmer. He pulled the trigger only after Mr. Palmer fired his gun at him. That was obviously an act performed without forethought. Mr. Brandt's act of firing his gun was a reaction done purely in self-defense." Trey had to be careful on this point as he was aware that the prosecutor could move to include a charge of manslaughter as an option for the jury to consider if they did not agree on second degree murder. Manslaughter was a more appropriate charge in a negligent killing and Trey wanted to leave in an element of intention in Terry aiming the gun at Palmer and pulling the trigger. He would possibly need that if the prosecutor moved for the inclusion of the manslaughter charge. Trey was also aware that the prosecutor may not be willing to include the manslaughter charge as it would decrease the possibility of a murder two conviction. Trey left the issue at that point and waited to see what the prosecutor and the judge would do.

The judge looked at the prosecutor and awaited his response. Jackson eagerly accepted the invitation to speak. "Your Honor, Mr. Brandt knew the gun was in the car positioned immediately next to him in the passenger seat. He had been advised to put it in the trunk of the car by his mother, yet he did not do that. He kept the gun out where it was accessible and that shows the premeditation that he intended or considered the possibility that he would have access to the weapon should the need arise. He has testified that he considered Tyrone Palmer a 'rough sort of fellow,' one that he would prefer to avoid. When Palmer approached the Brandt vehicle it was then that Terry Brandt was considering his options. He knew the gun was accessible and when Tyrone Palmer placed his hand inside his jacket or withdrew a gun, depending upon the scenario that you believe took place, it was then that Terry Brandt intentionally and with aforethought grabbed the gun to shoot Mr. Palmer. That is when Mr. Palmer feared for his own life. He could see where Terry Brandt's hand was moving to when it reached for the gun. Intention on the part of Mr. Brandt is present in this situation, Your Honor, and so is premeditation. Had he moved the gun into the trunk when he took possession of the car, premeditation would be absent. I further suggest, Your Honor, that an action being defensive in nature does not remove it from being an intentional act, or, for that matter, a deliberate action. I move that the defendant's motion be denied."

The judge said nothing; he just rubbed his chin looking at both attorneys. Finally he spoke. "I will have to think about this. I will give you my decision by telephone this evening. If you have any additional motions, we can handle them in the morning before we convene the jury." The judge advised the attorneys that he would call them by eight this evening with his decision.

Trey then said that he had another motion to make and the judge told him to go ahead. "Let's get them all out now and not later."

Trey said, "Your Honor, there is also a charge outstanding that is not supported by any evidence at all and that is the charge of illegal possession of a firearm by Mr. Brandt. There has been no evidence at all entered into the record dealing with this and I request that it be dismissed by the court."

The judge looked over at Fred Jackson and asked if he had any comment to make. Jackson said he supported Mr. Stark's motion and the charge should be dismissed. The judge noted the dismissal in the record and the charge was withdrawn.

Trey had submitted a number of proposed jury instructions as had the prosecutor, and it was anticipated that there would be some strong disagreements over some of the instructions. It was the judge's practice to use his own instructions, and when one of the parties wanted their own instruction, they could then discuss it. Frequently the proposed instructions by all three participants in this process were the same. It was the occasional exception that created the problem. In those cases, the judge usually went with his own selection and arguments from the attorneys were permitted only to a minimum. At the end of the conference, all of the instructions were approved for presentation to the jury when they were again seated.

The judge gave each attorney the jury form that he intended to deliver to the jury for their verdict. He asked if they had any proposed changes to the form. Trey examined the form and noted there was no mention of a manslaughter charge and the reduced charge of first or second degree murder was the only charge remaining. The prosecutor studied the form for some time and Trey was praying that he would not request the additional lesser charge of manslaughter. If he had, Trey was prepared to argue that it should either stand alone or the first or second degree charge should stand alone as the two charges would be contradictory by reason of the element of intentional killing that was in the first and second degree murder charge. Fortunately, the prosecutor was silent and both attorneys approved the form, subject to further order of the court regarding the charge of first degree murder.

That evening by eight p.m., as promised by the judge, the attorneys were informed by the court that the charge of murder in the first degree would be dismissed with prejudice and the charge of murder in the second degree would be allowed to proceed as the only charge against the defendant. The defense attorney would be allowed to argue that the reduction of Robert Simmons's charge from armed robbery to petty theft was the result of a quid pro quo exchange for his proffered testimony regarding Terry Brandt. Trey was not pleased with either ruling as the reduction to murder two still contained the possibility of a life term for Terry Brandt, and undoubtedly the prosecutor would argue for that in his closing. The prison time for conviction under a charge of murder two was ten years to life without the possibility of parole. As Trey explained it to Chris, a murder two charge was about the same as murder in the first degree. "The only difference is that it would probably sound better on one's resume if it read murder in the second degree, but then, what good is that."

The morning newspapers and radio news discussed in great detail the reduction of the charges against Terry Brandt, who had killed the hitchhiking student. The criticism was aimed at both Trey Stark, the debt collector, and the judge, who continued to give in to Stark's outlandish and unsubstantiated arguments. As the editorial phrased it, "How anyone could not be charged with first Degree Murder when they intentionally level a gun and fire it at a student who is seeking a ride to school baffles the imagination." The radio stations were equally inflammatory in their criticism of both Trey Stark and the Judge. Trey had Alice arrange for protection from the Sherriff's office for both himself and Chris at least through the end of the trial. He did not want to do that as it interfered with his privacy but the animosity created by the media was increasing daily.

In the morning, the attorneys had no additional motions to present and indicated they were ready to proceed with closing arguments. The Judge then recalled the jury and when they were all seated, he read the jury instructions that had been agreed upon the previous afternoon. He instructed the jury on their responsibilities as jurors and how they were to complete the jury form, explaining every blank space on the form that needed to be filled in by the jury foreman. He also explained that if they had any questions , the foreman was to contact the judge's clerk and have the issue submitted to the judge for review. They were again instructed not to review the case in any news articles in the paper nor were they to watch television news discussing the case. They were to discuss the case only among themselves.

After a fifteen minute break, the prosecutor began his closing argument which was, as Trey had predicted, an assault on the character and intentions of Terry Brandt. Jackson painted Terry Brandt as a vicious, hateful killer of a young man, troubled but striving to educate himself and gain access to economic independence. He spent a fair amount of time on the testimony of Robert Simmons, which he referred to as a 'window' into the thinking of Terry Brandt at the time of the killing of Tyrone Palmer. "We can actually see what was taking place in the mind of Terry Brandt as he reached for his weapon and coolly picked up the thirty-eight-caliber pistol, raised it up and leveled it carefully at Tyrone Palmer and squeezed the trigger. When we listen to what Terry Brandt said to Robert Simmons, we are listening to a recitation of careful, intentional, purposeful acts designed to take the life of another human being. We are not listening to someone describe how an accidentally dropped gun fired and took a life. Every movement by Terry Brandt in the seconds before Tyrone Palmer's life was torn away from him was designed to accomplish only one purpose, the killing of Tyrone Palmer. For taking that life, Terry Brandt should be found guilty of murder in the second degree with life-term imprisonment without parole." The prosecutor had taken forty-five minutes in delivering his closing argument. When he had completed his comments, the judge announced that the defendant's attorney would deliver his closing comments.

Trey was fully prepared to deliver his closing. He considered his closing arguments at trial to be his strongest trial asset, next to the cross-examinations. He could get very much involved in both of these phases of trial and his energy level was raised for both. His interest level in preparing for his closing was very high. He had spent much time in developing the closing and had worked closely with Chris in developing the points that both of them considered the most important. They also had to focus on the possibility that the jury could come in with a manslaughter conviction that could carry up to five years of prison time. That would be very damaging to the future career of Terry Brandt, not to mention what it would do to his focus on success in life. Fortunately, the manslaughter charge was no longer present, much to Trey's relief.

As Trey stood up to address the jury, all of these thoughts came to mind and added to the pressure of the moment. Trey worked well under pressure so this did not particularly bother him. He had learned long ago that he was more successful working under pressure than when he was too relaxed. He was quicker on his feet and could handle the organization of his closing better when the pressure was high and his energy level was higher as well.

Chapter 19

Trey studied the jury for a moment to get their complete attention before he began speaking. He again explained that he represented Terry Brandt, the defendant in this case, and this was Terry Brandt's final opportunity to point out to the jury the key points in the evidence that Trey wanted them to focus upon. It was very important that the jury focus on the separate actions that took place between these two young men that ended with the death of one of them in order for the jury to be able to determine the guilt or innocence of Terry Brandt with respect to the death of Tyrone Palmer.

What the jury decided in this case would determine the very existence of Terry Brandt's future. First and foremost, Trey told them Terry Brandt considered this an unfortunate loss of life. He regrets the events, as do most people who are familiar with the case. It was Terry Brandt who tried to revive Tyrone Palmer immediately after he had fallen to the ground. "Think what that means with respect to the mindset of Terry Brandt at that time. That is milliseconds after he had pulled the trigger that sent the bullet into Tyrone Palmer, taking his life. Is that act of attempted resuscitation the act of a person who intended to take the life of Tyrone Palmer? Clearly not. The message is clear and it is telling. Terry Brandt did not intend that Tyrone Palmer should die.

"His killing was a spontaneous result of a number of factors. First, Terry's mother had unintentionally left the weapon in the car when she turned the car over to Terry. It was there and was available for what happened. Tyrone Palmer was armed and it was his intent to use his weapon to criminally take by force the car that Terry was driving for his own intents and purposes. I do not believe that Tyrone Palmer intended to harm Terry Brandt in the process. However, he was prepared to do so if it became necessary. He was carrying his nine-millimeter automatic pistol for just that purpose.

"In Tyrone Palmer's mind it apparently became necessary to fire his gun at Terry when he saw Terry going for his gun. He missed when he fired his gun at Terry and that gave Terry the time he needed to fire his gun and to stop Tyrone Palmer from firing another shot. These final actions on the part of both participants took only milliseconds to perform. I question that intention to kill was present in either participant, other than the intent of Tyrone Palmer to carjack Terry's car using the threat of force. His firing of his weapon was a reaction to what Terry was doing, which was a reaction to what he saw Tyrone Palmer doing. The reactions of both individuals in this situation are not the same. Terry's reaction to seeing Tyrone Palmer pull a nine-millimeter automatic from his coat pocket telling Terry to get out of the car is not a criminal act. Terry Brandt had a recognized right to defend himself to the extent of taking Tyrone's life when he saw his own life threatened. The threat to Terry Brandt's life was a criminal act by Tyrone Palmer. The threat to Tyrone Palmer posed by Terry reaching for his revolver was not a criminal act—it was clearly an act of self-defense.

"I will now speak solely on behalf of Terry Brandt. He was proceeding lawfully in his automobile to attend college classes at Hennepin Community College when Tyrone Palmer approached his car and threatened him with a gun. Terry Brandt had every right in the world to defend himself in that situation. When Tyrone Palmer fired his gun at him, Terry Brandt was clearly within the law to fire his weapon at Palmer to prevent him from firing a second shot at him. The prosecutor has questioned that Palmer was in the act of an attempted carjacking. Remember, this is not the first carjacking by Tyrone Palmer. He had already been charged three times previous and was awaiting trial on those charges. His companion in two of those cases was LeRoy Carter, who was standing at the curb adjacent to Terry's car. We can only surmise what his intentions were.

"Let us now consider the issue of Tyrone Palmer being armed with a gun and whether he fired the gun at Terry Brandt. According to the police, no gun was found in the possession of Tyrone Palmer or near his body when he fell. While we do not have the gun, we do have two bullet holes in the driver's side window of the car Terry was driving. One bullet hole indicated it had been penetrated by a bullet outside of the car moving into the car and that bullet was found in the seat cushion next to Terry Brandt. This evidence clearly conforms to the testimony of Terry Brandt that Tyrone fired his gun at him through the window of the car."

Trey now used a diagram he had prepared for this phase of the closing that clearly depicted the path of the bullet through the hole in the window in a downward trajectory, narrowly missing Terry Brandt and impacting the seat cushion next to where he was seated. "As you can see, the path of this bullet came very close to striking Mr. Brandt. The clothing of Mr. Brandt also evidenced glass particles from the window and gunshot residue from the bullet fired by Tyrone Palmer. Our expert witness testified very forcefully that the evidence found on the clothing of Terry Brandt clearly proves a bullet had been fired from outside of the car, through the window and into the cushion, narrowly missing Terry Brandt. The expert also went into great detail as to the evidence the two bullet holes in the window showed with respect to the direction of travel through the window. The Palmer bullet entry hole was on the outer side of the car window and the Brandt bullet entry hole was obviously on the inner side of the car window. All of the evidence in this case supports the testimony of this case as presented by Terry Brandt.

"Now let us consider the testimony of Robert Simmons who was, in fact, housed in the same cell as Terry Brandt for five days after Terry was arrested. Terry says he explained to Robert Simmons the facts relating to his arrest identical to what he explained to you when he was on the stand either on direct examination by me or on cross-examination by the prosecutor. Simmons related to us a story that he said originated from Terry Brandt that was the complete opposite of what Terry said he had told Simmons. It was also opposite to all of the material evidence available in this case.

"Now, you ask who is telling the truth, Simmons or Terry Brandt? I will ask you, who received a reduction in charges from armed robbery, which carries a prison term of ten years to life reduced down to petty theft, which carries a maximum of one year in the county jail but normally carries no prison time whatsoever? Armed robbery is a felony. Petty theft is a misdemeanor, or a minor crime, usually punished with a fine. A traffic violation is a misdemeanor. Ask yourself, why did the State reduce Mr. Simmons' punishment from armed robbery to a misdemeanor? I suggest to you that such reductions sometimes happen when defendants who are in a position where they can assist in the conviction of another defendant on a more serious charge and are willing to offer such testimony for the purpose of getting their charges or sentence reduced. That is what clearly occurred in this case. Simmons sold his testimony for a reduced charge—clear and simple. All of the evidence in this case supports the explanation given by Terry Brandt. None of it supports the testimony given by Robert Simmons."

Trey spoke for another fifteen minutes on other aspects of the trial evidence and the need for the jurors to independently use their common sense in arriving at their verdict. He discussed the definition of reasonable doubt and clear and convincing evidence and their application to this case. Trey thanked the jurors for their attention given to the attorneys during the presentation of the evidence and for their service as jurors in the criminal justice system.

Trey's closing took forty minutes. When he finished and joined Chris at the defense counsel's table, she told him that Trey had laid out all of the key points and she believed the jurors had followed his argument. She said, "I say it will be an acquittal."

The judge then gave the jury additional instructions before returning them to the jury room for their deliberations. Trey was concerned they could have a hung jury as there were at least two or three jurors sitting in this case that he had not felt confident that he had their attention or support. It only took one juror to produce a hung jury, as a unanimous verdict was required for either a guilty or not-guilty verdict. If there was a hung jury, there were alternative proposals that could come up and he should be prepared to discuss them if that contingency arose. At the present time, the jury was comprised of twelve members, all of whom would have to vote for a conviction or an acquittal or there would be a hung jury. The defendant could opt for almost any alternative waving a unanimous verdict in favor of a majority vote or for a smaller jury. Trey was not in favor of reducing the jury size or giving up the requirement for a unanimous jury. Terry Brandt wanted out of there and was amenable to some changes but he was so far following Trey's suggestions. Chris agreed with Trey's opinion that they should stick with the requirement for the unanimous verdict with the twelve-member jury.

In the week following the day that the jury had retired to deliberate the fate of Terry Brandt, there was silence until the third day of deliberations. At that time, the foreman requested a transcription of the testimony of Robert Simmons. The judge informed the attorneys of the jury's request and asked for their opinions on whether the transcription should be provided to them or not. The prosecutor was in full agreement with the request. Trey was not. He would agree with it provided that his closing remarks relating to Simmons testimony were also released to the jury. The prosecutor objected to that and the judge agreed that Trey's closing comments would not be provided to the jury, as closing arguments were not evidence. Trey then objected to the release of Simmons' transcribed testimony and the judge took it under advisement. He said that he would consider the request and announce his decision the following morning.

The following morning when the attorneys were present in the courtroom and before the jury had been called in, the judge announced to the attorneys that he had decided to grant the request of the jury to have a copy of the transcript of the testimony of Robert Simmons and it would include both the direct testimony responding to questions from the prosecutor as well as the cross-examination from the defendant's attorney. The testimony was being transcribed and would be delivered to the jury before lunch break. Trey made a formal objection to the release on the grounds it was prejudicial to the defendant and did not include a delivery of a transcription of the defendant's testimony as well. In the absence of a request from the jury for this additional evidence, the judge said that he would withhold release of Terry Brandt's testimony pending a request from the jury.

Trey and Chris reviewed the direct and cross of Robert Simmons to see how they stood with respect to the delivery of the transcript to the jury. Both Trey and Chris were confident that the cross by Trey of Robert Simmons, as well as some of the direct, clearly showed the possibility and probability that Simmons testimony was traded for a major reduction in the criminal charge of armed robbery that he faced. They further concluded that it was not error for the judge to deliver the transcript to the jury, so they could not look for a successful appeal on those grounds.

The media were following the trial of Terry Brandt closely in the final weeks of trial. They were of the opinion that the court was granting virtually every request of the defense counsel and restricting the freedom of the prosecution to attack Terry Brandt. Trey Stark was the subject of at least one vicious attack a day in the local newspapers. They managed at least one reference in every article to the actions of the debt collector that represented Terry Brandt.

They had also managed to trail Terry Brandt back to his temporary homestead and listed the address in their newspaper. Terry had to find a new residence that afforded him the safety and security that he needed. It was not possible to provide this for him in the residence of a friend or associate and the decision was made to house him in a hotel in close proximity to the courthouse, where Hennepin County Sheriff's deputies could provide security. The walk from his residence to the courthouse through the enclosed overpasses with heavy security while wearing a bullet-proof vest was going to have to suffice until the trial was concluded. Trey was also very concerned that if Terry was found not guilty, that would inflame those who considered him to be a vicious killer of a poor child on his way to school. That would be the most dangerous time for Terry and Trey had already decided that he would have to leave the city for a period of time until feelings cooled down.

Trey also considered himself and Chris to be at heightened risk of attack, particularly as the trial was winding down and a verdict was near. The Sheriff's office had increased the protection for Trey's office, as well as for the residences of both Trey and Chris. He looked forward to the day when both he and Chris could board a plane and leave the state, if even for only two weeks. He was also becoming concerned that with the jury taking so long to come to a verdict, he would have to postpone his trip to California. He had built in a buffer on the reservation dates for his trip to the coast and that would probably suffice, even if the jury took longer than normal for their decision.

In the second week of jury deliberations, the foreman met again with the judge and informed him that they were deadlocked. The judge called the entire jury back into the courtroom and gave them the following instruction, which was generally referred to as an Allen Instruction—the accepted instruction for a hung jury. This instruction was developed following a string of instructions to hung juries that were determined on appeal to have been improper as imposing pressures on the jury to move in one direction or the other. There were no objections to this instruction by either Trey or the prosecutor.

The Judge delivered the following instruction to the jurors seated in his courtroom:

> *Members of the jury, you have advised the Court that you have been unable to agree upon a verdict in this case. I have decided to suggest a few thoughts to you.*
>
> *As jurors, you have a duty to discuss the case with one another and to deliberate in an effort to reach a unanimous verdict, if each of you can do so without violating your individual judgment and conscience. Each of you must decide the case for yourself, but only after you consider the evidence impartially with your fellow jurors. During your deliberations, you should not hesitate to reexamine your own views and change your opinion if you become persuaded that it is wrong. However, you should not change an honest belief as to the weight or effect of the evidence solely because of the opinions of your fellow jurors or for the mere purpose of returning a verdict.*
>
> *All of you are equally honest and conscientious jurors who have heard the same evidence. All of you share an equal desire to arrive at a verdict. Each of you should ask yourself whether you should question the correctness of your present position.*

I remind you that in your deliberations you are to consider
the instructions I have given you as a whole. You should
not single out any part of any instruction, including this
one, and ignore others. They are all equally important.

You may now retire and continue your deliberations.

As time dragged on without a verdict, Terry Brandt was becoming more discouraged. Trey had informed him that it appeared that a hung jury was growing more likely with each passing day. The last thing that Terry Brandt wanted at this time was to go through this process again, and he was certainly not going to accept a plea to a lesser offense when in his mind he had done nothing wrong. Trey was not pushing Terry to plead to manslaughter or any other charge—he knew where Terry stood on that issue. He did explain to Terry that he could consider accepting a non-unanimous verdict in the super-majority verdict range requiring at least ten jurors voting for a guilty or a not-guilty verdict. Trey was of the opinion that they would either be acquitted or remain with a hung jury if they agreed to this but he had no way to know which way the jury might go. Trey suspected that he had two or maybe three jurors who were voting for a conviction and were not going to change their vote. Trey discussed the possibility of the super-majority verdict with the prosecutor and he was agreeable to it as he saw only a hung jury with the present structure and the possibility of a guilty verdict was higher with a super-majority verdict than it was with what he was presently looking at.

Trey also explained to Terry that if they stuck to their guns with the requirement for a unanimous twelve-vote verdict and they ended up with a hung jury, it was possible that the prosecution could decide not to retry the case. Of course, there was also the possibility that they could retry the case with a lesser charge of say, murder two or manslaughter. In Trey's opinion, a manslaughter charge could succeed and would carry anywhere from three years to ten years in prison. This did not appeal to Terry Brandt. The decision to go with a super-majority verdict appeared to be his best option. If he went with the super-majority verdict and he was acquitted, they could not then retry him on a manslaughter charge. They could only do that if they had another hung jury. Hopefully that would not occur. Terry finally instructed Trey to try for the super-majority verdict option.

Trey met with the prosecutor and told him that the defendant would accept a verdict of ten of the jurors versus twelve. The prosecutor said that he would accept that and they could discuss it with the judge. Trey notified the judge's clerk that they requested a conference to discuss options. The jury had now been out nine days without a decision. The judge had the clerk notify the attorneys and the court reporter to come to his chambers for an immediate hearing. When they were all seated and the court reporter indicated she was ready to transcribe, Trey explained to the judge that he had explained all of the possible options available to his client. He did not attempt to convince his client to accept one option over another. He explained that among the options he discussed with his client was the super-majority verdict option whereby ten of the twelve jurors would be required for a guilty or a not-guilty verdict. He discussed the possible outcomes of this arrangement with his client as he had discussed the possible outcomes of the other options. After careful thought, his client said that he would agree to a verdict based on the vote of at least ten of the jurors. The prosecutor said that a super-majority verdict based on ten of the twelve jurors unanimously voting was acceptable to him.

The judge listened to what Trey had to say and then sat back thinking about the possible effects of the reduction from the normal requirement for a unanimous verdict in cases of the type that Terry Brandt was facing. He suggested bringing Terry into the hearing so that he could question him concerning his decision. The judge clearly did not want to agree to waiving a unanimous verdict and then have the defendant appeal for the court having denied him the protections of a unanimous twelve-person verdict.

The judge spent the next forty-five minutes questioning Terry Brandt on the record on this decision to waive the unanimous verdict decision. The judge did not end his questioning until the record was replete with Terry Brandt's testimony showing that he completely understood the decision that he was making in waving the requirement for a unanimous twelve-person verdict. As he concluded his questioning, he advised Terry that he would permit the jury to bring back a verdict based on the votes of ten of the twelve members sitting on the jury and that once the verdict was brought back, be it a guilty verdict or a not-guilty verdict, that would be the final verdict in this case and Terry could not set it aside claiming he did not understand some part or other of what had taken place. Terry stated on the record that the matter had been thoroughly explained to him by both the judge and his own attorney, Trey Stark, and that it was his decision to waive the unanimous twelve-man verdict and accept the unanimous ten-man verdict.

The prosecutor added his statement to the record acquiescing to the proposal for the super majority verdict option. The judge then called in the jury and when they were all seated, he explained to them what was required for a conviction or for an acquittal. While twelve people could vote either way as they saw fit, only ten votes in favor of conviction or acquittal were required. He asked if all of the jurors understood the new rules; all indicated that they did. The jury returned to the jury room to discuss the case and to again vote.

Following the departure of the jury from the courtroom, the team of reporters that were covering the case immediately departed as well and fled to the phone bank to call their editors with the news. That afternoon, the newspaper headlines announced that the court had given in to a request by the defendant's attorney, Trey Stark, to make it easier for his client to obtain an acquittal with a vote of ten of the jurors rather than the customary twelve. They did not discuss that it was also easier to obtain a conviction with ten votes than the customary twelve. There was a lengthy editorial criticizing the performance of the debt collector defense attorney, who was using every trick in the book to get his client out of jail and back on the street. Trey was tempted to write another letter to the editor objecting to his column but this time Chris successfully prevailed upon him and convinced him it would only produce more unwarranted criticism.

The jury remained out for three more days when they notified the judge that they had reached a verdict. The attorneys and the defendant were called back to the courthouse and soon were seated at their respective places awaiting the reappearance of the judge. He soon came in and the clerk called the room to attention rapping his gavel on the wooden sound block. The Judge directed the clerk to bring the Jury back and soon they were filing into the jury box.

Chapter 20

As the jury entered the courtroom both Trey and his client were trying to read their decisions in their facial expressions and were coming up with nothing. They looked exactly the same as they did at any other time they had entered the courtroom. Some would look over at the defendant but apparently only to see that he was there and some would look at who the spectators were that were seated in the courtroom. When they were all seated, the judge asked them if they had arrived at a decision. The foreman stood and indicated that they had. He handed the verdict form to the judge, who spent some time reading it to make sure that they had properly completed the form. When he was assured that they had, he had the clerk read the verdict form.

The clerk studied the form and then read, "With respect to the charge of murder in the second degree, we, the jury, find the defendant not guilty." The reporters again gathered their briefcases and cell phones and charged from the room, creating a sensation that caused the judge to slam his gavel forcefully as he demanded order in the courtroom. The spectators who remained in the room had a stunned look on their faces as they conferenced in small huddles voicing their opinions to one another as to the wisdom of the verdict. Some appeared pleased by the verdict and others were obviously disappointed. Trey shook Terry Brandt's hand while Terry appeared totally stunned by the verdict. He sat next to Trey with his head bowed over the desk obviously in total disbelief. Trey had known that Terry fully expected a guilty verdict in view of all the publicity from the media demanding that he be found guilty. There was silence for a few moments after the verdict had sunk into the courtroom staff and spectators.

Then the judge requested that the clerk poll the jurors to ensure that the requirement for ten not guilty votes were present. The clerk read the names of the jurors and before he had read four names, he already had two votes for guilty. These were from two of the three black jurors, and when he came to the third black voter and asked her what her vote was for, she responded, "I guess not guilty."

The judge intervened in the process and asked her to stand as he had questions for her. He asked her to restate how she had voted and she said, "I originally voted for guilty, but obviously we were going to sit here forever if I didn't vote for not guilty."

The judge thought for a minute and said, "That is not a sufficient reason to vote one way or the other. I cannot accept that. You must decide how to vote in this case based upon the evidence presented in this courtroom. Is that clear?"

"Yes, Judge. I understand that. I guess that is what I based my decision on. I just wanted some punishment for killing that poor kid but if I can't have that, I guess I can't."

"I must ask you again, did you base your not guilty vote only on the evidence you heard in this court-room?"

"Yes, Judge. What else would I have based it on? If I had found him guilty, I would have based it on the evidence here just the same."

"You said previously that you voted not guilty so that you didn't have to sit in the courtroom any longer. Is that the reason you voted not guilty?"

"That was just a fact. If I voted not guilty, it was based on the evidence. Can I sit now?"

The judge looked over at the attorneys. "Do either of you gentlemen have any questions for this juror?"

Trey did not want to stir up any more trouble with this confused juror so he abstained. The prosecutor saw the makings of a mistrial and eagerly accepted the offer. "Ms. Cole, had you talked with other jurors on the panel discussing how you would be voting in this case?"

"Yessuh. I talked with the other two black members quite often about the case and how we would be voting."

"Ms. Cole, had the three of you decided at any time that you would all vote for the defendant in this case to be found guilty?"

"Yessuh. We did that a number of times."

"And was one of the times shortly before you decided to vote not guilty?"

"Yessuh, we were going to vote guilty then."

"Why did you then change your mind and vote not guilty?"

"Da foreman said we'd be there till hell froze over if one of us didn't vote not guilty."

"Is that the reason you then decided to vote not guilty?"

"I guess so."

The prosecutor looked at the judge and said, "I have no further questions for this juror, Your Honor. May I inquire of the foreman?"

The judge thought for a moment and then said that he would question the foreman. The courtroom was absolutely quiet as the judge had the foreman move over to the witness box and be sworn in. Ross Adams, the foreman, swore to tell the truth and then sat down in the witness chair.

"Mr. Adams, you heard the testimony of Ms. Cole saying that you told her that hell would freeze over before they got out of there if either she or one of the other black ladies did not vote not guilty. Did you in fact say that to her?"

"I may have said that one of the three would have to change their vote or we would have another hung jury, which meant more time for us to argue and discuss the case. Your Honor, the entire panel with the exception of the three ladies that voted guilty was firmly, and thoroughly, convinced of the innocence of the defendant, Mr. Brandt. Frankly, we suspected there was an issue of racial bias in the votes of the three black ladies with their decision to vote guilty, regardless of the evidence pointing otherwise."

The judge pondered the statement by Adams and then told him to return to his seat with the other jurors. He again asked Ms. Cole if her vote was still to find the defendant not guilty. She again said, "I guess so."

The judge scowled at the juror and then asked her again, "Is not guilty your vote or is it not? Just answer the question."

Ms. Cole glared at the judge and said, "I voted not guilty yesterday and that is what I'm voting today."

The judge then polled the remaining jurors, all of whom firmly stated that they were voting not guilty. The count remained nine not guilty with one sort of not guilty and two guiltys. The reporters that had fled the courtroom with the foreman's announcement of not guilty had returned and were eagerly taking notes to record what was transpiring.

The judge addressed the defense attorney and the prosecutor. "I am going to dismiss the jury at this point and terminate proceedings for the day. At this point I am going to accept the jury's verdict as final. If either of you have any comments to make in this case, or motions, we can deal with them tomorrow morning at 9:00 when we reconvene." The judge stood up and left the courtroom. The reporters made a mad scramble for the phone banks to give their editors the latest on what was happening in the courtroom.

The morning papers and the radio and television news commentators were focused on what they referred to as the legal debacle in the Minnesota murder trial of Terry Brandt. One headline stated, *Brandt Jury Guesses He is Not Guilty*. The editorial in the morning paper went on to say that the judge appeared confused on how to handle the one juror who could not make up her mind on the verdict but who was voting not guilty in order to escape the courtroom. The other commentators used other sarcastic comments to get across the point that a major injustice was being perpetrated and a killer was about to go free.

As Trey, Brandt and Chris met for breakfast in the morning before the court session, Trey said, "This is a hell of a mess. The judge never should have polled the jury when they had come up with a not guilty verdict. You poll on the guilty verdicts. That was the first mistake. Now he may be forced to rule a mistrial. We shall see when we hear what he has to say. If he does not rule a mistrial, I'm sure Jackson will make a motion for a mistrial based on what has transpired. If the judge doesn't allow that, an appellate court most probably will." His comments were not pleasing to Terry Brandt, who was more than ready to return to a somewhat normal life.

As Trey entered the courtroom, it was already packed with reporters and the few sightseers that were able to gain entrance. There was another crowd out in the halls awaiting the judge's decision on how he was going to proceed.

Promptly at nine a.m., the judge entered the courtroom and the clerk gaveled the courtroom again in session. The judge had the clerk bring in the jury and they all filed in and took their normal positions in the jury box. When they were seated, the judge again called on Ms. Cole and asked her to stand. He said he had a question or two directed at her and then he would proceed with dealing with the problem at hand. "Ms. Cole, yesterday you indicated in this courtroom that you voted that the defendant in this case was not guilty of the charge of second degree murder. Is that still your opinion?"

"Yessuh. That is."

"And, Ms. Cole, is your opinion that the defendant is not guilty based solely on the evidence that you heard and saw presented in this courtroom during the trial of the defendant?"

"Yessuh. That's what I based it on."

"Very well, you may be seated." The judge addressed the courtroom. "This is my decision with respect to this matter. Ten of the jurors have voted that the defendant is not guilty as charged. I mistakenly requested that the jury be polled on their votes. There was no need to do that as the vote was for an acquittal of the defendant. Had I not polled the jury, we would not have had the issue come up. I am entering judgment in this case finding the defendant, Terry Brandt, innocent of all charges leading to his arrest and trial on the charge of second degree murder. I will allow the attorneys to comment if they so desire."

Trey said that he had no comment at this time. The prosecutor, on the other hand, indicated he did wish to comment. "Your Honor, I would request that we be given a few days to present a motion for reconsideration of your order entering judgment in favor of the defendant in this case. I believe the only order that should be flowing out of this situation would be an order granting a mistrial. I will be moving for such an order but request that a hearing on my motion be held in seven days or more from today to allow us time to prepare the motion."

The judge looked at the clerk and asked him to come up with a date in the next week or two. The clerk indicated that the judge's calendar was open for an afternoon hearing commencing at one p.m. on Wednesday, the 23rd. The judge then announced, "The jury is dismissed, court is adjourned," and he departed the courtroom.

Terry looked at Trey and asked him, "What happens now?"

"I believe there will eventually be a mistrial granted in view of the state of the record at this time and that could mean a retrial, offers to accept lesser charges or possibly no further charges. At this point I don't know. The fact that you were found not guilty by the jury would afford us an appeal of the issue to the court of appeals on the grounds of double jeopardy. They may just say that the judge's decision to respect the jury's decision should suffice. We will just have to see. We will keep you advised as we work our way through this business."

Later when Trey and Chris were back in their offices, Chris asked about the California trip. "Where do we sit with that?"

"As far as I'm concerned, that is still on. I built some extra time into the schedule and we should be able to get out there for a week, anyway. Let's hope. Now, moving right along. We have to prepare for this motion. That is going to require some research. I will get word to Walt to help us out here. Maybe there is some good law that will protect the verdict, but I don't know. I don't believe it was proper for the judge to put the foreman and a juror under examination on how the decision-making process went. I think that is a serious invasion of the province of the jury, as well. The privacy of the jury is sacrosanct. We shall see. I do not want to bring that issue up as I think it favors a mistrial.

"Our position should be to support exactly what the judge has ordered. Frankly, I think his position is correct under the circumstances. Keep in mind that a motion to set aside the verdict also violates the double jeopardy clause should another trial ensue. The strongest argument we have here is that the verdict as it stands supports the defendant. If this jury had voted the defendant guilty, that could be set aside on these facts but not a not-guilty verdict. Be sure and put that in our responsive pleadings."

Trey and Chris worked on the hearing of the prosecutor's motion for a mistrial throughout the week. Both worked on the drafting of the memorandum that would be submitted opposing the motion for a mistrial. The two attorneys worked up arguments supporting the court's voiced opinion on the state of the law. They also prepared arguments to the effect that the prosecutor's move for a mistrial was an attempt to gain a retrial, which would be prohibited by the Fifth Amendment prohibiting double jeopardy. Trey pointed out to Chris, "The key point here is that there must be a manifest necessity for a mistrial to be granted as opposed to no or minimal grounds for granting a mistrial. Many courts have denied a mistrial when there has been a hung jury in a case as there was no showing in that particular case of a manifest necessity to retry the case when the jury has been evenly divided in their verdict. The Brandt case shows even less necessity for a mistrial with a vote of the majority of the jurors in favor of a not-guilty verdict."

Trey was fairly confident that the trial court was thinking along exactly the same lines as he and Chris. Shortly after the hearing of the prosecutor's motion, the trial judge voted against the prosecutor on his motion for a mistrial and generally assumed all of Trey's arguments. Shortly thereafter, the prosecutor appealed the case to the appellate court, which rather quickly ruled against him on the same grounds as the lower court. After that, the prosecutor indicated to Trey that he was not going to proceed further on the case. The clincher for Trey was the fact that ten of the twelve jurors supported a not-guilty verdict, which had been accepted as decisive by the trial judge. With the appellate court order in hand, Trey told Terry that the case was finally over and he could relax.

The media had continued their disparaging attacks on the judge and the defense team of Stark and Sutton and after the passing of a number of days the attacks seemed to lose appeal for the readers. Regardless of the obvious lack of respect that the media had for the defense attorneys, the public had an entirely different view. The phones in the offices of Stark and Sutton were ringing constantly with requests that the attorneys represent the callers on all sorts of legal matters from personal injury cases to divorces, and included criminal defense. Most asked for Trey Stark but Chris Sutton received a large number of calls for assistance as well.

Chapter 21

Chris and Trey were worn out from being under the gun on the Brandt case for the previous eighteen months. It had been 24/7 everyday with no letup from the time they were initially retained to the present time. When Trey finally had some time to consider their California trip, he first purchased the two first class tickets from Minneapolis to San Francisco and then confirmed the room at the Mark Hopkins Hotel for ten days. The thought that he had ten whole days in Frisco—with Chris—was almost overwhelming. They would do all the things that he had done on the earlier trip and then a lot more. He had purchased some travel books on the city and had begun reading through them and making plans. Chris was going through the books as well and was becoming increasingly excited to be visiting a city that she had wanted to visit her entire life.

With all of the calls coming into the office seeking representation on various legal matters, Trey had to leave someone in charge to deal with the calls and book in the decent cases. Walt had continued to indicate an interest in working for the firm and Trey brought him on board, full time as a full partner, with authority to hire others if the demand for legal services justified the expense. He also instructed Walt to file claims for all expenses the firm was entitled to receive for the representation of Terry Brandt. That was a large accounting task and he was instructed to get Alice Bentley working on that project as well. Trey had his cell phone as did Chris and Walt and Alice were told to give them a call if either needed a decision made.

Trey had an open afternoon and he had some items that he wished to take care of before they made the trip to California. He located a wedding chapel in Reno by the name of "The Chapel of the Gold Ring." They had an advertisement on the internet along with about fifty other chapels in Reno. Trey considered the advertisement for the Gold Ring Chapel to be in good taste, although a number of the others seemed to deal with the matter in an acceptable manner as well. In fact, he was somewhat surprised and impressed by how they all dealt with it. He had expected far worse. In any event, he called the chapel and told them that he and his future wife were flying into San Francisco and would come to Reno by shuttle the following morning and he discussed making arrangements for a ceremony at eleven a.m. They were duly booked into the schedule for that time. Trey also learned what information they would have to provide the chapel and he inquired if the chapel would be able to obtain the license. They assured him they could handle all of the license requirements but would need certain information, which they passed on to Trey. Trey said that he would call them back later and would fax the information they had requested.

He called Chris and suggested they run out for lunch as they now had time to enjoy a quiet lunch. Chris was ready for that and in no time they were seated at Friday's enjoying the relaxing time. There were some brief interruptions as patrons stopped by their booth to congratulate them on their victory. Fortunately all of their comments were very positive. When they were again free, Trey told Chris that there were some things he had to talk to her about

"Am I about to be fired? I thought I did a pretty good job at the trial."

"You did, Chris. It's nothing like that. I just want to marry you and I wanted to talk about that."

"Well, we agree on that. Okay, let's talk."

Trey told Chris that he had made the arrangements for a wedding in Reno on the morning after they arrived in Frisco. He explained that they could take the nine a.m. shuttle the following morning from the San Fran airport to Reno for the eleven o'clock ceremony. It was all arranged. Trey had purchased the tickets on the shuttle and they would be back in Frisco by two in the afternoon. "Is all of this agreeable with you or would you like to make any changes or additions or whatever?"

Chris thought for a moment. "No. I am all for it."

"Okay, Chris. I thought that we could get married in the church later when we are back in Minneapolis so that we could have more of a wedding that our parents and friends would enjoy. What do you think about that?"

"Trey, I think that is a good idea. My parents would want that, for sure."

Trey obtained the personal information from Chris that he needed to deliver to the chapel, along with his own data, so that they could obtain the marriage license. Fortunately, there was no waiting period in Nevada but there was in California, which precluded their getting married in San Francisco. There were still six days before their impending travel to California and many of the radio and television stations, particularly in Minnesota, were clamoring for interviews. Both were sought for the interviews as both had been highly popularized during the trial. Chris scheduled four of these interviews before their trip and they all went very smoothly. All of the interviews were very complimentary.

Their flight to California went smoothly and in just a few hours, they were circling for the approach for landing at SFO International. They rented a car and drove to the Mark Hopkins Hotel. After they unpacked in their room, Trey suggested they visit Jack's Bar down in the theatre district and then after a drink or two they could find a nice restaurant for dinner. As they walked into Jack's it was about eight p.m. and the bar was already filled. There were some empty chairs and a table on the far side of the bar and as they walked past the piano player, he was just finishing a number and looked up recognizing Trey.

"Well, look who's here. I see you have returned. I was hoping to see you here again."

"Yes, thanks. I brought Ingrid back with me as I said I would. Can you play it again, Sam? We are getting married in the morning and we would both enjoy hearing your classic rendition."

"Well, congratulations. I would be glad to do that. Enjoy, Humphrey."

As they walked back to the open chairs, the melody of "As Time Goes By" came from the keyboard of the grand piano in the center of the room. Soon Sam's fine baritone voice filled the room, sending the lyrics out which brought all conversation to a halt. Trey and

Chris sat down and Chris's attention was focused on the piano man. She commented on what a fine piano player Sam was and that he was treating the lyrics with great respect and feeling.

"How do you know him, Trey?"

"I just met him here at Jack's. I was here on my first trip and asked him to play "As Time Goes By" when I was here. He asked me then where Ingrid was and I told him I would bring her out on my next trip and here we are."

"Yes. Ingrid Bergman. I was thinking Lauren Bacall was in Casablanca but it was Ingrid Bergman. Well, the piano man is a great talent. I will remember this forever. He even remembered the song you wanted him to play—amazing."

"Well, I did ask him to 'play it again, Sam,' which gave him a good clue."

When Sam had sung the final lyrics, he mentioned to the patrons that he had performed the piece for two friends who had just come in and were about to be married in the morning. He wished them well and saluted them with a wave. The patrons then gave Sam and the couple applause. Someone in the crowd then shouted out, "They are the attorneys from Minnesota. Congratulations on your victory there." Trey thought, *I hope the other patrons don't pick up on that.* To his chagrin, it became obvious from the increased applause that many of the patrons then recognized Trey and Chris from their pictures in the media following the story that had swept the nation. Some of the patrons stopped by where they were seated and congratulated them on their forthcoming wedding and their legal victory.

Sam came over to their table and said, "I thought you looked very familiar. I thought that I had seen you before when you were here on your first visit but when that fellow shouted out who you were, I looked again at Ingrid here and I immediately recognized her." Trey then introduced Sam to Chris and advised Chris that his real name was Porter Mayle, as he glanced over at the poster by the piano to make sure he had the name right. Trey asked Porter if "As Time Goes By" was on his CD that was advertised on the poster and Porter said it was not, but he was going to redo the CD and it would soon be on there. Porter took down Trey's address and told him he would send him one when it was available. Porter said he had followed the case every day in the San Francisco Examiner and also on the local TV channels. Porter said it was the hottest news item in the city all through the trial and everyone was talking about it.

"That was a gutsy move for you two."

"Porter, we really had no choice. We knew the boy's mother and she said we were the boy's last chance. It was the perfect case. He was, and is, a very fine young man and he was clearly innocent of all charges. What the media was doing to him got our hackles up and we had to take the case. Yes, we did put up with a fair amount of crap but we also had the support of many wonderful people."

"I will play your song again here in a few minutes. It has become my favorite song and it is not only a beautiful melody but also has great lyrics. You two enjoy your time in the city and please stop by sometime after the wedding. I would enjoy seeing you again before you return home."

"Porter, we will do that. Thank you and both Chris and I enjoy your performances here to the max. We will definitely return."

The high point of the trip to California, besides listening to Porter at Jack's Bar, was sitting in the rotating bar at the Top of the Mark as the sun set over the ocean to the west while the booth they were seated in moved at an almost imperceptible pace around to view the mountains to the east, and then very slowly, the city and again the ocean to the west. At first Chris, as Trey experienced on his first trip, did not notice that the booth was in fact moving. Fortunately, on this visit to the Top of the Mark, they did not have to be concerned about driving from the hotel to another hotel. Consequently, they were able to enjoy a few drinks and the view without worry.

While they sat in their booth at the Top of the Mark, Trey gave Chris her gift, a beautiful two-carat diamond engagement ring. He explained to Chris that the ring had belonged to his grandmother and was then passed down to his mother. She had suggested to Trey that he pass it on to Chris, as there was so much of the Stark family history involved in the ring. Chris was at a loss for words as Trey told her that the ring had been passed down through his family and that his mother wanted her to have it. Trey suggested to her that after they were married in Reno, they could buy their wedding rings in San Francisco upon their return. They stayed in the bar talking and watched the sun set over the ocean in the west. Later on the lights of the city were lit and the bar lights were turned down so they were able to enjoy a star-filled sky. Chris looked at Trey and said, "It has been an interesting trip."

Trey agreed. "It has been an interesting two years."

"It only gets better, Trey."

"Yes, Chris. I am very proud of what both of us have done in taking on the job of defending Terry Brandt. That was quite a challenging responsibility for us to take on, although I didn't look at it that way at the time. There was an old phrase associated with merry-go-rounds in years past that I have thought about after I had made arrangements with the chapel in Reno named "The Gold Ring." In years past, when they had painted wooden horses on the merry-go-round for the kids to ride, they used to have a gold ring hanging on a post that the children riding their wooden ponies would go by as the carrousel made its rounds. It was quite a stretch for the kids to reach out and grab for the gold ring and they would all try to get it as there was a prize for doing so. Of course, all parents were nervous their child was going to fall off the pony, and certainly some did, which is probably why they don't have the gold ring on merry-go-rounds anymore. Anyway, what we did in the Terry Brandt case was we reached out for the gold ring. We grabbed for it, and by God, we got it. We took a lot of abuse in the process but we also garnered a great deal of respect that we can take with us for the rest of our lives."

"Yes, Trey. We did reach out for the gold ring and we did get it. There were times when I did not think it was going to end as well as it did. Let's keep on going for the gold ring—I have enjoyed the trip so far."

"I totally agree, Chris. I promise you that I will do that and I think we should make it a point to come out here and sit in our booth at the Top of the Mark and renew our vows to always grab for the gold ring. We may not always succeed but the important point is we have to try. We have to go for it."

"We will do that, Trey. Same booth and the same time of day, at sunset, and you will have to tell our children the story of the gold ring at the carousel and how they too should always reach out for the gold ring."

Trey was silent for a moment and then commented, "Can you imagine being married to someone that had no interest in going for the gold ring?"

"I think we are pretty evenly matched, Trey."

The following morning Trey and Chris were married in Reno at the Chapel of the Gold Ring.

www.ingramcontent.com/pod-product-compliance
Lightning Source LLC
Chambersburg PA
CBHW070005260626
47159CB00005B/1672